MARTIN À BECKETT BOYD was born in Switzerland in 1893 into a family that was to achieve fame in the Australian arts. His brothers Merric and Penleigh, as well as Merric's sons Arthur, Guy and David, were all to become renowned artists, while Penleigh's son Robin became an influential architect, widely known for his book *The Australian Ugliness*.

After leaving school, Martin Boyd enrolled in a seminary, but he abandoned this vocation and began to train as an architect. With the outbreak of World War I, he sailed for England where he served in the Royal East Kent Regiment and the Royal Flying Corps.

Boyd eventually settled in England after the war. His first novel, *Love Gods*, was published in 1925, followed by *The Montforts* three years later.

After the international success of *Lucinda Brayford* in 1946 Boyd decided to return to Australia, but by 1951 he was back in London. In the coming decade he was to write the Langton Quartet: *The Cardboard Crown*, *A Difficult Young Man*, *Outbreak of Love* and *When Blackbirds Sing*. In 1957 he went to Rome, where he lived and continued to write until his death in 1972.

BRENDA NIALL lives in Melbourne. She is the author of a number of award-winning biographies, including her acclaimed accounts of the Boyd family. In 2004 she was awarded the Order of Australia for services to Australian literature. Her most recent book is the best-selling *True North: The Story of Mary and Elizabeth Durack*.

ALSO BY MARTIN BOYD

Fiction
Scandal of Spring
The Lemon Farm
The Picnic
Night of the Party
Nuns in Jeopardy
Lucinda Brayford
Such Pleasure
The Cardboard Crown
A Difficult Young Man
Outbreak of Love
When Blackbirds Sing
The Tea-Time of Love: The Clarification of Miss Stilby

Under the pseudonym 'Martin Mills'
Love Gods
Brangane: A Memoir
The Montforts

Under the pseudonym 'Walter Beckett'
Dearest Idol

Non-fiction
Much Else in Italy: A Subjective Travel Book
Why They Walk Out: An Essay in Seven Parts
Autobiography
A Single Flame
Day of My Delight: An Anglo-Australian Memoir

The Cardboard Crown
Martin Boyd

Text Publishing Melbourne Australia

textclassics.com.au
textpublishing.com.au

The Text Publishing Company
Swann House
22 William Street
Melbourne Victoria 3000
Australia

First published by The Cresset Press, London 1952
First published by The Text Publishing Company 2004
This edition published 2012

Cover design by WH Chong
Page design by Text
Typeset by Midland Typesetters

Printed in Australia by Griffin Press, an Accredited ISO AS/NZS 14001:2004
Environmental Management System printer

Primary print ISBN: 9781922079411
Ebook ISBN: 9781921961717
Author: Boyd, Martin, 1893–1972
Title: The cardboard crown / by Martin Boyd ; introduction by Brenda Niall.
Series: Text classics
Dewey Number: A823.2

CONTENTS

All History Is a Little False
Brenda Niall

It's one of the set pieces of nineteenth-century fiction and painting: the exile's return. A long-lost uncle, bearded and careworn after penitential years in Australia, is restored to a joyful family whose problems will all be solved by a sackful of nuggets from the goldfields.

In some such tableau, its English setting transposed to mid twentieth-century Melbourne, Martin Boyd might have taken centre stage. Having led a nomadic life in England for twenty-seven years, making a meagre living as an author, he came home in 1948, aged fifty-five, with fame and money earned at last, eager to regain his place in the famous Boyd family of artists, restore an ancestral house and rescue his needy, talented nephews—painter Arthur, sculptor Guy, painter and potter David, architect and writer Robin. But ironic comedy, not melodrama, was Martin Boyd's style and in that spirit he had to play his part. Nothing went to plan; nothing was as he had expected it.

Yet the brief return of Martin Boyd had its reward. This was the splendid, witty, poignant series of novels known as The Langton Quartet. In *The Cardboard Crown* (1952), *A Difficult Young Man* (1955), *Outbreak of Love* (1957) and *When Blackbirds Sing* (1962), Boyd reinterpreted a century of family history. His homecoming prompted the first in the series, *The Cardboard Crown*. The subtle shadings of light and dark in the interplay of his own childhood memories, and the perceptions of the middle-aged expatriate narrator Guy Langton, make this one of the finest Australian novels—as fresh and funny, sad and shrewd as when it was first published in 1952.

Historical novels are often weighed down with period detail. Not this one. Martin Boyd knew his family so intimately that he did not need to persuade his readers, or himself, of the texture of life in Melbourne from the time of his grandparents' marriage in 1855 to his own departure for service in World War I. The shock of return to an almost unrecognisable world gives *The Cardboard Crown* its sharp focus; it also sets the mood of rueful acceptance.

The creative impulse often works mysteriously. For Coleridge it came in a dream. Tolstoy's chance reading of a newspaper report suggested the tragedy of *Anna Karenina*. By contrast the catalyst for *The Cardboard Crown* was specific and immediate. A moment in time, a familiar place and a hoard of family papers prompted Boyd to write something quite unlike his earlier work, more accomplished in tone and more personal. Its narrator, Guy Langton, is a version of the author, seen with wry detachment as well as understanding.

Martin Boyd's *Lucinda Brayford* was published in 1946, while he was living in Cambridge. He was already an established author but nothing in his earlier work had prepared him for the rapturous reviews and astonishing sales of this novel, in which his experiences as a young officer in World War I, his pacifist leanings and his sense of cultural displacement, found their appropriate form. A bestseller in Britain and the United States, it was greeted by the influential critic Richard Church as one of the three great novels of the twentieth century.

Martin Boyd had not wanted to return to Australia as a failure or an indifferent success. He had always been restless, and with the success of *Lucinda Brayford* he had the means to make a home wherever he pleased. He had no close personal ties and seems never to have contemplated marriage. Some of his friends were sure he was homosexual; others disagreed. A few discerned inner loneliness in this witty, sociable, generous man whose private life was closely guarded. In middle age he felt the need for permanence. He began to think of family life, imagining himself as a generous uncle, helping his young nephews to a start in their creative lives. Spinning a fantasy of homecoming he arranged to buy and restore The Grange, his maternal grandparents' house at Harkaway, near Berwick, Victoria, and once again make it the family centre it had been in his childhood. It was a beguiling dream, but the homecoming was a failure.

Lucinda Brayford, as Martin Boyd soon discovered, was unknown in Australia: few copies had reached Australian bookshops and no one had reviewed it. His Boyd nephews, then in their twenties, were better known than Martin himself. Robin Boyd was making his name as an architect and writer. Arthur's paintings were critically acclaimed, even though they did not yet sell; and in Sydney, Guy and David Boyd had established a business which, without consulting their uncle, they called the Martin Boyd Pottery. There were no accolades for *Lucinda Brayford*. Instead, Martin Boyd was asked how he found time for writing as well as pottery.

Stubbornly, but with growing unease, he began to transform the old house. Nostalgia for his Australian childhood mingled with a yearning for the English country life he had left; and in an oddly contradictory act of reclamation he turned his grandparents' unpretentious house into an English gentleman's residence, furnishing it with elegant eighteenth-century furniture ill-matched with the overgrown garden and neglected paddocks. Even the verandah, which gave the house its authentic Australian character as well as much-needed shade, was removed to give the facade a Georgian look. In the Australian bush it seemed very odd; and although the nephews were too polite to say so, they thought it was absurd.

The house needed an heir and Martin needed company.

Arthur Boyd was invited to bring his wife Yvonne and their two young children to live at The Grange, and to paint biblical frescoes in the dining room for a substantial fee. Arthur, however, was too independent to be woven into his uncle's design. The frescoes, a brilliant artistic achievement, seemed likely to be the only gain from an ill-advised venture.

The house itself saved the day. Stored in one of the outhouses, forgotten for half a century, the diaries of his grandmother Emma à Beckett were discovered. From the time of her marriage in 1855 until her death in 1906, Emma had recorded the life of the family. Martin read the entry on his own birth in 1893, and the sad, stoic words written three years later when his oldest brother Gilbert was killed in a riding accident. The diaries took him back in time to discover much that was unexpected. Urged on by Arthur (who was always saying 'Why don't you?' to his uncle), Martin saw the makings of a novel in his grandmother's diaries.

If he had merely turned the diaries into narrative, *The Cardboard Crown* might well have been an unremarkable period piece. But as Martin read Emma's daily entries he reflected on the family stories he had been told as a child, which were sometimes sharply contradicted by the diaries. His grandparents—the amusing, terrifying and eccentric W. A. C. à Beckett, and the serene, beloved Emma—were not easily reconciled with the images of the young Willie and Emma and the circumstances of their marriage, which once rattled the teacups of polite Melbourne and caused

Willie's father, Chief Justice Sir William à Beckett, the deepest embarrassment.

The diaries confronted Martin Boyd with the truth of his grandmother's parentage and the source of the prodigious wealth she had inherited from her father, John Mills. Even after huge losses in the financial crash of the 1890s, and the division of the remaining assets into smaller shares as the family increased, there had still been enough to keep Martin's artist parents Emma Minnie (nee à Beckett) and Arthur Merric Boyd in modest comfort, with no urgent need to sell their paintings. It was the Boyds who helped the impoverished Arthur Streeton by taking his now famous canvas *Golden Summer: Eaglemont* to London. They entered it in the Royal Academy show of 1891, where it was accepted, as were two works of their own. Returning to Australia they brought up their children in a 'golden summer' landscape at Sandringham, on Melbourne's Port Phillip Bay, and at rural Yarra Glen. The Boyds gave small allowances to their sons Penleigh and Martin, and they supported Merric in his financially unrewarding pottery. The family's roller-coaster ride from riches to poverty reached bottom in the 1920s depression. When Martin returned to Australia, Merric's sons, Arthur, Guy and David, were beginning again, inheritors of nothing except their talent and the certainties of art.

As everyone knew, the bounty which had sustained the Boyds and other family members was based on Melbourne city property acquired before the gold rushes. Known to some, but seldom mentioned, was the story of Emma à Beckett's father, John Mills, founder of Melbourne's first brewery and owner of several public houses. Mills died in 1841, leaving these assets to his only child. Behind the shameful brewery fortune was the real family secret. John Mills came from a family of Gloucestershire labourers who had busily engaged themselves in burglary and theft. William Mills was hanged at Gloucester Gaol in 1826 while his brother, sixteen-year-old John Mills, was transported to Van Diemen's Land where he served a seven-year sentence before sailing to Melbourne in 1837 to buy land and set up his brewery. Because Emma's inheritance was contested by several Mills uncles as well as her disreputable stepfather, the story was common knowledge in the Melbourne law courts and therefore well known to her future father-in-law Chief Justice Sir William à Beckett. To add piquancy to the inevitable gossip when Emma married Sir William's eldest son in 1855 was the fact that Sir William often railed in public about the evils of the liquor trade. With his imposing new house in East Melbourne not long completed, he resigned from the Supreme Court on the grounds of ill health and returned to England. There he resumed his crusade against the liquor trade.

If Martin Boyd did not know his convict heritage, the discovery of the diaries gave him the clues he needed. Some living witnesses—aunts and cousins—may have been indiscreet enough in old age to add their testimony. The diaries offered Boyd a wonderful story, rich in irony, which he was perfectly equipped to tell. Yet, even half a century ago it was unthinkable for him to expose the convict stain. Social shame, clan loyalty, and reverence for his grandmother's memory stayed his hand. Packing the fifty-odd volumes of diaries in his luggage, with the first pages of his novel, Boyd sailed for England in 1951. He never returned. The experiment of the old house had failed. It was exquisitely done but no one wanted to live in it.

How to rework the family story without using the convict element? How to do justice to Emma's strength and independence without revealing the shameful burden she had carried into the cultured, upper-class à Beckett family? The diaries themselves offered an alternative dramatic centre. At the time of Martin's birth in Lucerne in 1893, Emma left the family party and went alone to Munich. There she renewed a friendship with a Herr Weiger whom she had met in Paris.

He took her to the opera, sent golden roses to her hotel room, gave her small, expensive gifts. The lines of a wistful song, transcribed by Emma, suggest a sad acceptance of the impossibility of changing her life:

La vie est brève:
Un peu d'amour,
Un peu de rêve,
Et puis—Bonjour!

La vie est vaine:
Un peu d'espoir,
Un peu de peine,
Et puis—Bonsoir!

At fifty-five Emma was still beautiful, in love with art and Europe and perhaps with Herr Weiger too. But there was also her feckless husband Willie à Beckett, her six children and many grandchildren, all financially and emotionally dependent on her. Emma made her choice and returned to Australia. In her grandson's novel, Alice Langton commmits herself to carrying the family burdens. Alice's strength, clear-sightedness and generosity of spirit make her one of the great women of Australian fiction. She is never a victim.

To drive the plot of his novel Boyd had to devise a family scandal to take the place of the convict story. His answer was to develop Emma's reticent diary entries into a strong and central love story, to which he added an imagina-tive element: an outrageous series of infidelities on his grandfather's part. The story of rapacious Hetty, with whom Austin Langton, the fictional counterpart of W. A. C. à Beckett, has four sons is almost certainly Martin Boyd's invention. This sustained betrayal sets Alice Langton free to contemplate divorce, as perhaps Emma à Beckett did. Emma's diaries, however, are seldom reflective and although Martin Boyd reproduced many entries word for word, Alice's confession of love belongs only to fiction.

'All history is a little false.' So the narrator of *The Cardboard Crown*, Guy Langton, warns his readers. The strategy by which Martin Boyd transformed his grandmother's story into a work of art was his use of an unreliable narrator. Guy corresponds in many ways with Martin himself. The return from England, the old house, the young painter Julian (based on Arthur Boyd) are all instantly recognisable. So is the reckless old gossip Cousin Arthur—a version of the Boyds' cousin Ted à Beckett. Some of the best comic scenes are those in which Arthur is torn between ribaldry and family piety. In his account of the first voyage to England, the ship is at times a version of the *Mayflower*, filled with grave, high-minded pilgrims. After an extra glass of burgundy it becomes 'a kind of nautical brothel'.

Guy Langton never says 'Trust me'. In countering one family voice with another to show the impossibility of ever knowing the truth of any human heart, he deliberately undermines his own authority. Self-characterised as a loner, an aesthete, probably homosexual, Guy shows the reader how he would be most inclined to interpret the story. The character of Aubrey Tunstall, with whom Guy and Arthur Langton have obvious affinities, is one example. We are told that if Guy's brother Dominic had written the Alice–Aubrey romance, he would have had Aubrey tormented by conscience, spending his nights in prayer. It occurs to Guy, however, that Aubrey might not have relished the thought of half a dozen Australian stepchildren sliding on the marble floors of his Rome apartment.

After a number of novels in which the point of view is conventionally omniscient, Boyd was prompted by the impossibility of truth-telling to write a modernist work. He would have agreed with William Faulkner that 'the past is not dead. It's not even past.' *The Cardboard Crown* is at one level a story of Melbourne's colonial past and an exploration of the Anglo-Australian relationship. Unlike most novels set in this period it ignores bushrangers, bushfires and outback privations. The dramas of love, money and class in the new society are set against a landscape which Boyd evokes in loving detail, in the spirit of the Heidelberg School painters. His novel is also a finely shaped story about storytelling: a meditation on truth and memory.

Writing in the London *Observer*, David Paul compared *The Cardboard Crown* with Anthony Powell's wonderful twelve-volume series of novels *A Dance to the Music of Time*. Paul and other English critics had a surer sense of its quality than the Australians who saw Boyd's novel as an Antipodean *Forsyte Saga*. Published by Cresset Press, it was a 1952 Book Society Choice in Britain, where it had excellent sales. And in the United States the *New York Times* and the New York *Herald-Tribune* gave Boyd celebrity treatment, with his photograph beside the lead review. Yet, like Patrick White, whose 1955 novel *The Tree of Man* was misunderstood or derided by Australian critics on first publication, Boyd had to wait for serious attention in his own country. Not until 1971, when Melbourne's Lansdowne Press reissued *The Cardboard Crown* in a handsome new edition, was there widespread recognition of Boyd's subtlety and narrative skill. Judah Waten's review for the Melbourne *Age* acknowledges that Boyd's novels 'have won both praise here and abroad, perhaps more abroad than at home', then adds that 'the publication of this new edition of Martin Boyd's four novels in Australia once again suggests that however limited the home base might be it is in the long run the Australian writer's mainstay'.

The old house, The Grange, was sold to a quarry in the 1960s and later demolished. Attempts to salvage Arthur Boyd's superb frescoes failed: they exist only in fragments. Emma à Beckett's diaries survived many journeys with Martin Boyd, who died in Rome in 1972. No longer the rich uncle, he was helped financially in his last years by his nephews. The diaries came home to Australia in the 1990s, when Arthur Boyd gave Bundanon, his house and land on the Shoalhaven River, New South Wales, to the Australian people. Safely housed again, the fifty pocket-sized volumes are a permanent record of the life of a remarkable woman whose love of art and reverence for creativity transformed her legacy of convict gold into something far more enduring. *The Cardboard Crown*, and its successors in which Martin Boyd continued the story of the Langton family, are part of that legacy.

Author's note

While the plot of this novel is founded on fact, the characters and certain episodes are fictitious. This is most particularly true of the characters of Hetty and her children, and her relationship with Austin.

Thanks are due to Messrs Chatto and Windus for permission to make the quotation from *The Captive*.

M.B.

The Cardboard Crown

1

'When we have passed a certain age, the soul of the child that we were, and the souls of the dead from whom we spring, come and bestow upon us in handfuls their treasures and their calamities'.* The realisation that I had reached this age came upon me one night in 1949. It was after midnight, and I was driving through pouring rain from a dinner party in Toorak up to Westhill, my home in the country, thirty miles from Melbourne. My thoughts were accompanied by the dreary whining of the windscreen wiper, and occasionally and dangerously interrupted by the blinding lights of a timber lorry, driven presumably by a drunkard or a criminal.

* *La Prisonnière* by Marcel Proust, trans. by C. K. Scott-Moncrieff.

Not that my thoughts were very coherent. It had been a rather dull party, with the champagne more stimulating than the conversation, so that one's mind was buzzing like a motor engine that is pulling nothing, except for one incident, when a fashionable doctor made an outrageous reference to Dominic, my poor dead, mad brother, who had been his patient. I shall not repeat it, at any rate not yet, as although an incident may be true, it is not necessarily credible, and I do not want to give at the outset an impression that I am not telling the truth. Nor shall I give my retort, which was brief, impersonal and very restrained, but which shocked the millionaires and their wives as much as if I had used an obscene word, because of its preference to a standard of values of which they did not seem to have heard.

At last I left the Princes Highway, and roared up the hill, where my grandfather eighty years earlier had driven his four-in-hand and blown his coaching horn. I passed the smart new gate of Burns the dairy farmer, and came to my own, which was removed from its posts, one of which was knocked askew, while the gate itself, old and weather-stained, leaned against the stump of a fallen tree. At this height I was above the rain and I could see only too clearly, as I bumped up the stony drive, the general disorder of this property which I had inherited from Dominic a year ago, and which it would take at least another two years to put straight. The naked white branches of the gum trees, broken and hanging at strange cubist angles, were illuminated eerily by the headlights, while tangles of blackberries and fallen fencing made my back ache at the thought that even if I could find labourers, the heaviest and dirtiest jobs would still be left to me.

I drove through the tall brick gateposts, from which the gates made by my father had also gone, into the stable yard, and left the car in the dilapidated coach house. My labrador retriever raced from the house, like a lion roaring after its prey, and leapt against me with such force that my foot slipped on a cobble and I fell over. He was delighted to find me prone at his mercy. He put his foot on my shirtfront and joyfully licked my ear. I put my arm round the soft golden neck of this noble and beautiful creature, partly to lift myself up, but also to embrace him, for nowadays when we are hardened to endure so many evil things, the sight of the innocent melts and disarms us. My dog seemed to me a higher order of creation than the fashionable doctor, or than the smart lady who sniggered at the tale of Dominic delirious, and wandering lost in the back passages of a hospital. With the superb integrity of animals he decided his demonstration was adequate, and drew away until I stood up, when proudly waving the banner of his tail, he led me into the house.

In the lobby by the side-door I found Julian Byngham, one of my young cousins, who is a painter.

'Hullo, Julian,' I said. 'When did you arrive?'

He said that he had come up after dinner, and was just leaving. This was a polite fiction, to provoke an invitation to stay, which I gave, though I knew that it was almost certain that Mrs Briar had insisted on his staying and that his pyjamas were already laid out on the bed. His family are like that. Words have little relation to reality. It was even possible that Mrs Briar had given him dinner, and that he had drunk the rest of the liqueur brandy which I was keeping for a bishop who was coming up to luncheon the next day. But it was probably true that he had arrived after the dinner hour, and only speculating on a meal, and therefore from a vague delicacy wished me to understand that he had not deliberately dined in my house in my absence.

'I'm sorry I'm so late,' I said, becoming affected by this polite, quasi-Chinese divorce from reality, as there was no need for me to apologise, seeing that I had no idea that Julian would be here, 'but I've been to a dreary dinner party. At least it wasn't dreary, as it was very well done and everyone was very nice except a doctor who said a frightful thing about Dominic.'

'What did he say?' asked Julian.

'I won't tell you, as you wouldn't believe it. I might tell you my reply, as it seemed to shock everyone, more than what the doctor said, and you can tell me if you think it in very bad taste.'

'But I shan't be able to judge unless I know what the doctor said,' Julian objected.

'Well you must promise to believe me if I tell you. It is extremely improbable.' He promised and I went on. 'They were talking about good-looking men, and a Mrs Vane, who did not seem to know about Dominic's last years, or even that he was dead, said that he looked very distinguished. He had, you know, a kind of El Greco gloom about him and obviously "une hérédité très chargée". The doctor burst out laughing and exclaimed: "Distinguished! He looked very distinguished when I met him in the hospital, a hundred yards from his room and carrying an armful of bed-pans. He thought he was helping the nurses. Distinguished!" and he laughed again.'

4

'And what did you say?' asked Julian.

'I said, sounding I hope as cold as death: "He doubtless thought that he was St. Simon of Cyrene, helping our Lord to carry the Cross."'

'Didn't they like it?'

'No. I feel that I've blotted my copy-book.'

'It doesn't matter,' said Julian, and he turned to some pictures he had been examining when I came in.

'Who painted these?' he asked.

'Arthur Langton,' I told him. 'They're not very good. I only hung them there out of piety, using the word in the Roman sense. I found them out in the stables.'

'Who is this man in the pink coat?'

I was a little startled. The hungry generations had at last trodden into oblivion my grandfather, whose forceful and highly-coloured personality, even after his death had dominated the scenes of my earliest childhood.

'Your great-grandfather,' I said.

'He looks very important, but not quite at ease with himself.'

I was more startled. If when I was Julian's age I had spoken of my grandfather in that detached and critical tone, my father, easygoing as he was, would have been angry. It is disconcerting to find a younger generation assuming, with justifiable impunity, critical privileges which were not allowed to oneself. My grandfather Langton died when I was about six. For fifty years his image had remained immense in my mind, but fading, like those gods of whom Aldous Huxley writes, who have actual existence, but who die when men no longer worship them. At Julian's remark the faint balloon-like ghost of my grandfather suddenly shrank to its proper size in history. With the collapse of the bubble, I felt that I began to see him as he really was, and that in his shrunken image I began to perceive the nature of the treasures and calamities he had left us. But I was still shocked at Julian's unawareness of his identity.

'Creation only comes from an inner tension,' I said, 'and in a way he lived creatively. He tried to make his outer things accord with those which were within. The difficulty was that he was not sure what was within.'

'Is this his wife?' asked Julian, turning to the portrait of my grandmother. 'She has a good face, kind and strong.'

'She was very kind, and she certainly was not weak-minded. I should think that she was not at all an easy person to lie to.'

'You wouldn't think she was his wife,' said Julian. 'Their faces don't seem related to each other.'

Again I felt like a fundamentalist listening to higher criticism.

'I have an idea that she didn't lead a very happy life,' I said. I was so used to this portrait, having known it since my earliest childhood, that I had not given it close attention. I saw now how clearly it revealed those qualities which I had remembered in, or heard attributed to, my grandmother. Her sense of justice and her kindness were shown in the broad forehead, the gentle, well-placed eyes, and the firm but pleasure-loving mouth. 'She not only had to endure her husband's eccentricities,' I went on, 'but to act as banker to the whole family. She was rather like Baron Corvo's onion woman.'

6

'Who was she?'

'A woman who had lived a life of unrelieved wickedness, except that once she gave an onion to a beggar. She died and went to Hell. As the mercy of God is infinite, an angel let down an onion and told the woman in torment to grab it, which she did, and was pulled up towards Heaven. But a lot of other damned souls hung on to her skirts. This is the only part that is applicable to Grannie. She always had this weight on her skirts. The onion woman kicked them off, so the angel let go of the onion and they all flopped back into Hell. But Grannie never kicked them off, and it's the remains of her fortune, divided up, that still keeps us more or less out of the gutter. Her life might make a novel.'

'Why don't you write it?' suggested Julian.

'Make a novel about the sorrows of my grandmother!' I exclaimed. 'It wouldn't be decent.'

'How long has she been dead?'

'About fifty years.'

'If you can't write freely about someone who has been dead for fifty years, you can never write the truth at all,' declared Julian. 'Fifty years is just the right distance. It's near enough to know what they were like, and far enough off not to hurt anyone by what you say.'

'I should be cut by everyone.'

'By whom? By the people you dined with tonight?'

'One has to know somebody,' I replied. 'It's no use sitting down in the Australian bush and waiting for a beautiful genius with perfect manners to come along. Anyhow the people I dined with tonight are quite nice. I've never known them be unkind to anyone, unless of course he had no money.'

Julian was not to be side-tracked. 'It's better to write a good book,' he said, 'than to know a lot of rich people.'

'Of course it is,' I agreed. 'But it is not only a question of knowing rich people. One has other friends, people like Aunt Maysie, who may hold the old-fashioned views of their generation—one can't expect them not to—but who are kind good honourable people. I don't want to offend them. Suppose that I went to Aunt Maysie and said to her: I want to write a book about Grannie. If it is to be truthful, either literally or artistically, I may have to put in it things which you will think unpardonable. But please don't mind. If we are to have any writing that is worthwhile we must ignore these objections. Surely it is better to be held up even to ridicule, and be crystallised eternally in a work of art, than just to keep your skeleton respectably in a cupboard? What would Aunt Maysie say?'

'If she's any sense, she'd say go ahead.'

'And then supposing I sacrificed all my friends and the book didn't turn out to be a work of art after all?'

'You have to take risks,' said Julian, and turned again to the portrait of my grandfather. 'At a first glance you would think that a brutal arrogant face, a sort of Prussian general, but when you look into it you see that it's really sensitive, with an almost guilty look. I'm sure he's the subject for a novel.'

'I'll leave it to you then,' I said, 'as you feel the inspiration.'

'I'm not a writer.'

'Everyone can write one book. At least, so they say.'

All this time Dudley, the labrador, had his nose pressed against the door into the passage, while he looked at me sideways with an affectation of pathos.

'Let us get something to drink,' I said, and opened the door. Dudley, waving his tail, trotted before us into the dining-room. It was as I had thought. There was half an inch of brandy left in the decanter, and the pineapple had been cut. Julian, though he stood with me at the sideboard, was not at all embarrassed, but he seemed satisfied when I offered him only lemon squash. I had had enough alcohol for that evening, and so, judging by the decanters, had he. We took our drinks and some biscuits and went into the little drawing-room.

'This is a lovely room,' said Julian, and my annoyance about the brandy evaporated, as I had painted the walls myself. They were pale grey, with ivory rococo panels. Compared with Julian's own painting they were trivial, which made his praise more welcome. There was nothing here later than 1780, and in the soft light from the chandelier its beauty was a little deathly, the grey walls only relieved by the velvet and satin in bewigged portraits, and the rusty pink and pale gold of the aubusson carpet, on which Dudley now sat, dribbling horribly at the biscuits, but looking as if the whole room had been designed only as a setting for his golden coat. Julian pointed this out, and Dudley, at the mention of his name, put his wet chin on my knee. I lifted his brown plush ear and stroked it.

Julian looked about him, at the smug faces on the wall, whose blood was mingled in his own, at the stylised decorations, and he smiled faintly, a little amused, a little mystified at the almost surrealist incongruity of this room, set down in the midst of a derelict garden in the Australian bush. I began the restoration of Westhill with the inside of the house, so that I could continue operations from a base of comfort and order. Now at night, with the curtains drawn, we might have been in a room in an English manor house, or a French *gentilhommière*. Julian's smile was his response to the atmosphere of the past, of which this was his first experience, as he had never been out of Australia.

'You could bring this house into the novel, too,' he said. 'They lived here, didn't they?'

'Yes, but apart from everything else, I don't know enough about them.'

'You saw them when you were quite young. If you set your adult experience to work on your youthful memory, you would know what they were like. Or if you looked at those portraits long enough you could imagine it. Besides, there must be other things, photographs and letters and things, poked away in old cupboards?'

'I might possibly find some in the laundry,' I said. 'Dominic seems to have amused himself by scattering his penates in the outhouses. Actually there is some material of the sort you mention. Yesterday I found a uniform case in the harness room. It was full of old parchments, some seventeenth century, one from the Herald's College, and with them were my grandmother's diaries almost complete from her marriage to her death.'

'There you have the whole thing!' exclaimed Julian.

'They tell nothing exciting. I glanced at them. The entries are mostly things like "Hetty came to luncheon. Mildred wore her new dress, a rather ugly blue". Even if there are other things I couldn't possibly use them. I should have to leave this place which I have sweated to bring back to life, and return to England, or to France or Italy. And yet that is what I've always longed for, the literary freedom of the outcast—to be like Verlaine or somebody who did not have to worry when he sat down to write, whether he would offend Aunt Maysie, or whether it would lose him an invitation from Mrs Vane. It would be a profound satisfaction not to bother about this any more, but to write exactly what one believed to be true about the things one knew best. I suppose that is what I know about best, all the events and influences of the last eighty years which have made us what we are and which culminated in this house in Dominic's final rack of mental anguish. It's what I said to you just now. Everyone can write one book. This would be my one real book. I'd go on writing it till I die.'

In spite of myself I was taken with the idea.

'It would be wrong not to do it,' said Julian.

'Your idea of right and wrong is not the same as Aunt Maysie's,' I said, 'although, changing the meaning of the word a little, you are more Right than she is. I am supposed to be extremely snobbish, even in Melbourne, the most snobbish place on earth. The reason is that my snobbery is of a different kind. It is not concerned with the horizontal divisions of society, but with the vertical, which is down the middle, "*per pale*" as the Heralds say on that document in the harness room. At the top on the Right is the duke, and at the top on the Left is the international financier. At the bottom on the Right is the peasant—on the Left the factory worker. On the Right between the duke and the peasant are all kinds of landowners and farmers, all artists and craftsmen, soldiers, sailors, clergymen and musicians. On the Left side are business men, stockbrokers, bankers, exporters, all men whose sole reason for working is to make money, and also mechanics and aviators. We on the Right cannot make money. When we have it, it has only come to us as an accident following on our work, or from luck. There are those whose place is on the right of the *pale* but who express the ideas of the Left. They are traitors. They imagine that by breaking down the pale, giving that word a slightly double meaning, they are releasing humanity into wider fields, when in reality they are letting in the beasts of the jungle. One could enlarge on this, explaining how doctors are on the Right of the *pale* because they put their work before money, but near the Left because of their materialistic conception of life. Lawyers are on the Right because of their concern with justice, but near the Left because they serve business interests. Scientists are not concerned with money, but they are the supreme servants of the Left. In satisfying their vicious curiosity they are prepared to deny all we know of good, and even to destroy the world. This division *per pale* is also not unrelated to the political division between Right and Left, but do not imagine that the big business Tories who have wrecked Europe are on the Right. It also has some connection with the heraldic term "sinister" for the Left side of the shield. Again, if you are clumsy in spirit you are *gauche*. Even at the Last Judgment the division is *per pale*, and those at the Left Hand of God are plunged into Hell. There is also I believe a term in boxing—the dirty Left.

'This is not really true, of course,' I went on, 'but one must talk a great deal of nonsense to arrive at a little truth. If you go mining, you must dig up a great deal of quartz to find a little gold. If you only dig as much quartz as you want gold, you will have hardly any gold at all.'

'I've always thought the Left was right,' said Julian. He was smiling but a little truculent.

'Nonsense,' I said. 'You don't believe it at all. If you did you couldn't paint as you do. Your painting would damn you at once if the Communists had power. It's traditional, rooted in nature, Catholic, it breathes the inescapable sorrows of the human race. It denies flatly that science can cure the soul of man. Otherwise how could I have asked you to decorate a room in this house?'

'You're trying to get away from the novel.'

'Not at all. What I have been saying has to do with it. All these people you want me to write about were far on the right side of the *pale*. One must understand what that means before you can understand them. I might write this book, and let all the skeletons come tumbling out of the cupboards, but allow only you to read it. Then you would bear our curse in your heart, like that Scottish family whose eldest son never smiles after his twenty-first birthday.'

'What curse?' asked Julian.

'Doesn't it appear to you that we are cursed? I don't know where it comes from, probably the duque de Teba.'

'Who was he?'

'You haven't heard of him? Then I'd better not tell you.'

'I promise not to believe you,' said Julian smiling.

'Then what's the use of telling you? By the way, the patterns have come for the chapel. You might as well choose them now, or at any rate see what they look like at night.'

I pulled open a drawer and took out some squares of

13

gold and soft red damask and brocade, and we went to that room which always filled me with such great depression that I was turning it into a chapel, in the same way that the Church of S. Maria del Popolo in Rome was built over the tomb of Nero, to scatter the devils gathered there. My mind automatically went to the chapel on the mention of the duque de Teba.

In that room all flippancy left me, and I was subject to the heavy influences of the place, though these were not so great since Julian had done his murals. I looked first at the huge crucifixion painted by Dominic, the tortured body, the face hidden by hanging hair, the conspicuous genitals. It was not a thing that could properly be shown, except perhaps to Carthusian monks on Good Friday, and yet I could not bring myself to paint it out. Dominic must have been a kind of throwback to that Spanish forbear of whom I had not yet told Julian. With his *anima naturaliter Catholica*, but brought up in dreary low-church Anglicanism, he had painted as it were on the cross formed by his inner desire and his habit of mind, this terrible figure. Apparently he had used this room as an oratory. When I arrived there was no furniture in it beyond a hard wooden chair and a Bible. I could not use it for any other purpose with that painting on the wall. Julian also had something dark in his imagination, probably derived from the same source, though in him the Spanish passion was blended with both German brutality and the Langtons' weeping tenderness of heart, which gave his work a sombre beauty. I thought that he would be able to paint murals round the entire chapel which would incorp- orate the crucifixion and so make it appear less starkly horrifying. He did the other walls splendidly, but when he came to Dominic's painting, and tried to think of some way of relating his own to it, he admitted himself beaten, so we decided to frame it off in a separate panel, in a large empty eighteenth-century frame which I had found in the stables, and to have it normally covered with a damask curtain. It was for him to choose a colour related to his murals that I had brought in these squares of stuff. Before considering them our eyes turned automatically to Dominic's painting.

'It is pure duque de Teba,' I said. 'So is yours. Those murals could only be painted by someone whose ancestors had looked into hell.'

'Well, really . . .' protested Julian.

'It's the highest praise I could give you. All I mean is that in your blood is the awareness of evil combined with an obsession with the good.'

'And does it come from this thingummy Teba?'

'It's more likely to have come from him than anyone else.'

'But who was he?'

'He was my mother's and your father's direct ancestor. When his wife died he had himself ordained priest, but he was executed for strangling his altar-boys after Mass in the cellars of his castle in Aragon.'

Julian looked at me incredulously.

'It's just quartz,' he said. 'You're making it up.'

'Unfortunately I'm not. His two daughters went to England to escape the scandal, and one married beneath her a Suffolk squire with nine thousand acres, and the other an Irishman named O'Hara. The squire's daughter married beneath her a naval officer called Masterman. Her daughter married beneath her your great-grandfather, Captain Byngham, the nephew of an Irish viscount. Her daughter married beneath her Steven Langton, my father. Because of the duque de Teba they had this habit of mind, that they were always marrying beneath them.'

The wine I had drunk at the dinner party was having a delayed action. Apart from my retort to the doctor I had not been able to give voice to any of the conceits which occurred to me, and was so occupied in making up for this, that I did not at first notice the effect my disclosures had on Julian.

'They were proud of being descended from a monster like that,' he cried. 'They must have been mad.' He glanced at his hands and then looked away with almost a shudder. I was surprised, as when this particular skeleton had been unveiled to myself and my brothers, we had been more amused than shocked, except Dominic. Neither Bobby nor Brian nor I had much taint in our blood from the ogre. Whatever vices we may have had, cruelty was not one of them. We were incapable of deliberately and in cold blood inflicting pain, and so this hideous tale only seemed a fantastic legend to us, like one of Grimm's fairy tales. But Dominic and Julian had a darker knowledge which was denied us. To them the tale was vivid, and so Julian recoiled from it more violently, even though he was a generation farther away from the wicked duke.

'If you can't be proud of the monster,' I said, 'you can at least be grateful to him. It's your Teba blood that gives you your passionate impulse towards forms of art, that makes you see in the Australian landscape not only sunlight and dreamy distances, but dark forces lurking in the trees. When you feel that creative tingling in the tips of your fingers, you have the same impulse as the duque. He could not create beauty, so he could only release his impulse in destroying it. Then for two or three generations this impulse lay dormant in the blood of Suffolk and Sligo squires. It probably only gave a greater zest to their fighting and foxhunting, until we come to my mother and your father, who both married Langtons. The Langtons are witty, immensely agile in mind, but not creative. They can express ideas with great lucidity, but their ideas are shallow. However, though sterile themselves, they could fertilise the Byngham blood into creative activity. All that vigour, that appreciation of life, that enjoyment of form and movement and colour, which hitherto could only express itself in gallop-ing after foxes, or more experimentally, a stage nearer the blossoming of art, in the murder of altar boys, was by this mercurial infusion released from the state of being into the state of knowing, as if the brain of Zeus, before Pallas Athene could spring from his head, had been fertilised by Hermes. The result was you and Dominic, and even I when young felt faint gusts of this desire to pierce truth to the heart, to see what she was made of, or perhaps myself to be pierced by the eyes of a god. It is this which makes me so tempted by this dangerous idea of writing the truth about all of us, about all I know, not merely putting it in a light which will be acceptable to Aunt Maysie. And if I did it and she read it and didn't like it, she would be unreasonable, for she and all of us in a few years, if our souls survive, must face the truth. In twenty years I shall be dead or dithering. How idiotic to shirk reality for the sake of a few dinner parties!'

Although I was, like a true Langton, especially one who was slightly tipsy, letting fancy control, or rather release, my mind, Julian was looking at me seriously. His pupils were enlarged. Behind him was one of the walls he had painted, the harsh Australian landscape, the branches of the trees blackened with fire, the distant hilltops glistening with dead trunks, and against this background, in the soft deep blues and reds of renaissance clothing, Christ dining *al fresco*, with the publicans. Behind me was Dominic's terrible crucifixion.

Suddenly I felt that I had gone too far, that although I half meant what I said, I had been guilty of the hideous vulgarity of talking facetiously about things that involved great human suffering. I said, completely changing the tone of my voice:

'Really one shouldn't talk about this sort of thing at this time of night.'

'Now you are spoiling yourself,' said Julian.

This gave me a curious sensation, partly of annoyance that anyone as young as Julian should criticise me, partly of satisfaction that he should recognise that I had some basis of seriousness to spoil. I had thought that his generation regarded me as an amiable but obsolete frivolity, like an ornate glass shade to a gas lamp.

'We had better choose the stuff,' I said, and for ten minutes or so one of us held up squares of material against the wall, while the other went to the other side of the room to judge the effect. We did not take long, as it was obvious that a soft old gold damask was the most suitable.

'Oh well, it's bed time,' I said, 'but I don't feel at all sleepy.'

'Why not bring in the diaries,' asked Julian, 'and see what's in them?'

'We can bring them in if you like,' I said. 'The cool air may do us good, but we can't read them tonight.'

I opened the door and disturbed Dudley lying against it. When he saw us going down the passage instead of to bed, he stared after us in consternation, and then followed in silent protest. I picked up an electric torch in the lobby and we went across the stable yard to the harness room, where, lying among some old picture frames and a broken music stand, was the dented black tin uniform case, with my grandfather's name painted on it in large white letters. Julian took one end and I the other, and we carried it indoors.

As we went past the portraits we had discussed and up into the other drawing-room, where the carpet was less fragile, I felt as if we were carrying a coffin, which held not a body, but the ghosts of the past, of those who had so often walked in this passage, of my grandfather who for fun had chased us here with horsewhips, of my grandmother who in the room where we brought our mystical load, had sat writing cheques for her numerous relatives, of Aunt Mildred who, while her parents were in England, had learned here to speak in that flat-vowelled nasal whine which ruined her hopes of marriage, and here too twenty years later, she would stop me if I were eating an apple, and cry with great archness : 'Apples again!' trying in her loneliness to establish, through the repetition of this senseless exclamation, an intimate relationship with a boy of six. Some ancient peoples had a rite, performed in the spring, of 'carrying out death' from their houses. Dominic may have had something of the same idea. The things which he had put out in the stables and the laundry were all those which had to do with the past, particularly the past of our family. He may have been trying, in a desperate, negative and superstitious way, to find new life. He may have been pouring contempt on all his pride. I felt, a little uneasily, that Julian and I were putting the process in reverse.

We dumped the uniform case by the fireplace. I swept off the dust and cobwebs with the hearth-brush, and then opened it. Julian was attracted by the long red leather box, stamped with gold cyphers, from the Heralds' College. He took out the parchment backed with red silk, and unrolled it. It was about twelve feet long and at the bottom was emblazoned the family shield.

'There it is,' I said, '*per pale* argent and sable, divided straight down the middle, white and black, and the black on the left, the sinister, the gauche side, and over it all a cross counter-change. We couldn't have a more suitable or symbolic coat.'

'It looks very mediaeval,' said Julian, 'but it's all too long ago. Are these the diaries?' He lifted out a handful of the books in varying dark shades of Russian leather.

'Yes, but we can't begin to read them now. We might go on till dawn. If it's raining we'll go through them in the morning. I'll play you something to soothe your mind, so that you won't lie awake consumed by curiosity.' I took a record from a book and put it on the gramophone. It was the marvellous Palestrina 'Improperia', the introit to a requiem, sung by the Sistine choir. It startled Julian. He had never heard any music of this kind before. He stared at the gramophone for a moment, and then sat back with his head bowed. I felt that there had been suddenly revealed to him in a different medium, the ancient sorrow of mankind, which he tries to express in his painting. I thought that if Dominic could have heard this music, which actually he may have heard, but not after the age of five, he might have been stirred by the same recognition, and have been helped to resolve his conflict. He might not have thrown out the past, but have interpreted it.

It was odd the effect these sounds had on Dudley. He lay on the floor as if dead, as if he could not bear them, but wished that they might pass above his prostrate body, yet when I played more cheerful and innocent music he would lie on his back with his four legs stretched upwards in delight.

I too was affected. I had brought these records out, like some of the old furniture in this room, to console myself in those moments, when, although this house was my home, I might feel myself in a country that was less my home, not only than England, but than France or Italy. The inevitable click of the gramophone stopping itself brought us all back from Rome to Westhill. Julian wanted to hear some more, but I said I was going to bed and I took him to his room, where as I had expected Mrs Briar had put out his pyjamas before I came home. I said goodnight and went to my own room. Dudley, his patience at last rewarded, flattened out his hindquarters, and with one last wave of his glorious tail, squeezed himself under the bed.

Although it was so late, I could not sleep, and after about half an hour of punching the pillows, and rearranging the sheet round my neck, I sat up in disgust and switched on the light. I thought if I went out and heated myself some milk I might be able to sleep. Instead I went to the drawing-room, collected half a dozen of the diaries, and put them on my bedside table. I imagined they would be fairly soporific.

I moved the lamp and took up the diary for 1892, the year before I was born. My parents and grandparents were then living at Waterpark, our old family home in Somerset. In my grandmother's angular Victorian writing were accounts of the usual mild country activities, with occasional visits to London to buy clothes or to see a play. On 28 March there is an entry:

'Went to the gallery to see Mr Whistler's pictures. They looked very strange at first, but the more I looked at them, the more I liked them.'

On 25 January they went to a meet at Boyton Manor. 'Austin had his horse taken by the groom and drove with Laura, Bobby and me.' There was some writing in French on this page, but it was rather small and I did not bother to read it.

On 5 May: 'Steven and George practising archery. I tried but the bows are too strong. The children picking cowslips. Bobby gave his bunch to me. Austin, Laura and I drove to Warminster in the wagonette. Saw some lime-burners at work on the downs. The smoke very pretty.'

I read on, but this was all I could find. It made a pleasant enough picture, a rather thin watercolour, but was hardly material for a novel. There was one skeleton of which I knew. I had heard of it from Uncle Arthur who had painted the portrait in the lobby, but I doubted that it would be referred to in these pages, where there seemed to be nothing more than a little tepid local colour of the period. I certainly did not want to write a book in which the women were only dummies to hang with crinolines, their feet only something to rest on beadwork stools, and it appeared that poor Grannie could provide nothing more robust.

I picked up the diary for 1893 to read about the day I was born, but the only thing of interest was the fact that my mother ate for luncheon some fish which had been caught by a Russian. This again, no more than Mr Whistler's exhibition, or the meet at Boyton, or the lime-burners' pretty smoke, was the subject for a novel.

I glanced idly through the rest of the book, thinking that now I would be able to go to sleep, when I found that for a whole fortnight in October it was written in French, some of it in very small writing. I took the trouble to read a page or two, and then I could not stop. There were references to events twenty years earlier, and I went back to the uniform case for the diaries of the early eighteen-seventies. At the same time I fetched a magnifying glass, possibly the same one which my grandmother had used for this minute writing, as I had known it from infancy, and like so many of my possessions here, had seen it also on the other side of the world.

In the morning I told Julian that I would try to write the book he wanted.

2

It is said that all mankind looks back to the golden age of Saturn; to most of us the golden age is not so remote. It is more likely to be our own childhood. Perhaps my own was here at Westhill, before at the age of thirteen I was taken to England. And yet the other night when with Julian I walked up the dark passage, carrying the uniform case, it did not seem only to contain the ghosts of the dead from whom we spring, but also the ghost of the living, of the child I was, equal bestower of treasures and calamities. Here I had been brought dripping and covered with leeches after I had bathed in the dam. Here I had suffered measles and chicken pox and had shed my first teeth. Here I had endured at the age of eleven, the pangs of apparently unrequited love for a governess. Here the body of my eldest brother had been carried and laid on his grandmother's bed.

I think then, that the golden age for me must have been before this, the earliest days of the country in which I then lived, Australia, the only place I had known since I left the cradle. There is no country where it is easier to imagine some lost pattern of life, a mythology of vanished gods, than in this, the most ancient of all lands, where the skeletons of trees extend their bleached arms in the sun, and giant lizards cling to their trunks. But my imagination only went back as far as the first European settlers in Victoria. They provided my mythology and I was as closely connected with them as the heroes of Homer with the gods from whom they claimed descent. The gods, too, were my grandparents. I saw them as living always in one of those Australian mornings of the early spring, the mornings of the golden age. Then the leaves of the gum trees hang in the air, so still and pure and fresh that their beauty is completely revealed, without any veil of atmosphere or confusion of movement. In this crystal air the shouts and laughter of the children are as liquid as the falling notes of the magpies in the field. The still morning absorbs all the sounds and turns them into music. The sun is not scorching but sparkles softly on the bridles of the ponies. The mountain ranges are of a blue so peaceful and mysterious that they are an invitation to adventure, and against this sunlit land one would not be surprised to see a frieze of naked Spartans. However, in this scene the first human being I visualise is not a Spartan boy, but the small black figure of Cousin Hetty.

It is not on a spring morning that I see her, but on a winter afternoon in the schoolroom of the deanery, that grey gabled house, something like Kilawly, with the little pseudo-romanesque cathedral, of which her father was dean, on the other side of the garden. It was too wet to go out and the Mayhew children, with their cousins the Langtons and their friend Alice Verso were amusing themselves with historical charades. At the moment Hetty was standing with her back to the fireplace, holding a cardboard crown, and shouting defiantly: 'If I can't be queen, I'll burn the crown.'

This created so much commotion that Mrs Mayhew came up to see what was the matter. All the children explained at once: 'Hetty wants to be queen again.' 'She's been Eleanor with the burghers already.' 'Now she wants to be Queen Elizabeth.' 'It's just because Austin's to be Sir Walter Raleigh.' 'It's Alice's turn to be queen.'

Alice, the only one who was not a relative, stood apart with a faint embarrassed smile.

'You must play some other game,' said Mrs Mayhew. 'There's far too much noise. Hetty, you mayn't have any jam for tea. I'll tell Miss Tripp.'

Hetty, without any preliminary protest or whimper just opened her mouth and roared with rage. Mrs Mayhew shrugged her shoulders and left the room. Austin, smiling with half-brutal good-nature, took the crown from Hetty's hand and jammed it on her head.

'There, you may have it now,' he said. 'It's torn anyhow.'

This is what Arthur Langton, my grandfather's younger brother told me, but, although he was present, he was only eight years old at the time. He was a colourful, though never a very reliable witness, as I shall explain later, but he is almost the only authority I have for these early days, which must therefore remain partly mythological.

Arthur said that when Hetty was seven years old, Austin kissed her under the mistletoe and that she never forgot it. She regarded it as a betrothal and Austin as her private possession. This was understood by everybody all through their childhood and adolescence. The understanding arose simply from Hetty's own grim determination that it should be so. Austin, a good-natured boy, flattered and amused by her attitude towards him, and regarding her as of a different generation—she was four years younger than himself—acquiesced in it. When her brothers wanted to tease her they called her 'Mrs Austin,' but this only provoked an expression of fatuous smugness, like that of a cat which has eaten all the cream. I have seen a daguerrotype of her as a young woman. Her eyes were dark and flashing, her mouth full and voluptuous, and her jaw as square and strong as a sergeant-major's. Though she was not conventionally pretty, even this faded photograph gives an impression of tremendous vitality. In her old age, though she was not genial, she suggested a Buddha or a Gong. Her massive build seemed an affirmation of willpower rather than a result of good-living.

The Langton and the Mayhew children always played together, but when the Langtons were not there, Hetty would go and sit by herself in a remote corner of the garden, meditating on the subject of Austin, her dark eyes glowing with joy in her square, determined face.

Alice also played with these two families. She had her lessons with the Mayhews, but she learnt more from her aunt

Miss Charlotte Verso, who, like her name-sake and contemporary Charlotte Brontë, had once taught in a school in Brussels. Alice's father was the younger son of a Lincolnshire vicar. He had come out to Australia to make his fortune. He bought for a few pounds some blocks of land in Bourke Street and Collins Street, and then died, leaving a widow and one daughter, Alice. At first they were very poor, but the land increased rapidly in value. Mrs Verso was married for her money by an engaging and dissipated young adventurer named Drax, who then discovered that the property had all been left to Alice. Miss Charlotte Verso, hearing in her Lincolnshire vicarage of the rackety household in which her little niece was living, came out to rescue her. The Draxes willingly handed her over—Mrs Drax probably for the child's own sake—and went off to Sydney, where every quarter they squandered Drax's remittance from England in bars and on the racecourse, and then starved till the next instalment arrived. Miss Verso bought a little house in East Melbourne and settled there with Alice.

Arthur said that when Drax was drunk he used to put his wife, who was, I am afraid, my great-grandmother, across the table, lift up her skirts, and beat her with a broom handle, but that she enjoyed it. Because of rumours of this sort of thing, Miss Verso was anxious that Alice should only form the most respectable associations, and although it was unnecessary, as she was a far more competent governess than Miss Tripp, was glad for her to share the lessons and games of the dean's children, and through them of the Langtons, whose father was the Chief Justice. She was also careful, as Alice's income increased, not to make any display of wealth, so that she should not be classed with those dreadful people who had recently made fortunes at the gold diggings, and now drove in fine carriages about the streets of Melbourne, where a few years earlier they had walked as kitchenmaids and pot-boys. The result was that a large part of that income went back to increase the capital.

The state of affairs between Hetty and Austin, of fierce emotional possession on the one hand and kindly tolerance on the other, lasted until he left for Cambridge. It is possible that Austin felt a little more than tolerance for Hetty, as he always liked people who amused him, and although she was quite humourless, she was often very funny. She could imitate the bishop or a bucking pony with equal virtuosity, and the fact that she did not know how funny she was made the other children shriek with laughter.

Austin was indignant when told he was to go to Cambridge. His father said that he must have a gentleman's education. Austin said:

'I've been to the Melbourne Grammar School.'

This astonished Sir William, as he had only sent Austin there from necessity, and hardly considered it a real school.

'You must have what in England will be thought a gentleman's education,' he said.

Austin said that he did not live in England—that he was an Australian.

'What is that?' exclaimed his father contemptuously. 'A convict—a gold digger. You were born in England. It is your home and we shall go there when I retire.' As he looked at Austin, he must have been dismayed to find that although he had been successful, he could not pass on to his son the fruits of his success, as the conditions which had made it possible also made Austin unable to enjoy them properly. This did not prevent his insisting on his leaving for Cambridge.

Before Austin left, his mother gave a farewell party for him. He must have been very upset at the prospect of leaving every friend he had, to go among strangers, even if some of them were relatives, on the other side of the world. Because of this his brothers and cousins would all have been especially dear to him on the night of this party, and perhaps because Hetty made it more obvious than anyone else how much she would miss him, their association was less one-sided than before, and he told her, half as a joke, much in the same tone as he had told her she could have the cardboard crown: 'I'm going to marry you when I come back.'

She was then fourteen and the next morning he had already forgotten that he had said it.

All the relatives went to see him off at the ship. At the last terrible moment of farewell he went round kissing them. When he kissed his mother, Hetty was standing beside her, the tears streaming from her eyes down into the corners of her grimly closed mouth. It was the only time that he had seen her cry without roaring with rage. He was so surprised and touched that he bent and kissed her too. She was the last person he kissed and she gave this enormous significance.

It was nearly four years before Austin returned. I have little idea of what the lives of the Langtons and Mayhews were like during that time. It would be possible to reconstruct it from the accessories, crinolines and beadwork and croquet, but that would not tell us what Hetty and Alice were feeling.

When an English mail ship had arrived, the Langtons and Mayhews would foregather to compare news from home. If Mrs Mayhew went to the Langtons, Hetty managed to go with her. There was not always a letter from Austin as he was not a good correspondent. He did not once in the four years write to Hetty, but twice he sent her a message, and as she was the only Mayhew he mentioned by name, again she gave this great importance.

When Austin returned, his parents were living at Bishopscourt, the blue stone building still standing in East Melbourne, which they had rented for a year, until Sir William went home on leave, after which he thought of retiring, as his health was poor. Because of this he had taken advantage of a good offer to sell his house. Only Austin's father and brothers had gone to meet him at the ship. The rest of the clan were gathered in the Bishopscourt drawing-room. Austin, a little shy at the change in his own physique, but full of boisterous affection, in the midst of his general greetings, catching sight of her exclaimed: 'Hetty!' and kissed her again after a four years interval. She entered this as another item on her small but solid credit balance with him.

A few days later his mother gave an evening party with dancing to welcome him home. Hetty had known for months beforehand of this dance, at which she had arranged to make her debut. She had also formed in her mind for this evening other intentions that were unrelated to any probability. She would dance more dances with Austin than was convention-ally permissible. People would begin to talk about them, saying they were too much together. She would be indifferent to this, would flaunt her daring behaviour, and then at the end of the evening their engagement would be announced, and she would be triumphant, the queen of the party. She had a new dress, folds and folds of white muslin. She wore a crown of white roses on her glossy hair, and an expression of determination on her square glowing face, of which the only beauty was in its vitality, in the texture of her skin, and in her rather too magnificent eyes.

The Mayhews arrived early, and in the role she had designed for herself, Hetty stood beside Lady Langton and Austin at the drawing-room door, where they were greeting their guests. Lady Langton suggested that she joined the other young people, and Mrs Mayhew tried to lead her away, but without success, feeling herself blackmailed by the threat of a scene.

Then Alice was announced. She was a girl of fourteen, reserved and not very noticeable when Austin left. Now she was a young woman and a very pretty one. She was far more agreeable to look at than Hetty. She had not Hetty's splendid Savonarola eyes, which were a rather frightening asset, but neither had she her massive figure nor her grim jaw. Her eyes were grey and level, her hair fair and shining, and her nose straight. The curves of her mouth made charming a face which otherwise might have been a little stern. It was as if Jupiter, who had given her wealth, had bestowed with it other Jovian qualities, a bearing and a look in the eye which would make any liberties dangerous.

Austin always liked the best of everything and naturally assumed that he should have it. It was inevitable that as soon as Alice came into the room, he should have eyes for no one else. Everything about her attracted him, he liked being surprised and she was a great surprise. Her clothes were very good, being made for her in London. He always noticed things like clothes, the harness of horses and carriages. He danced with her as much as possible, and ignorant of the grotesque anticipation seething in Hetty's head, he forced on Alice the role which his cousin had designed for herself.

It is from Arthur that I learnt what I know about this period and it must contain a good deal of conjecture and mythology, but I remember him at the age of seventy or more, standing in a Toorak ballroom, in that brief decade when it was my turn to be a young man, and shrugging his contemptuous shoulders at the jazz and the dancing of 1913, while he described to me this very evening at Bishopscourt, at which he had been present.

'I remember your grandmother then,' he said. 'She was like some shimmering fairy, a sylphide, so modest and so graceful and with such a charming dignity. No one would have dared to touch her as that young man over there is grabbing that young woman who appears to be clad in gold plate, which is doubtless necessary for her protection. I hope he hasn't a tin-opener in his pocket. How different these young people are from those beautiful girls, with their billowing white skirts which swayed as they danced to real music, not to a negroid din.'

'Did Cousin Hetty look like a sylphide too?' I asked, as I knew that Arthur had disliked her.

'She looked more like one than that young woman in armour,' said Arthur gruffly.

Even if Hetty looked like a sylphide, she did not feel like one, for a sylphide which had received such a terrible blow would surely want to fade and die, whereas although she was suffering a pain which was almost physical in its intensity, she by no means contemplated defeat. She was one of those who are quite oblivious of their own attractions or lack of them, and who rely more upon will-power than on love to secure the object of their affections. When this hideous evening, which my great-uncle saw in retrospect as full of graceful girls and roses, came to an end, and Hetty in her wreath and her muslin went out to her parents' carriage, she was less like a sylphide than a nun who is dressed as a bride only to pass to a symbolic death. But, unlike a nun, she had no intention of renouncing anything.

She was tormented by her obsession. The young Langtons and Mayhews met less frequently than when they were school children. How Austin behaved to Hetty at one of these meetings regulated not only her own peace of mind until their next meeting, but that of all her family. If he showed her some cheerful chaffing attention, she was in heaven. If he went out riding as soon as she called with her mother at Bishopscourt, and just nodded a casual goodbye from the door, she was in hell, and when she was in hell she saw to it that the rest of the Mayhews shared her situation. She nursed the instrument of torture which she had created in herself.

This lasted for three months. Whether she was in a state of elation or of gloom from their last encounter, her heart began to beat when she knew that she was to see him again, and she always counted on the next meeting as one that would fix their relationship. Austin had no idea of the effect he was having on her, that his most casual words or absent-minded glances were flinging her from heaven to hell and back again. He was much too occupied with his own affairs and he simply thought of her as a slightly comic moody character. So the situation remained always the same, and she might have spared herself her passionate broodings. She was the only actor in the drama which was played nowhere but in her own agonised heart.

Why Austin behaved in such a secretive fashion is hard to know. He may have been afraid of the disapproval of his elders, or he may simply have enjoyed the fun of hood-winking everybody. It is just conceivable that his love for Alice was so tender that he could not bear it to be assessed by his relatives, or the subject of coarse chaff from his brothers. One day he heard his parents discussing the Versos.

'I should think it would be difficult for Alice to find a good husband,' said Sir William, 'as no decent man would make her an offer unless he had a fortune approaching her own.'

After this Austin was more than ever careful to conceal the amount of time he spent with her. Nearly every day when she had no other engagement she went out riding, attended by a groom. Austin would meet her at an arranged point some way from her house, bribe the groom to go and amuse himself for an hour or so, and he and Alice would ride off alone into the country.

It is also hard to understand how Alice, normally so straightforward and so kind in all her ways, could have acqui-esced in this concealment. Probably she felt uneasy, but could not bear to disagree with Austin, with whom she was in the throes of first love.

Then came that evening from which spring so many of our treasures and calamities, not all of them, not Dominic's nor Julian's which have their origin in the dying cries of the altarboys at Teba. They come later in this story. Our more external destinies were fixed on that evening at Bishopscourt, about which Arthur was extremely eloquent.

3

The Langtons were having a dinner party. By a piece of
luck, perhaps hardly luck seeing that his presence was due
to an integral part of the plot, Arthur was brought down
to fill in the gap made by Austin's unexpected absence.
Otherwise he would have been having high-tea in the
schoolroom, and I could never have met an eye-witness,
not at least later than my childhood. Unfortunately, as I
have said, Arthur was not a reliable witness. He embroidered all his tales beyond recognition, and frequently to
a male audience decorated them further with startling
improprieties. If Arthur had written a novel it could have
been safely given to a girl of twelve for Christmas, but his

conversation was almost too much for me, who had just returned from four years in the trenches of Flanders. Often, after his listeners had enjoyed his wildly improbable account of what had happened, say, to Aunt Mildy in an omnibus, they would demand: 'Now tell us what really happened, without the embroidery.'

If I give his account it will make this more a work of fiction and the reader may himself have the satisfaction of searching for the reality beneath the embroidery, whereas if I attempt to make the separation, I may remove some of the foundation material and so in the long run give a less true account than Arthur's. All history is a little false. It is only fair to remember this when judging the characters in my book. You see them only as they exist in my imagination. To go back to the last chapter, I write of 'the small black figure of Cousin Hetty.' She was not black at all, neither her skin, nor at that age her clothes. I am not even sure that her hair was black, as when I knew her it was grey. It may originally have been bright red but I imagine her as somehow black against the bright landscape. If Dominic had described these characters you would not recognise them. They would all be shown as tormented by their separation from God. If Aunt Mildy had done so, they would be shown as having the sweetest thoughts about sex. I shall try while writing a history which is inevitably a little false, to point out the parts least worthy of belief. They will not, I am afraid, be the most incredible. It is also important to remember that my view of Hetty is through the eyes of Arthur who disliked her, and she may have been far more attractive than I show her.

According to Arthur, and this is most likely true, it was an exceptionally grand dinner party, that is in the choice of guests, and his mother was very annoyed at having to insert a scrubby schoolboy amongst them, instead of her eldest son, fresh from Cambridge. Arthur said that he was at the age when he kept growing out of his clothes, and that there was a gap between his waistcoat and his trousers which caused him miseries of humiliation. The chief guest was some important Englishman who was making a tour of the colonies, and Lady Langton had collected the most presentable people she could find in Melbourne to meet him. They included Captain Byngham, the Military Secretary, and his wife who radiated an air of untouchable nobility, being a great-granddaughter of the monstrous duque de Teba, also the dean, Mrs Mayhew and Hetty. It was the last occasion on which the Langtons would wish for any awkwardness.

I sometimes wonder whether Arthur in describing this dinner, did not mix it up with the dance a few months earlier. The effect must have been the same on Hetty, but more devastating. According to him she had also been looking forward to this dinner party for some time, and building up in her mind another romantic sequence. She was certain that, as the two youngest people present, she and Austin would be sent in together. When instead she found herself next to Arthur, she knew that one of those evenings had begun when clouds of misery enveloped her, though she always refused to admit their existence till she was seated in the carriage on the way home.

'It was the most ghastly dinner party,' said Arthur. 'I was trying to hide the gap between my waistcoat and my trousers with my table-napkin, but it kept slipping onto the floor. Hetty made a conspicuous fool of herself by loudly expressing her anxiety for Austin's safety. "Oh Aunt Emma," she said to Mama every three minutes, "do send a groom to look for Austin. He may have had an accident." Mama had that thin smile which she wore when she was pretending that someone was behaving well, who was really an infernal nuisance. At last Papa said to the table at large: "Austin went out driving this morning. It is tiresome that he's not back in time for dinner, but I know no one for whom there is less need to feel anxiety when he is dealing with horses." I suppose that when one has ordered a number of people to be hanged, it gives a kind of authority to one's voice, and Hetty shut up for the time being. But she was determined to make clear her proprietory interest in Austin. She said to the man on her right: "I'm so worried about him," as if he were already her husband, so that when half an hour later Austin appeared in a very different role, not only did jealousy turn her blood to poison, but she looked a fool—not that this worried her. She never minded how she looked. If she could bring her prey to bed, she wouldn't have cared if she had mutton fat in her hair and a smut on her nose. That's why she always got what she wanted. She went straight for it, regardless of manners or appearances.

'We didn't stay long in the dining-room as Papa's complaint didn't let him drink much. The babble of reunion had just begun when it was silenced by Sparrow, the butler, throwing open the door, not to bring in the tea tray, but to announce, very loud and clear:

' "Mr and Mrs Austin Langton."

'There stood Austin, looking unspeakably smug, with Alice on his arm. Although she was in an unusual situation,' said Arthur emphatically, 'you must understand that your grandmother had great dignity. She was perhaps a little shy, but it was the shyness of a spring flower, which does not detract from its perfect poise. Anyhow there we were, all gaping at them, when Papa said quietly: "Is this a joke, Austin?"

'Austin said, no, it wasn't a joke, and that Alice was his wife. Poor Mama was dividing her swift mind how to carry this off with as little immediate discomfort as possible, to save the wreckage of her elegant dinner party, as in those days the most disastrous family event could not be allowed to embarrass a guest.'

Arthur was as usual, torn between the desire to tell a racy story with the conflicting one to impress upon me the immense superiority of his own generation.

It is thirty years since Arthur told me about this party, and that was sixty years after it had happened. Even so he left a very vivid, if embroidered picture of the evening in my mind, so if I tell it in my own words they will not be very different from his, as we both used the same idiom. According to him, Hetty bellowed in a furious contralto voice, like a cow in pain:

'It *is* a joke!'

The eyes of the guests, almost with one movement, turned from the door to stare with even greater astonishment at Hetty. Her eyes were glowing black. The bones of her face and her square jaw seemed more prominent and masculine than usual, and the wreath of pink roses round her head simply an arbitrary, irrelevant and unconvincing statement of her femininity.

'I should think Austin knows best, Hetty,' said Lady Langton, who had not much sense of humour, though oddly enough her husband, who had a very keen one, might have made exactly the same remark. She turned to Austin and added:

'Perhaps you would explain, dear.'

'We were married this morning,' said Austin, 'and we drove out into the country this afternoon.'

'What a fine way to be married,' cried Hetty, 'with a honeymoon in a ditch!'

Lady Langton ignored her and said: 'This is a considerable surprise to us. I hope you will tell us later why you could not take us into your confidence.'

'He knew you wouldn't let him marry beneath him,' shouted Hetty. 'Everyone knows that her stepfather's a drunkard.'

'She has £4000 a year,' Austin shouted back, while the carefully selected guests gaped, unable to keep up their pretence that this was a normal interlude. This is the part that I do not believe, but I must record it, as it is the only available evidence of an eye-witness. I used to think that Arthur disliked Austin because he was jealous about Alice, with whom he had a close life-long friendship. I found later that his attitude was very different. He concealed an intense loyalty beneath an affectation of malice. He used to say outrageous things which no one would believe about his brother, so that he might be counted as an enemy. Then, when he denied those true facts which were to Austin's discredit, people would say: 'It can't be true, because Arthur denies it, and he would never deny anything against Austin if he could help it.' Anyhow, I do not believe that Austin mentioned Alice's money on this evening. But according to Arthur Sir William said:

'I hope you did not let that influence you.'

'I didn't know of it until an hour ago,' Austin replied.

'He did know. I told him long ago,' cried Hetty.

'Liar!' shouted Austin.

Dean Mayhew flushed at hearing his daughter called a liar, but said: 'It would be wiser, Hetty, if you didn't intervene.'

'To go off and be married like an animal! I could never bring myself to do such a thing!' Hetty spoke with such passion that it was evident there was nothing she would like more. Lady Langton gave her sister a vicious glance as much as to say: 'If you can't control your daughter, for Heaven's sake take her home.'

Mrs Mayhew put her hand on Hetty's arm, at which she burst into tears, not of gentle grief, but the same loud, raging, roaring sobs which she used to bellow forth in the school-room. Fortunately she allowed her mother to lead her away. Alice stood aside from the door to let her pass. She was a good deal shaken by the scene.

Lady Langton came forward and took her by the hand. 'I must now welcome you as a daughter,' she said and kissed her on both cheeks, and then kissed Austin. Sir William shook hands with Alice and put his hand on Austin's shoulder and murmured a wry congratulation. One of his maxims was: 'Never make a fuss unless there is something to be gained by it.' Austin was unlikely to be able to make a habit of eloping with heiresses, so there was little use in showing a deterrent displeasure. Hetty providentially had acted as a scapegoat, drawing the disapproval of the company onto her own head. Now that she was gone, all was gentle and pleasant gaiety, and it seemed quite an agreeable thing for the son of the house to bring home an unexpected bride in the middle of a dinner party. Lady Langton said with a deprecating smile:

'I'm afraid my drawing-room has turned into a vestry.' She led Alice round introducing her to those guests whom she had not already met. Sparrow brought in the tea tray and Lady Langton was just going to tell him to bring two extra cups, when she realised that as Mrs Mayhew and Hetty had left, it would be unnecessary. What the distinguished English visitor thought of it all is not recorded. Incidentally, this butler, Sparrow, cleared out suddenly and went prospecting for gold.

That is the story according to Arthur. If it is not true as to what Hetty said, it is very likely true as to what she felt. Seeing what she did later, it is even possible that she did behave as Arthur said. And so, to change the metaphor back from embroidery to quartz, it seems best to bring up the whole load, from which the gold of truth may be picked to suit individual taste.

It is only fair to give as well Aunt Mildy's account of that party. She was not of course present, but she must have heard about it from people who were.

'It was so sweet, such a touching evening,' she said. 'Papa looked so strong and loving, and Mama so maidenly in a turquoise blue mantle. She was dreadfully shy, but Grand-mama was so sweet to her. It wasn't really a surprise, as everyone knew they were very attached. And it was such a delightful coincidence that there was a dinner party that night, as it made a little impromptu wedding reception. They say that Cousin Hetty was a tiny bit sad, as she had once had loving thoughts of Papa, though of course she was much too well-bred to show it, but she went home as early as she could without its being noticeable. That was the only tiny cloud on an evening which must have reminded everyone of the troubadours. There was such a wonderfully sweet and loving atmosphere. Whenever I go to the Bishopscourt Annual Garden Party, I go into the drawing-room and think of what a very sweet thing happened there on that evening long ago, and I say a tiny prayer.'

Whichever account is true, it is still difficult to understand how Alice could have lent herself to this escapade, and whatever Arthur and Mildred may say, she must have hated this dramatic appearance in the middle of Lady Langton's party, and the exposure of herself as someone who had offended against the conventions. She always had a strong sense of decorum, though she was also very romantic. She had been taught French and some Italian by her aunt, and she was steeped in poetry and picturesque legend. It is possible that she found in stories like *Isabella and the pot of basil*, and in *Romeo and Juliet*, precedents which put her adventure not below but above the conventions of early Colonial society.

Another consideration is that I myself only saw Alice with the eyes of a child, and that was when she was old and stood for all that was impeccably dignified. I have only heard of her early days from people like Arthur, who idealised her. It is possible that when she was young she enjoyed the follies of youth, and enjoyed giving society a slap in the face. After all, under those crinolines, the bodies were the same as under a pair of flannel trousers and a polo sweater. We know little of her father except that he must have had an adventurous spirit and plenty of courage, but Alice also had in her veins the blood of her mother, who at that time was kicking over the traces in Sydney.

Shortly after his marriage Austin was prosecuted for abducting a ward in chancery, or something of that kind. The court was filled with the people who had been at the dinner at Bishopscourt and their intimate friends. Sir William was on the bench, so that it was more like a family party than a legal proceeding. When Austin stood up to make some statement his father said impatiently: 'Sit down, Austin.' Everybody laughed. It was impossible that in this atmosphere anything unpleasant should happen, and Austin, in the carriage of the judge who had tried him, drove home to enjoy his wife and her wealth.

It was more difficult to appease Miss Verso than the Langtons or the law. She felt that Alice and the name of Verso had been treated with disrespect. She would have been very pleased with the match if it had been normally arranged. Austin was a fine-looking young man, and as the eldest son of the Chief Justice was as eligible as any other in Melbourne. But the implication of the elopement was that the marriage was one of which his family would disapprove, and being sensitive on the subject of Alice's mother and stepfather, she attributed their imagined disapproval to this undesirable association. Even when the Langtons welcomed Alice with the greatest affection, she did not become reconciled to the marriage. She did not see that Sir William's only reason for disapproving was that he did not want his son, who already showed too great a love of pleasure, to have his gingerbread so soon and so heavily gilded. It was some months before Miss Verso would see Alice and Austin, except on necessary business. A year later, she returned to England. She refused the allowance offered her by Alice, and lived economically on her own small income, and after two winters she died. My father used to say that it was only the strong streak of conscience we inherited from the Versos that kept us all out of the jails and the lunatic asylums, so it seems that Alice brought us not only money, but enough character to enjoy it without too great a deterioration. My father of course may only have said this to give some credit to his mother's rather broken and tarnished family, which Hetty never ceased to describe as one of drunkards and gamblers.

Austin had conversations with Sir William about his future. He said that he wanted to breed horses and when any comment was made on his idleness, he went off to inspect a site for a stud farm, but he always came back and said that it was unsuitable. He had originally wanted a stud farm so that he could have good horses, as a child might say: 'When I grow up I'm going to have a sweet shop.' Austin could now afford what sweets he wanted without the shop. In the meantime he and Alice were living with his parents at Bishopscourt.

Austin was never an idler, and it is unlikely that he married Alice for her money, or that, as in Arthur's story, he knew of it before the wedding. He must have known she had some money, but Miss Verso's menage gave no indication of wealth. Also Alice was attractive enough to need no bait. When he learned the extent of her income he was frankly more delighted than embarrassed. He was untouched by the nineteenth-century middle-class idea that it is dishonourable to marry a girl with a great deal more money than oneself, though his father apparently believed this. Austin was more like the saintly Alyosha Karamazov, who was indifferent as to who paid for his food and shelter, though he was a quite unconscious parasite, and would not have sponged on anyone who could ill afford it. Also he would not have cared to live with the poor.

Now he was much too interested in revealing to Alice the connection between money and this world's goods to think about burying her and himself in the country. Miss Verso had regarded her niece's growing fortune merely as a mathematical increase in security, not as something that could be converted into horses, fine clothes and carriages. Alice enjoyed this revelation as much as Austin enjoyed making it, and it increased her love and admiration for him. She felt that her security had not lain in Miss Verso's thrift, but was in Austin's capacity to spend.

A few months after their son's marriage, Sir William and Lady Langton prepared to leave for England on a year's furlough, to be followed possibly by retirement if his health did not improve. The children were to remain in Australia in case he did return, and so save the expense of a double journey for them. They were to live with the Mayhews at the deanery.

There are some entries and accounts of conversations in Alice's diaries at this time from which I am able to make up a fairly coherent story. The diaries and Arthur are my two main authorities, but I have heard numerous details of various incidents from different members of the family. From now on, I shall not often interrupt myself to quote my reference, unless there are conflicting accounts.

Meanwhile Hetty was turning the deanery into a miniature inferno, throwing plates at her brothers who teased her, or bursting into paroxysms of sobbing and dashing from the dinner table. Certainly I remember one of the Mayhews, then quite an old man, with a scar across his forehead which was said to be caused by Hetty's throwing a decanter of port at him when he was a boy. Aunt Mildy said that Hetty went into a decline, and stayed all day in her room, reading religious books about love and death, so that her parents became anxious about her health and feared she might develop the wasting disease. Whether it was the desire to rid themselves of a raging wounded tigress, or anxiety to save a wilting snowdrop, it is true that they asked the Langtons if they would take charge of Hetty on the ship, if they sent her to England for a change. They must have been very anxious to be rid of her, as the expense of this trip deprived their eldest boy of a university education.

Alice and Austin, who had been out shopping, came in just as Lady Langton had written to Mrs Mayhew agreeing to chaperone Hetty to England. She told them what she had done.

'Oh, I would love to go to England,' exclaimed Alice. Austin said that there was no reason why she should not.

'But what about the stud farm?' asked Lady Langton.

'I can't deprive Alice of the sort of life she's entitled to,' said Austin.

'Then dear, you might choose an occupation which doesn't conflict with that life,' suggested his mother.

'I could read for the Bar, I suppose,' said Austin doubtfully. 'That's what Papa has always wanted me to do.'

'It would please him very much if you did.'

'Then you won't object to my taking Alice home?'

'As long as it isn't Alice taking you home,' said Lady Langton.

Alice had the uncomfortable feeling that they were going to talk about her money, and she went up to take off her bonnet, so the rest of the conversation is lost, but apparently, there was a good deal of discussion among the Langtons as to whether it was advisable for Alice to go on the same ship with Hetty, who had taken such a violent dislike to her.

'It's not Alice,' said Austin. 'I'm the one Hetty doesn't like, and I can take care of myself.'

To Lady Langton's surprise, her husband welcomed the idea of the young people coming to England with him. He was tired, had become indifferent to ambition, either for himself or his son, and he was depressed at the prospect of parting from all his children for a year. Mrs Mayhew, when she heard that Alice and Austin were going, went with trepidation to warn Hetty, but Hetty said nothing and appeared more satisfied than otherwise.

The fact that Hetty was allowed to travel with the Langtons rather discredits Arthur's account of the Bishopscourt dinner party, for if she had revealed her passion for Austin with such devouring rage, surely no one in their senses would have let her accompany him and his wife on what was almost a honeymoon. It is hard to explain, but then if we look at history we find it full of far worse idiocies on a far greater scale. We must accept that people do behave idiotically, and that this was one of those occasions.

4

Arthur was not a very consistent character. When he was quite sober and had been listening to the music of Brahms, he would speak gravely of his own generation as the noblest creatures ever made, with an implication of contempt for the weedy moderns born after 1870. The women were sylphides, and the men models of whiskered chivalry, a kind of cross between Mr Gladstone and Sir Philip Sidney. But after dinner, when he had taken enough wine to dissolve his always slight sense of propriety, and he wanted to make a young guest laugh, nothing delighted him more than to strip off the crinolines and the moss roses, the peg-top trousers and every rag that gave a semblance of decency to the family skeletons. It is not possible to print, even today, all the things that he said about Hetty on the ship—though thirty years ago, he denounced modern novels as too disgusting for any decent man to read. He had not the same standards for the written and the spoken word. It was on one of those evenings when he had drunk most of a bottle of burgundy that he told me about this voyage. The worst things he said have to do with a later part of this story, where they will be in due course disclosed. At present, I shall give his more general description.

'She didn't care a damn,' he said, 'about leaving her family. Everyone else was weeping bucketfuls. It was like a funeral to see one's parents go off on a dangerous voyage, and know that they had to do it twice before one saw them again. You people who go home as safe as houses in a liner, don't know what your grandparents had to endure, or what courage they showed.' His voice took on a sonorous and sacred note, and I was afraid that he was going to switch off onto sylphides and splendid pioneers, but the burgundy won. His noble expression faded, a gleam of savage delight came into his eye and he exclaimed:

'I don't believe that woman had a bit of decent feeling in her whole bloody body. She had appetites, and because they were as strong as a bull's, she thought she was a heroine of romance—a kind of Colonial Sappho. Her heart was as cold as a bit of pig's liver, left out on a marble slab on a frosty night. Mama told me that she had a devil of a time with her on the ship. She walked up and down waggling her behind at the sailors, advertising the fact that she was the only young virgin on board, like Orberosia in *Penguin Island*. It's always people whose virginity is entirely valueless who seem to treasure it most. Not that Hetty treasured hers, of course.'

'But behinds wouldn't show under those crinoline dresses,' I objected.

'That wouldn't stop her waggling it,' said Arthur. 'Unfortunately she wasn't seasick. She stood by the gunwale in a stiff breeze and imagined herself to be some sort of splendid sea queen, riding the storm, and I've no doubt that she had a damned silly smug expression. The sea went to her head. She met Percy Dell on that voyage. At first she wouldn't look at him. She liked men large and vigorous and he was a miserable worm. He was never a real husband to Hetty, but like that piece of jelly, protoplasm or something which I believe some primeval animals had in place of the male sex. Then, a few weeks before they landed, she turned all her batteries on him—literally took him by assault. It must have been terrifying for the poor devil, though he always was very fond of her.' Arthur paused and looked at me suspiciously. 'D'you know about that?' he asked.

'No,' I said, trying to make my voice sound indifferent.

'H'm.' He was evidently considering whether to tell me more. The gleam in his eye showed that he was itching to make some monstrous final disclosure, when the telephone rang.

'Answer it, will you, my dear boy?' he said, a little irritated at the interruption.

I went out into the hall, picked up the receiver and heard the stern throaty voice of an elderly gentlewoman asking to speak to Mr Arthur Langton.

'He's at dinner,' I said. 'Could I give a message?'

'Who is that?' she demanded testily.

'It's Guy Langton.'

'Oh, Guy!' The voice sounded deep and kind and old. 'This is Cousin Hetty. Would you ask Uncle Arthur if he will come to luncheon with me at the Alexandra Club on Thursday to meet Mrs Sprigge?'

I felt awful, as if I had been caught taking part in some shameful indulgence. Cousin Hetty was vivid before me in her black taffetas and her black bonnet relieved as always with a jaunty tuft of four white feathers. There were jokes made about the feathers. She was never without them, and when one tuft became shabby, she had another made, exactly the same. Everyone knew they had some meaning, but no one knew what. It could not be that of Mr Mason's novel, as whatever doubts people may have had about Cousin Hetty, no one questioned her courage. It was said that the feathers stood for her sons, four feathers in her cap. But she had five sons.

Now, I was only aware of her as an object of great respect, with the impressiveness of a slightly shrunken Mussolini, someone who without much money and by sheer willpower, had made herself of social importance in Melbourne. And I had just been laughing about her virtue and her anatomy, and she must have been nearly eighty. I had the same dreadful sensations as when a fat middle-aged woman standing in front of me on the beach at Lavandou, began to undress with a modesty which only had regard to those whom she could see. I went back to the dining-room and said in a sickly voice:

'Cousin Hetty wants you to lunch on Thursday at the Alexandra Club to meet someone called Sprigge.'

Arthur was even more upset than I was. His old resentment and his pleasure in malice had surged up, making him forget that the person he was 'throwing to the wolves' as he called it, was someone whom he now, as the result of life-long association, though much of it was hostile, thought of in his sober moments, as a close friend. He was also ashamed and angry that he had betrayed one of his own superior generation, one of the sylphides, though the least graceful, to a miserable modern weakling. He dropped the nut-crackers on the floor.

'Very well,' he said.

'Thank you very much. He'd like to, Cousin Hetty,' I said into the telephone.

'And how is your dear mother?'

'Very well thank you, Cousin Hetty.'

'Is she in Melbourne?'

'No. She's up at Westhill, Cousin Hetty.'

'Well, goodnight. Tell Uncle Arthur one o'clock on Thursday.'

'Yes. Goodnight, Cousin Hetty.' I was like a schoolboy who tries to placate a master by frequent 'sirs.'

I sat down again at the dinner table and from embarrassment gave a vulgar snigger, which I detested even as I uttered it. Arthur ignored it. All the lively malice had gone from his eyes. The lids were heavy and he looked very high-minded.

'Your poor grandmother,' he said, 'was unwell for the whole voyage, which lasted sixteen weeks, as they were becalmed off Nigeria. She was expecting her first child, and although she travelled so much during her life, the sea never agreed with her.'

He could not change the subject immediately. That would be an admission before a young man, which he would never make, that he had behaved badly. He was trying to reinstate himself in his own good opinion by continuing the same subject from a lofty angle. He talked about his father's illness and his mother's patience. The ship in his imagination was at once converted from a nautical brothel into a kind of *Mayflower* full of grave and reverend pilgrims. We both found it less entertaining under this aspect, but I knew it was hopeless to expect him to return to his former mood tonight, and we moved into the drawing-room. Here Arthur lighted a little lamp behind a miniature of Alice painted on glass, or in some way transferred to it.

'Your grandmother,' he said, excusing this ceremony, 'was a saint, but a saint who loved the world, the only true kind.'

He sat down at the piano and played Brahms's cradle song. After that he sat still for a minute or two, his right hand with its huge signet ring resting on the keys. His face was immensely sad and noble. Then softly he began to play a little Chopin prelude which I knew well. He had once told me that it was Alice's favourite melody, but he did not play it often for fear of deadening his response. As he played I felt dreadfully sorry for all these old people, and tried to imagine how I would feel if I were seventy-seven, and the only one of my generation left was a cousin whom at the moment I cannot stand, but with whom I would be compelled to associate as she would be the only evidence that I had lived.

But after all, this embarrassing evening was thirty years ago. If Hetty were alive today, she would be about one hundred and eight. Seeing that she has become all dust and flowers, surely it is permissible now to refer to any part of her anatomy. Part of her may be the daphne in the garden, or Dudley's silken ear.

I had to dine several times with Arthur before I could lead him back, by silences and suggestions, to the subject of the voyage. As I have stated, much of it was unprintable, and the rest will not be relevant till later, but I may give here his description of Percy Dell.

'Percy,' he said, 'was one of those unfortunate creatures to whom the Almighty has granted no other sign of manhood than a large Adam's apple. He was five foot four and I must say I am very glad that I never saw him with his clothes off. He would have compared very unfavourably with the Hermes of Praxiteles. Your grandfather used to declare that he was what Casanova called *uno bello castrato*, but it is difficult to see how this could have been so, as Austin was compelled to admit. Percy the Protoplasm is a more accurate description. He was very anxious to appear important and was always exercising himself in great matters which were too high for him. He would make sententious criticisms of political speeches. He mouthed his words and dragged down his wretched little chin and said things like "I am of the opinion that it is a most imprudent utterance." Hetty's full-blooded rampaging vigour drew him like a white moth to a furnace, but she couldn't stand him. At least that's how it looked. When she stood posturing as a sea queen and felt his watery pink eyes fixed on her, she would toss her head

(Arthur here inserted a piece of pure embroidery):

'Papa used to say—"I wish to goodness Hetty would stop tossing her head, she's not a pony." Then just before the end of the voyage she did stop. She turned and snatched up her piece of protoplasm. She went round telling everyone that Mr Dell was so refined, such a gentleman, though for the past two months she had been saying that he couldn't possibly be a gentleman as his family neither owned land nor was distinguished in the church. Actually he was a solicitor, the son of a solicitor, very respectable people in Dorking or somewhere. He had a little money and had gone out to Melbourne thinking the climate would suit him, but he found the life too rough.'

The events of the following year were much talked about in the family. I have always been acquainted with them and the diaries have freshened up my memory. They all disembarked at Plymouth. A Reverend Frederick Mayhew, an uncle of Hetty's, met them at the ship, to conduct her to his house at Datchet, where she was to stay. The four Langtons were to rest at Waterpark for a few days, before going on to London. They parted from Hetty and Mr Mayhew at Frome. Mr Dell also was in the train.

Waterpark, where the Langtons lived for many centuries, is four miles from Frome. Our Australian relatives who have never been there are apt to speak of it as if it were one of the great houses of England, but it is only a modest manor, though a very pleasant one. I may think this because I spent the happiest years of my life there, probably happier than my childhood here at Westhill, where I felt the countryside to be large and frightening with so much dead timber, with snakes and scorpions, with magpies which snapped their beaks like a pistol shot close to one's ear when they were hatching their young. Sometimes in the summer to go out of doors was like entering a vast scorching oven, and I felt my head would burst. The doctor said we all had thin skulls, particularly my eldest brother Bobby.

Waterpark on the other hand is, or was, embowered in elms and horse chestnuts. No scorching winds came near its lawns. It was deep-meadowed and happy. It did not display its dignity to the world but only to its own garden. One drove there through steep-banked Somerset lanes, and the first sign of it was a simple white gate, with a notice: 'Wheels to Waterpark House only' meaning there was a right-of-way for pedestrians. Beyond the gate was a short avenue, in summer a green tunnel under the chestnuts, and at the end on the left was a door in a high wall. Above this carved in stone, was a shield, chipped and stained and covered with lichen. One could hardly see that it was *party per pale.* By the door was an iron bell-pull, but when it was rung and answered, one came, not into the house, but only onto a stone path which led to the front door. The lawn stretched across to a stream, and beside it were three oak trees. Across the stream were meadows full of buttercups, which shed their golden dust into the seams of one's shoes. Phrases from Tennyson crowd in my mind when I think of Waterpark. It was the land where it was always afternoon. How far away they seem, those summer holidays, when we played tennis with the Tunstall boys, and had tea under the tree by the stream. How irre-coverable, not because I was young then and cannot be young again. One would not mind that if there were other young people, Julian or his children, playing on those lawns. But the life is gone. This was finally brought home to me on the morning after my arrival here a year ago. There our old kind butler and the fresh-cheeked footman brought out the silver trays. Here the cook I had before Mrs Briar, wearing an old dressing gown and with a row of black glossy ringlets round her forehead, which recalled one of King Charles II's mistresses, handed me a cup of tea slopped over into the saucer, and explained: 'The bloody kettle took an hour to boil.'

It was hard to say where the original house at Waterpark began. The cellars were supposed to be Saxon. The red brick facade to the garden was Queen Anne, the latest and largest of a series of small additions and alterations which had been going on for hundreds of years. From this front one went into a square hall with good panelled rooms on either side, but behind them was an extraordinary conglomeration, a maze with steps every few yards, with some rooms six feet high and others going up into the raftered roof, and the stone-floored larders smelling like a church. The bathrooms were large with fireplaces. In the drawing-room, the panelling was painted white and decorated with gilded carving, but the furniture was less formal than the decorations, with comfortable chintz sofas, though there were also old looking-glasses and walnut chests. This room faced west, and gave most the impression of eternal afternoon.

Waterpark was the magnet which drew my family back at intervals across the world, whisking them away just as they might have been thrusting their roots fruitfully into Australian soil. This distraction went on for four generations.

With Julian at last the umbilical cord is cut. Not only were the family themselves whisked backwards and forwards—to Westhill when they felt the cold, to Waterpark when they felt the heat and sighed for that restfulness in their surroundings which only comes after centuries when nature is utterly conquered. I write at a table which was once at Waterpark. Over the chimney piece is a portrait of a Langton in a green velvet coat and a wig which hung in the same position there, and in a tin shed down below the coach-house, tipped out years ago to make way for the first motorcar, is an old rat-infested landau, with brambles climbing up the wheels, which at one time, highly polished, with coachman and footman and shining bays, rolled through the Somerset lanes and along the elegant streets of Bath.

At the time of Alice's first visit to Waterpark, it was owned by Thomas Langton, a cousin of Sir William's. The entail had been broken and he had no children, so it was uncertain to whom the place would come next. Of recent years Thomas had kept up a regular correspondence with Sir William, and he was expected to inherit. The only obstacle was that he might die first. Austin had stayed there during some of his Cambridge vacations, but Thomas was not much taken with him. The invitation to stay was most likely due not only to hospitable impulse, but to the wish to have another look at Austin, to see how long Sir William was likely to last, and also to see how suitable was Austin's Australian wife to become the future mistress of Waterpark. To Alice, arriving on a fine June afternoon after sixteen weeks at sea, it appeared the most desirable place on earth, far more a haunt of ancient peace even than when I knew it, half a century later. She writes:

'We arrived here about an hour before sunset. There is nothing in Australia that has the quality of this place—a wonderful peaceful mellowness. Everything indoors and out is in harmony. The house makes one feel that it has a soul. We walked in the garden and the low sunlight slanting across the lawn made the old bricks a glorious soft, rich red. I have never before felt such strong emotions awakened by a place. I should have thought that these feelings could only be aroused by a *person*. It may be partly due to relief at being on land again.'

Then comes the first of those passages in tiny French, in which Alice only wrote when she was feeling grief or anxiety or intense joy, and did not want to betray herself at a first glance to some inquisitive person who might happen to come across one of her diaries. They are rather like scars on the record of her life.

'A. est redevenu ce qu'il était,' she wrote. 'Pendant les dernières semaines, je craignais qu'il ne m'aimât plus. Quelquefois it était gentil, mais quelquefois, assis près de mon lit, il me regardait presque avec méfiance. Cet après-midi, quand nous avons quitté Hetty and M. Dell, il me semblait que le ciel est devenu clair. Peut-être était seulement qu'il n'aimait pas M. Dell, qui est vraiment ignoble. Et je crois qu'il commençait à détester Hetty. Mais pourquoi moi? Je prie pour qu'il reste sain et heureux dans cette très belle maison.'

They stayed there some weeks as it agreed so well with Alice and also with Sir William, whose health had not improved on the voyage. He was reluctant to move, and the Thomas Langtons appeared pleased to have them and urged them to stay. They were delighted with Alice, and when they learned that she had money, and would be able to keep up the place, they finally decided to leave Waterpark to Austin. They could only leave the property. There was not much to go with it. So Alice, in addition to providing Austin with a good income, brought him ultimately if indirectly, an ancestral estate.

Austin now liked England much better than he had as an undergraduate with a small allowance. He added an interest in genealogy to that in horses. He drove about inspecting churches and tombs in the neighbourhood, and when he discovered a connection or colateral, he would call and ask them rather abrupt questions about their houses and their pedigrees. Occasionally he went to London by himself, as Alice was unfit to travel, and there was no point in her buying new clothes before her baby was born.

One day Alice made an entry in her diary:

'This morning Lady Langton had a letter from Hetty in which she announced her engagement to Mr Dell. The most surprising part of this was its effect on Austin. I have seldom seen him so vexed. He called Mr Dell the most dreadful names, not exactly swearing, but making up disgusting combinations of words at which he is very clever. Sometimes they are quite amusing, but I was glad that Mrs Langton was not present. A. says Mr Dell will be a disgrace to the family, of which he has recently become very proud. I am sorry for Mr Dell, though he is not attractive.'

To the further surprise and dismay of Lady Langton, Hetty wrote that she was to be married quite soon, within a few weeks of the announcement of the engagement. She explained that as Percy Dell had enough money for them to live on if they were economical, there was no need to delay, and as she had no home in England except with her uncle, there was every reason to hurry on the wedding. Her uncle Mayhew was to marry them, so she asked if Sir William would give her away.

Sir William supposed he could not refuse, but he grumbled at having to make the journey to Datchet. When the time came he was not well enough, and he told Austin he would have to act for him.

'I won't give one of my relatives to that white maggot,' growled Austin.

'You can't refuse,' said Lady Langton. 'It may not be a very grand alliance, but he knows how to behave himself, more or less. He'll be quite a gentleman in Australia if they go back there. If they don't we need not meet them. Personally I am relieved to have Hetty married to anybody, and would gladly give her away if I were qualified to do so. I would perform the duty as a thank offering.' Again Lady Langton said without humour exactly what her husband would have said with a witty intention.

A few weeks later Alice wrote:

'Austin left this morning to give Hetty away at her wedding to Mr Dell. He was very angry. I sent them a silver teapot.'

Arthur once said to me: 'Apparently two nights of a honeymoon with Hetty knocked Percy Dell flat. He must have felt like a puny Hercules faced with the fifty daughters of King What's-his-name. She had to take him to Switzerland to recuperate, though they said it was because of the cheap living.' Arthur knew when he said this, that neither of the reasons he mentioned was the true one, but he was at that time engaged in drawing red herrings across the trail of family scandals, and even of drawing further different-coloured herrings across the trail of the red ones. For quite another reason, which Arthur told me later, Percy Dell and Hetty did spend the first year of their married life in Zurich.

Late in September my father was born at Waterpark, and at the same time his grandfather became very ill, as if the new life demanded the extinguishing of the old. At the same time as his relapse Sir William was offered a baronetcy for his services in helping to found the colony of Victoria, which, because of some grievance in his sick mind, he refused. He had just learned that Austin was to inherit Waterpark, and he thought perhaps that was good enough for him, or that a new baronetcy would not enhance his ancient name. Arthur said he knew that Austin would always be flamboyant and that he did not want to make him more conspicuous than necessary. Alice was hurt at his refusal. She would have liked a title, both for herself and for the heir whom she had just provided. She thought that the offer could not have come at a more appropriate time. She was not stupid and she could not help realising, especially as the years passed, how much she did for the Langtons—how heavily they clung to the onion woman's skirts. This one thing they could have given her in return was meanly withheld.

Perhaps it is a good thing Sir William refused. Austin as a baronet would have splashed himself about even more than he did, and attention might have been drawn to scandals which as it happened were largely ignored. My father, who was very retiring, would have been irritated by the

66

distinction, at any rate in Australia. If Dominic had been a baronet he would hardly have noticed it but his peculiar life would have had much more publicity. If it had come to me I should have felt frustrated, when, on Mrs Briar's day out, I have to wash up. In my youth I used to be angry when I thought of my great-grandfather's refusing this honour. Now I think that perhaps it was all for the best, especially when I remember that after me the heir would be a Queensland cousin with a frightful accent.

It is absurd to suppose that Sir William's refusing the baronetcy had any effect on anything, and yet it did seem that by this gesture he had offended the benevolent gods. On the morning the offer came, good fortune appeared to be showering on the family. They had recently learned that Austin was to have Waterpark. An heir was born. Alice was recovering rapidly. Sir William himself felt a little better, and then there was this letter from the Prime Minister's secretary. Sir William refused it, and put the process in reverse, turning the tide of fortune outwards. He may of course have been short of ready cash, and did not want to pay the patent fees, or to borrow the money from Alice.

The next morning he was not so well, the baby had a slight upset, and Austin returned early from the hunt, bespattered and gloomy like a large sulky child, and told them that his favourite hunter had fallen and broken its leg and had to be shot. A week later the doctor said that it would be suicide for Sir William to spend the winter in England, but neither was he fit to undertake so soon the long voyage back to Australia, and he said: 'I'm damned if I'll be buried at sea.' The only alternative seemed to be for him to go to Naples.

Then another blow fell. Alice's lawyers in Melbourne wrote to say that her mother, presumably instigated by the rackety Mr Drax, was bringing an action to recover from Alice most of her first husband's estate and that he could not send any further funds until the case was heard. The lawyer did not think that Mrs Drax had much chance of winning but they had to be prepared. Fortunately Alice had enough money in her London bank to keep them for some months ahead. Even so the news was disconcerting to the household at Waterpark, and made them feel that the bottom was falling out of their world. Sir William was not rich. He said that he did not think it right for a man in his position to make speculative purchases of land, as Alice's father had done. If he had been less conscientious I might now have been a millionaire.

The immediate result of the lawyer's letter was a family conference on Austin's earning capacity, which did not appear to be great. His father said that he should at once begin to read for the bar, even though the hunting season had just started. Thomas Langton suggested that as he had a degree he might take orders, then he could have the living after the present vicar, who however was only fifty-two. Austin did not respond very gratefully to this offer.

The discussion went on for a fortnight, when it had to be put aside as Austin had to conduct his parents to Italy. Part of Sir William's illness was an affliction of the legs, and he often had to be lifted up steps and in and out of carriages. Austin was able to do this with greater strength and efficiency than the valet, and Lady Langton refused to go unless he came too. As his father's life was in question he had no choice, but Alice refers several times to his reluctance to leave her and the baby.

'Austin grumbled a great deal when we were going to bed about his trip to Italy. He said that Herbert was as strong as a horse and could easily lift his father. Then he pretended to be a little boy and cried. He was very funny. He said that foreign countries were full of popery and that he'd be burned at the stake. I wish he need not go, but think he must.'

In the middle of October he set out with his father and mother for Naples. It was necessary for Sir William to rest frequently to recover his strength for the next stage of the journey. It took them a month to reach Rome, and Sir William refused to go any farther. It is doubtful whether he could have done so. The whole journey seems to have been one of those imbecilities which people commit when the gods are determined to destroy them. They settled in an apartment in a narrow street in the centre of the city. It had to be on a lower floor as Sir William could not be carried up many of the long flights of stairs, so that, though it faced south, the sun never reached it. He would have been better off at Waterpark, where the rooms drew all the sun there was, and the floors were not icy marble. Neither Lady Langton nor Herbert the valet could speak Italian. They were swindled and the food disagreed with them.

As soon as they were installed Austin hurried back to his wife and his horses. Thomas Langton occasionally made vague references to his reading for the bar, but no one seriously thought he should begin this before the end of the hunting season, especially as he had lost a month in taking his parents to Rome. He and Alice spent a pleasant winter with their cousins, but a little subdued by the two Damocletian swords over their heads, the impending lawsuit and Sir William's health.

In early March when the ash-buds were black in the hedgerows, and a few furtive daffodils bloomed in the sheltered but rougher corners of the lawn, the swords fell. Alice's mother had been awarded two-thirds of the estate which presumably would be squandered in riotous living, so that Alice would not only suffer the loss of the money, but would gain reflected notoriety from the way it was spent. This was not as bad as it might have been. If they could no longer consider themselves rich, they were by no means penniless. There was no immediate need for Austin to take Holy Orders, or to dash off to eat his dinners at Lincoln's Inn. Also Alice's lawyers lodged an appeal.

At the same time they heard from Zurich that Hetty had given birth, prematurely, to a baby boy.

Then the second sword fell, this one more accurately. Lady Langton wrote from Rome, on note paper with black edges a quarter of an inch wide, that Sir William had died. Again it was assumed that Austin must leave at once for Italy to settle their affairs and bring his mother home. This time he did not hesitate, but asked Thomas for the carriage and drove to the station within an hour of receiving the news.

In a few days Alice had a letter from Zurich saying that he had seen Hetty and her baby and that it was a fine boy, weighing ten pounds. Alice was amazed.

'Is Zurich on the way to Rome?' she asked Mr Langton.

'Not directly, I think,' he replied.

'But Austin has written from Zurich. Surely he would go

by the shortest route?' She was going to add, 'To his mother when she is in such distress,' but thought it would imply a criticism. 'He says he has seen Hetty Dell and her baby. But he dislikes the Dells. You heard what he said at the time of their marriage.'

'He certainly did not sound attracted by them,' agreed Mr Langton.

'He probably thought,' said Mrs Langton, 'that they would want one of the family to rejoice with them over their first child. That was a kindness he could perform without delaying his other duty more than a few hours. I have noticed that Austin is often very kind in those ways.' Mrs Langton always put the best interpretation on any action.

Lady Langton and Austin returned to Waterpark at the beginning of April. Everyone was shocked at her appearance. She had always been thin, but now she looked ravaged. Her life, without warning, or rather with warnings she had not understood, had collapsed. She felt she must be somehow to blame, and tried to find what mistake she had made. She kept saying that they should not have left Australia. Everything had gone wrong since then. She did not remember that in their first weeks in England it appeared that everything was going right. But she had not attempted to relate herself to England. She had perhaps been full of hubris, of that elation which angers the gods. When she went up to London to see her relatives, people of no great social pretension but in some ways more civilised than herself, and who, in twenty-five years, had changed almost to different people, her manner had been that of a great lady. This created a falsity and irritation in reunions

71

which she had long anticipated as wonderfully happy. But she was not putting on her manner. For many years she had been the second most important woman in the country where she lived. When the Governor was away, her husband represented the Queen. Her manner had grown from the deference to which she was accustomed.

Now that Nemesis had followed, she half recognised what had happened, but she could not wholly resolve it in her mind. To do that it would have been necessary to accept the idea of divine injustice. She was forty-five years old. She had twenty-five years of married life behind her, and ahead were perhaps thirty or more years of widowhood. The proportion was cruel. When she left Melbourne she achieved the ambition of more than half her life. Her long exile was over. Now she saw her departure as only a terrible mistake, her advent in Europe as an immense defeat. She could talk of nothing but an immediate return. Above all things she wanted to be in the country where she had spent nearly the whole of her happy married life. The Thomas Langtons offered her the little Elizabethan dower house at Waterpark, which was then empty, but she said she must go home. 'Home' had switched again to the antipodes.

'We have all decided to return to Australia,' wrote Alice. 'Lady Langton and I had a long discussion about it this afternoon. She seems calmer now that we have made this decision. She spoke with sad resignation, but much more sensibly than of late. She said that we have to accept the inevitable changes in our condition—that our life at first is full of hope and beauty. Then comes a period of fulfilment, but it is very short. The same thing happens to every form of life, to trees, and animals and men. The branches fall, the fur becomes less glossy, and we feel pain in our joints and in our hearts. She also said that apart from these natural processes we enter periods of misfortune, when the fates turn against us. Wisdom lies in recognising when this has happened. It is no longer of any use trying to impose one's will on life. I did not agree with this and said: "Surely no adverse fate can work against us if we are Christians?" She replied that God Himself may send us misfortune. I disagreed even more strongly. I said: "All evil must come from evil. Evil cannot come from good. If we do not ask God's help against misfortunes, instead of accepting it as His Gift, it may overcome us." She did not answer that. Although I did not agree with her it was a very interesting conversation, and certainly this has not been a fortunate trip.'

Alice did not realise until ten years later how unfortunate it had been.

5

When the William Langtons first set out for Australia their ship was wrecked between London and Plymouth. They came ashore in a lifeboat, bought new equipment and went on by the next ship. The ship in which Austin with his family now embarked also ran into a storm and Lady Langton thought that she was going to be wrecked a second time. It is a curious if irrelevant fact that nearly every outward voyage was stormy and difficult, and nearly everyone back serene. As if to compensate this their years in Australia seem to have been less complicated, and freer from unexpected misfortunes than those in England.

Alice was glad to be back in Australia. She did feel that

the large light landscape was her natural element, and that the gum trees were more friendly than the winter oaks. But she felt defrauded. She had actually been, if not defrauded, deprived of more than half her income by the Draxes. This was only a partial cause of her feeling. Another perhaps was Sir William's refusal of a baronetcy, but the chief cause was that she had endured these two long sea voyages and had seen practically nothing of Europe. She had longed to travel in France and Italy. Austin and Lady Langton had done so, though without any pleasure, while, apart from a few days in London, she had seen only the countryside round Waterpark, delightful for the first three months, but after that brown and cold and dark, unless it was covered with snow.

Since her marriage she had had no home of her own. Now she was determined to have one. Bishopscourt had returned to its natural occupant. Even if it had been available they could not have afforded it. Sir William had paid a thousand pounds for eleven months tenancy. Rents everywhere were still very high. Alice wanted to buy some land and build a house on Toorak hill, but then they were told of a nice house vacant in East St Kilda. It had two added attractions. There was in the same road another smaller house vacant which would do for Lady Langton and her three unmarried sons, and it was only a few hundred yards from the Bynghams, who had settled in a grey gabled house like a large English vicarage, with gothic touches in the chimney pieces and the windows. It is still standing, but shorn of its acres and squeezed among red villas. It was and is called Kilawly, after a seat of the Bynghams in Co. Sligo.

It may be as well to explain the significance of Melbourne suburbs. Most of the early colonists of the better sort, the judges, army officers and gentlepeople who somehow found themselves in Victoria, lived in East St Kilda, which remained an 'exclusive' neighbourhood up to some time in the 1920s. But long before that it had been over-shadowed by Toorak, where the first large Government House with its fine renaissance drawing room was built, and where, as the wool-growers became richer, they raised their Italianate mansions. Toorak with its neighbour South Yarra became the Mayfair of Melbourne, and the descendants of the St Kilda gentry, as they felt their social importance in danger, fled to any cottage in the shadow of the mansions of the squatters, many of whom their grandparents would have refused to know, in the same way that people would rather live in two rooms above a delicatessen shop behind Berkeley Square than in a house with a ballroom in Putney. It was also possible to live in Kew, Brighton and other suburbs, but this was only done by people who preferred the river and the sea to 'society.' It is necessary that the reader should understand the character of these different suburbs, partic-ularly the potent meaning of the word Toorak. If Alice had decided to build in Toorak instead of buying the house in East St Kilda, this story would probably have been very different. In fact I might not have been born, as it was that decision which brought about our close association with the Bynghams.

Alice had just settled in her new house and was begin-ning to enjoy having a home of her own, when Hetty and Percy Dell arrived in Melbourne. They did not want to spend their lives economising on the Continent, and she had persuaded him to return to Australia and follow his original intention of practising there as a solicitor. They took a cottage which was separated from Alice's house only by a two acre paddock. None of the families already settled there appeared very pleased to welcome them, but Hetty was unaware of this, or indifferent to it.

There followed what was probably a very happy period, one of those when babies burst, like squalling pink flowers on the younger branches of the family tree. The three couples, the Langtons, the Bynghams and the Dells produced twenty children between them, half of them Bynghams. I might almost in the language of Holy Writ, put: 'Captain Byngham begat . . .' But it is only confusing to give the names of people before they are concerned in the story. We have numerous relatives whom I may not even mention.

It is usual to think of these large mid-Victorian families as slightly comic, and sometimes it is difficult not to caricature them. Arthur himself did so. When one considers what their lives were really like, they were not a joke. Mildy, the most comic had the most tragic life of all, as she did not once achieve a true sympathetic understanding with another human being, though she went on to the end trying to see every darkening night as a spring morning. Even if the large Victorian families were not funny, they are rather surprising in the confidence of the parents that they were conferring a benefit on these children whom they brought into the world, though if they judged by their own circumstances they were justified in thinking so.

Captain Byngham had a sheep station in the Riverina,

but it was run by a manager and he seldom went there. It did not occur to anyone until after the 1914 war that there was any obligation to work unless it was necessary, and they may have been right. If a man has an unearned income of £5,000 a year, and goaded by his puritan conscience takes a position at £500, he has still failed to justify his drawing an unearned income of £5,000 from the community. My grandparents had no qualms about their incomes.

When I was a child I used to be taken by my mother to sing 'Good King Wenceslas' to Grandmamma Byngham at Kilawly on Christmas Day. At that time the group of houses where the Langtons, Bynghams and Dells lived was much the same as when they first went there, so I can fairly easily visualise the outward circumstances of their lives. I can even remember some of the furniture and the pictures at Kilawly, apart from those which have come down to me, and are now here at Westhill, mixed with Langton belongings.

Except for the frequent pangs of childbirth, theirs must have been as agreeable a life as it was possible to lead. Oceans lay between them and countries afflicted by war and serious poverty. The climate was excellent. Their slow means of transport gave them leisure and dignity. Mrs Byngham and Alice had their carriages, Lady Langton drove herself in a pony phaeton, while Hetty and Percy Dell trotted about in a jinker, Hetty driving and Percy beside her, looking like a minor accessory of the equipage. Where their style of living fell below that of their relatives, Percy prided himself on their freedom from vulgarity. They all gave frequent entertainments, lawn parties and dinner parties. I have seen the equipment for these functions at Kilawly, monstrous epergnes and candelabra—and finger bowls weighing each about two pounds. They had brought out with them their English style of living, but it was tempered by a pleasant colonial informality. They had to satisfy no one but themselves. They did not follow the social pattern, they set it. The men rode, went to the races, shot, hunted and sat in the Melbourne Club.

Austin alone seemed dissatisfied. At times Alice found him difficult and irrational in his moods, but never really bad tempered. He had joined the volunteers to give himself something to do, but that did not cure his restlessness. He said he wanted to live in the country. It might have been thought that East St Kilda at that time was countrified enough. The milk, butter, fruit and vegetables were all produced on the place. It was only necessary to drive a mile or two to shoot and fish, or in the hot summer to go to the sea to bathe, but Austin had there no scope for his pioneering instincts. He wished to leave some mark on the country. As will be seen later he had other reasons for wanting to move from that neighbourhood.

Alice was reluctant to give up her pleasant social life, but she agreed to buy a place in the country, even to carve a new estate out of the virgin bush, if this would cure Austin of his discontents. She was more willing to do this as she had just won a round in her long drawn-out series of lawsuits against Mrs Drax, and had some extra money to invest. As soon as he had her agreement, Austin hired a covered wagon from the grocer, filled it with camping equipment, and taking his youngest two brothers set out in the direction of Gippsland. When in the evening they were near any habitation, a farm or rough hotel, he would choose a camping site, leave his young brothers to pitch the tent and prepare a meal, while he went off to have a yarn with the farmer or innkeeper, though the latter seems an inaccurate word to apply to these men whom he would sound about the land available in the neighbourhood.

On their second day, at a hamlet some miles beyond Dandenong, a man told Austin that there was both very good grazing land, and very beautiful wooded country, up in the hills towards the ranges, and he turned the grocer's wagon in that direction. It was not a good road, up hill and then steeply down into a gully, where they had to ford a brook, or creek as they are called here. By the creek were tree-ferns and the aromatic sassafras, and the cool air was full of the sound of bellbirds. They stayed here to water the horses and to bathe. From the creek they drove up a very long steep hill where the grade was one in six. They had to stop at intervals to rest the horses, and the boys put large stones behind the wheels to prevent the wagon rolling back. After five miles they came to a clear space with magnificent views, to the north across the valley to the ranges, to the west across twenty miles of plain to the bay, an expanse of pale gold in the evening light, beyond which could be seen the delicate purple peaks of the Youyang Mountains, ninety miles away.

Austin told the boys to pitch the camp, and he walked about the open space to different vantage points, giving grunts of satisfaction. Then he went to ask for water at a little whitewashed cottage by the roadside. A house in Australia, the first of its kind built only a hundred years ago, may suggest the antique more than a sophisticated palace built centuries earlier. There are in the country outside Melbourne little cottages built of bark and tin, whitewashed, with vines along their walls, and the fowls pecking at the hard earth under the fig tree, where one feels the disguised Ulysses might have asked for shelter and a bowl of goat's milk, while one cannot possibly imagine him calling at Waterpark, with its far greater antiquity. But this may be partly due to that feeling one has in the Australian countryside, that it has known the morning of the world. This cottage, where Austin asked for water, had the appearance of belonging to all time. When the man brought him his full bucket he asked him:

'Have you much land here?'

The man said that he had about a hundred acres. He was rather gloomy. He said that his wife was ill, and that he wanted to sell the place and get work in Melbourne.

'There's no neighbours,' he said, 'and they're all Germans like. Some of them have run away from ships and they've settled in the bush round about here. They seem decent folk but I can't understand their talk.'

Austin thanked the man for the water, gave him a shilling, and went back to the camp. He was excited. Certainly there was not much land but he had no doubt he could extend the boundaries, and he was not concerned with a revenue-producing property. He wanted a country house where he would not see suburban roofs two hundred yards away— particularly one suburban roof—but where he would be monarch of all he surveyed. While his brothers grilled chops, holding them on long forked sticks over the gum-scented fire, he walked about on the grass plateau, and visualised the mansion from the windows of which he would look out on these serene and splendid panoramas.

In the morning he asked the man, whose name was

Darke, how much he wanted for the property, and he named a reasonable price. Austin asked what it was called.

'Westhill we call it,' said Darke, 'because it's on a hill to the west, like.'

Austin gave him a guinea and asked him not to sell it until he heard from him, which was hardly necessary, as the man had been trying to sell the place for eighteen months.

When they had packed their tents and equipment into the wagon Austin turned the horses' heads towards Melbourne. The boys were disgusted that the fortnight's camping expedition had lasted barely three days, but he promised to bring them back later. Alice was surprised that they returned so soon, but she was also relieved that Austin was enthusiastic about a site only thirty miles from Melbourne, already cleared and with a cottage on it. She was afraid that he might have chosen somewhere hundreds of miles away in the depth of the virgin forest.

As soon as the purchase was completed and the Darkes had moved out, Austin and Alice went up to camp in the cottage and to plan their future home. There began for them two years of struggle and frustration. Their worst defeats have proved of the greatest benefit to me. They found it would be too difficult to cart bricks up those hilly unmade roads, so they had to be baked on the place, with the result that I have a house of handmade bricks of that soft red which one sees in old houses in England. They had a tiresome old-fashioned builder whose ideas were still Georgian, and who put in round arches, six-paned windows, and plain classical chimney pieces, thwarting Austin's grandiose Gothic ideas. Best of all, half-way through the building, Mrs Drax brought another lawsuit and they were afraid that they might not have the money to finish it. At the same time the man making the bricks died, so they decided to reduce the size of the house by leaving off the top storey. If this had not happened, I would not have attempted to live here.

At the end of two years they moved in. Still only half the rooms were ready, but Austin was full of the spirit of the pioneer. He put his arms in stained glass over the front door and above them in Latin: 'Unmindful of the tomb you build houses.' As well as struggling with his own property, he worked hard for the improvement of the countryside. He blazed a track from the sea to the ranges, which passes Westhill gate and is still called Langton Road. He became a member of the Legislative Council, Alice providing the necessary £500 a year. This gave him the title of 'honourable' with which he was very pleased. It is on the uniform cases and many other of his possessions lying in the outhouses.

Three weeks after they moved in, Aunt Mildred was born, very suddenly, probably owing to the exertion and discomfort of living in a half-finished house. In the room in which she was born, later the night-nursery and now the painted chapel, only half the windows were glazed and it was thick with the buzzing of bush-flies, a species of blowfly. One always associates the more acute Australian discomforts with Aunt Mildy, possibly because of her voice. She was always very proud of being the first of the family to be born at Westhill.

It is hard to know whether this can be counted a fortunate house. There are those like old Miss Vio Chambers who speak of it as an earthly paradise, but when one remembers the two years of worry and anxiety its building cost my grandparents, that Aunt Mildy was the first to be born here, and that her birth brought Cousin Sarah into the household, one can hardly imagine more inauspicious beginnings. Alice's East St Kilda servants would not go with her to the country, and when Mildy was born she badly needed more help than the rough local domestics who spoke only German. Dean Mayhew had recently died, leaving barely enough to support his widow, who went to live with her sister, Lady Langton. The boys were earning their livings on sheep stations and in banks. Sarah was to find a situation as a governess, but Alice asked her to come to Westhill as a kind of companion-housekeeper. She was given slightly higher wages than the cook, which was thought generous, as at that time most people expected their poor relatives to slave for them in exchange for their keep.

Another effect of the move to Westhill, one that can hardly be considered fortunate, was that Lady Langton again returned to England. Arthur, her second and favourite son had unusual talent and for some time had been saying that it would be wasted unless he could go to London and Paris to study painting. Lady Langton had been reluctant to move away from the neighbourhood of Austin and his family, whom she saw every day. Now that they had moved to the country she became restless and at last agreed to take Arthur home for a few years, 'home' having again moved back to the northern hemisphere. This also would enable her to visit her husband's grave in the Protestant cemetery in Rome, and to see that the instructions she had given for it were carried out. She had to magnify things of this kind into importance to satisfy her emotional needs. Mrs Mayhew was to stay on in the house in East St Kilda and look after Walter and Freddie, the two younger boys. Walter was at the Melbourne University and Freddie when he left school was to go as a jackaroo on Captain Byngham's station in the Riverina.

But the most unfortunate effect of Westhill was to strengthen the association with the Mayhews, a disintegrating family possessed by a sort of dreary meekness, a mildew of the spirit. In fact as children we used to call Aunt Mildy, who came most under Mayhew influence 'Aunt Mildew.' Since I have been back at intervals I have been accosted in the streets of Melbourne by various seedy individuals called Mayhew who have claimed me as cousin. Yet they have all had an air of gentleness and good breeding about them, and they have greeted me so warmly, not because they wanted to borrow money, but because I was a symbol of a happier past, and these timid shabby Mayhews are still more presentable than half the 'Leaders of Toorak society.' As Arthur said: 'No one can help having relatives who have come down in the world. It is a process of nature. What would be utterly humiliating would be to have relatives who have come up.'

The most mildewed of them all was Cousin Sarah. Austin could not stand her and made forcible objections to her coming, but Alice had to have help and there was no one else. Austin called her 'the Jinx' and throughout the remaining forty years of his life protested against her intermittent attachment to the household. Long after she was an unavoidable necessity she remained, spreading a grey blight over all the opulence of their lives. If in later years, Alice was just setting out for some function in Toorak, at the last minute Sarah would scramble into the landau with a dipper full of eggs, or something wrapped in newspaper which she was taking to a sale of work. She always had the wrong wines brought up for a dinner party, not from stupidity but with the intentional malice of a tee-totaller. She could not order the most elaborate meal without giving it somehow the atmosphere of a schoolroom tea. Her words were always gentle and righteous and her deeds always full of spite. As a child I saw her, this black alpaca spinster, as a kind of dam holding back all she could from the stream of good things our grandmother delighted to pour on us. Mercifully, like the blowflies, she was a purely Australian affliction. She never reached Waterpark.

If Sarah was the most mildewed of the Mayhews, Hetty was the least. She was entirely free from any blight of meekness or dissembling. She did not practise germ-warfare, but used instead a bulldozer to disintegrate the Langtons. She would invite herself and one of her children to stay at West-hill, leaving her mother to see that the general servant looked after Percy and her other boys. Herself impassive, like a large fowl squatting in a smaller bird's nest, she created quarrels and tensions all about her. One day Alice wrote:

'Hetty has now been here for over a fortnight. It is her third visit since Christmas. It is extraordinary of her to leave her husband for so long and it is not entirely agreeable having her here. Though with three children and only one servant she must have to do a share of the housework in her own house, here she makes no attempt to lessen the work she causes. She makes her room very untidy and the nurse complains about the extra child to mind.' Then Alice changes into French and continues: 'That is not really what worries me. I feel there is something peculiar about Hetty. At times I feel a sudden irrational dislike of her, almost a detestation which shocks me. I did not know I had such feelings. I wish she would go before I reveal it. The whole household is upset. Austin is in a very moody state. This evening I saw him staring at Hetty as if he hated her. I have never seen such an expression in his eyes and it quite frightened me. I could not stay in a house where my host disliked me. I am sure I should feel it, but she seems quite indifferent to our feelings. Once or twice Austin has grumbled to me, but at other times he will say nothing. It is almost as if he were afraid of her because she knows something about him. But what could she know that he would mind revealed? He has never done anything dishonourable. It would be impossible for him. Of that I am sure. But that is what worries me. All the time Sarah apologises for Hetty's being here, but she does not ask her to go.'

They had regular letters from Lady Langton in England, written on black-edged 'foreign' paper, criss-crossed in angular writing. At first everything seemed to go well. She had taken a small house in Brompton Square and they stayed at Waterpark for long periods in the summer and at Christmas. Arthur loved life in England. Long afterwards he would tell me incidents of those six years as if they were the only time he had really lived. He had good enough connections to bring him invitations to the kind of houses he liked. He was very presentable and amusing. His mother in her letters gave an exaggerated impression of his popularity in the artistic world, and of his brilliance as a painter. We always had the impression that he had known all the greatest writers and painters of the nineteenth century, but the only encounter of which he actually told me was that when leaving a club, he asked Swinburne to return him his hat which the poet, who was drunk, had taken in place of his own.

Then came the spectacular announcement of Arthur's engagement to Damaris Tunstall, the daughter of Lord Dilton, a neighbour at Waterpark. This might have been expected to please Austin, with his sense of family importance. On the contrary, it made him anxious about his inheritance. Although he spent so much thought and energy on Westhill, he had not forgotten that he was the heir to Waterpark. He thought that Arthur, with his charm and polish, might easily supplant him. Now that he was marrying a peer's daughter he felt that he was almost certain to be considered a more suitable heir than his elder brother, and Austin was confirmed in this view when he heard that Thomas had let Arthur have the dower house at Waterpark, so that he might make some pretence of keeping his wife.

The last of the long series of the lawsuits against the Draxes had just been won by Alice, and they were once more fairly wealthy. Austin suggested another trip to England, and Alice agreed. She wanted to see Europe, and she was even influenced by the prospect of escaping Hetty's visits to Westhill. The children were to remain here in charge of Cousin Sarah. All arrangements were made for their departure when startling news came from England. The black edges on Lady Langton's writing paper widened again.

I do not know exactly what happened. Arthur when exposing all the skeletons to me, naturally did not include his own, and Alice's diaries give only the bare facts of this tragedy. There may have been nothing behind it, no skeleton, and yet from the reserved way in which people spoke of it I always had the impression there was. Perhaps there was nothing shocking, but it may have been thought that the affair was not very creditable. The family may have taken the attitude of those Italians mentioned by Samuel Butler, who say they are disgraced when they are only unfortunate.

Damaris Tunstall was six years older than Arthur. She was a clever, ugly, artistic woman, and seems to have taken the initiative in courting. They went sketching together round Waterpark. It was probably thought discreditable because it was imagined that Arthur could not possibly be in love with her and that he must be fortune-hunting. Lord Dilton was very rich. So was Aubrey Tunstall, Damaris's brother, who had been left a fortune by a maternal uncle and lived in Italy. So was her sister, who had married a rich man and also lived in Italy. But Damaris only had a sufficient income to keep them modestly. The allowance Lady Langton could give Arthur did not pay for more than his dandified clothes and his paints, and he sold few pictures. The Diltons were not very pleased about the match, but as Damaris was thirty-three they did not think her likely to do any better for herself, and Arthur did at least belong to a good local family, and one much older than their own. They regarded her marriage as just another eccentricity, as when she had made a voyage to China.

Arthur and Damaris went on a honeymoon to Cornwall. There, three weeks after the wedding, she went out one afternoon, alone in a hired dogcart, and drove over a cliff. Herself, the horse and the cart were smashed on the rocks two hundred feet below.

It was assumed that the horse had bolted, but Damaris was a good driver, and surely she could have headed it away from the cliff. There were hints at something, but I do not know what. Alice could not believe that Austin had done anything dishonourable and it is even more impossible to believe it of Arthur. He had of course no Teba blood in his veins, and he had from no other source any Teba instincts. He might say the most outrageous things to entertain one, but even when he was 'throwing Cousin Hetty to the wolves' he did so because she herself had been cruel, and his reference was always back to the standard of the angels. Also judging from Damaris's portrait, if there was any cruelty practised, it was more likely to have been by her than by Arthur, and it is likely that there was no skeleton in his cupboard at all.

I do not want to insist too much on the influence of heredity, and so have withheld until after the account of Arthur's marriage a fact about the Tunstalls, which by another thread draws them into the orbit of this story. They were related to Mrs Byngham. Again the connection was only dubiously gratifying as it was through Mrs O'Hara, Damaris's maternal grandmother, who was the second daughter of the monstrous duque de Teba. This lady had quarrelled with her sister, each declaring that the other had married beneath her, and the two families had no contact. Seeing that not only Damaris, but later her brother and sister come under our notice, it is worth remembering that they were not free from Teba blood. There are some coincidences in our family, and some symbols almost too appropriate to be credible, and therefore I am suppressing them, but I shall give this example. The charges on the Teba arms are six snakes emerging from a basket. In the passage here hangs a shield with sixteen quarters, which Arthur emblazoned to remind us of our illustrious forbears, a rather mischievous gift to a family of young Australians who were already far too aware of them. In one of these quarters are the Teba serpents. They are the first things I see every morning as I go to the bath.

To return to Lady Langton, she felt that again a period of affliction had come upon her, a recess of the tide of fortune. She felt a blow to Arthur more keenly than if it had been aimed at herself. She urged him while he was sitting stunned amid the wreckage of his world to continue with his painting, and to try to forget his loss in creative activity. It was then he admitted that he could never be a painter, that he was colour-blind. It was very slight and only confused pale blues and pinks. By avoiding those tints as much as possible and by following more the labels on his paint tubes than his eye, he had managed to conceal the defect until now. Once or twice he had nearly been caught out, as when a fellow student said: 'You never see a sky as pink as that.' If he had looked at Arthur, he might have added: 'And I've seldom seen a face so red.'

Arthur told his mother he could not continue the effort any longer. His defect was sure to be discovered soon. The tragedy of his marriage had destroyed his spirit for the time being. Again Lady Langton thought it best in misfortune to retreat to Australia. This became a habit of the family, to use Australia as a refuge in time of trouble. Westhill particularly became a bolt-hole when things went wrong, so nothing much was ever done to the place after Austin's first burst of activity. When here they were either depressed or practising economy, which was ultimately fortunate, as if they had been here in their periods of opulence they might have made the place uninhabitable with new wings and Gothic towers.

After he had arrived back in Melbourne it did not take Arthur long to recover his spirits. The scene of his dreadful experience was far away, in another world, and so it became less real to him. There was no association here to recall it, and the whole incident had been too short to leave a very lasting impression. Also he could not fail to be aware that he had no further worries about money. Perhaps that was why some people spoke with reserve of Arthur's marriage. They thought he should not have made on it. Actually he did offer to return Damaris's income to Lord Dilton, but he would not take it. Not many of those who were so honourable on Arthur's behalf would have made the same gesture of offering a few hundreds, all he had, to a man with many thousands a year. It also suggests that Lord Dilton knew his daughter, and thought that Arthur had earned the money by his experience. In later years, when the circumstances of Damaris's death were forgotten, Arthur gained a perceptible increase in importance from being the son-in-law of a peer. He returned with his mother to their house in East St Kilda. He tipped Mrs Mayhew out to live with Hetty, and arranged the portières and objets d'art he had brought out from Europe. There he settled down to a life of ordered routine which he followed for sixty years, gathering every kind of moss.

Austin and Alice had postponed their departure to see Lady Langton whom otherwise they would have passed in the Indian Ocean. A few days after their arrival, Arthur and his mother came up to stay for a week at Westhill. One day during this visit they were all going for a picnic to that creek where Austin and his younger brothers had bathed on the day they first came there. Lady Langton wanted to hear the bellbirds. Austin had driven the wagonette round to the front door to collect the party, but only Arthur was ready. Austin asked him to hold the horses while he made some fixture to the harness. Arthur who was still bubbling with lively comment on Melbourne and everyone in it, began to amuse himself on the subject of the Dells.

'What beats me,' he said, 'is how on earth Percy Dell fathered those children of Hetty's. They're like young bulls. I only hope they have more intelligence than either of their parents.' Austin looked annoyed and Arthur thought that the groom had made a mistake in harnessing the horses. 'Of course,' he went on, 'Percy isn't really a man. I believe that among certain primitive creatures the male is just a bit of protoplasm, a piece of jelly that the female uses to fertilise herself. Percy is just Hetty's piece of male jelly, and I don't suppose a piece of jelly can transmit its characteristics to its offspring, so Hetty has a clear field in which to reproduce her own bovine charms.'

Austin, his eyes blazing, suddenly turned on Arthur.

'Be quiet, damn you!' he shouted.

At that moment Alice with Lady Langton and the children came out of the house. They stood amazed, as though Austin often growled at them, it was half buffoonery. None of them had ever seen him so violently angry. His anger passed almost immediately. He gave Arthur a curious glance, suspicious, shame-faced and quizzical, as he climbed onto the box and took the reins from him. No one referred to the incident. The conversation was a little stilted until they came down the steep hill to the creek, and chose a site for their tea. While Austin saw to the horses, Lady Langton and the children went to gather twigs for a fire to boil the billy. Arthur stayed to help Alice to spread a cloth on the ground, and to put out the cups and the cakes.

'Why was Austin so angry?' asked Alice.

'I have no idea,' said Arthur. 'It knocked me flat. I was being funny about Hetty's enormous children. He says much worse things himself and he loathes the Dells.'

'I don't understand his attitude to them,' said Alice. 'He hates Hetty coming up so often to stay, and yet he won't tell her not to. I suppose he was angry simply at the thought of them.'

Lady Langton came back with her hands full of long strips of dry bark, and they did not continue with the subject.

6

A month later Austin and Alice sailed for England and for eighteen months Cousin Sarah reigned supreme at Westhill. I have already given some indication of her character and may give more later on, when I come to my own contacts with her. At present I shall only mention her effect on Mildred, who was about six years old when her parents went to England. Although there were four children left behind, it was on Mildred that Sarah lavished all her affection. Hitherto she had been a pretty little girl nicknamed Moo. Sarah called her her own little girl, and changed her pet name to Mildy, which somehow stuck. She encouraged her in ways of nauseating sentimentality, and worst of all she did not correct the accent

Mildy caught from the servants. It is even likely that she encouraged her in this hideous twang, as she liked everybody to be humble. If she kept Mildy as common as possible, she would remain superior to her and able to retain her love. She would not lose her in a fashionable marriage. Sarah was not as unlike Hetty as she appeared on the surface. Her concentration on Mildy was fortunate for the other children as they were spared a great deal of unpleasant and mischievous attention, which even I, a generation later, did not escape when we stayed with our grandmother.

Arthur used often to talk about Sarah and Mildy, using his favourite illustration.

'All the Mayhews were conscious of their behinds,' he said. 'Hetty was proud of hers, but Sarah tried to pretend she hadn't got one. She used to hold it in and the effort made her hold her chin in as well. I used to feel I was ravishing her even when I shook hands, she was so modest about her fingertips. The real trouble of course was that Sarah taught Mildred to hold in her behind, but she only taught her to do it physically. In Mildred's mind her backside was as prominent, rotund and provocative as ever, and this conflict between the way she held her behind and her intellectual conception of it nearly drove your poor aunt off her head.'

It may sound callous to go off to the other side of the world, leaving one's children for so long, but it was a thing Australian women had to do if they were not to cut themselves off entirely from the country they called 'home.' Alice was certainly not indifferent to her parting with the children and she had thought of cancelling the trip at the last moment, but she hated any form of weak-mindedness, and she would have endured far worse things rather than show herself as vacillating.

Owing to the delay in their departure, they did not arrive in England until August, instead of in the early summer as they had intended, when Alice had hoped to remedy the omissions of her last trip to Europe and to make a Continental tour. But after a week or two in London, they went to Waterpark, just before the cubbing and Austin said it was not worthwhile going away. It did not occur to Alice to expect him to give up any of the hunting to fall in with her wishes. The Thomas Langtons obviously wanted them to stay, and it would have been difficult to refuse people who had shown them so much kindness.

Alice enjoyed living at Waterpark, and would have been contented there if she had not wanted to go abroad, and if she had not missed her children. She gives frequent appreciations of the restful, dignified house with its well-trained servants, and yet she never made any attempt to reproduce this at Westhill. She thought it admirable in Somerset, but she also thought it would be out of place nine miles from Dandenong, and there she allowed Sarah to continue with her dismal housekeeping. She had perhaps better taste than the Langtons, but was less of an artist. Arthur, if he had had the money, would have set out with the enthusiasm of a stage manager to have reproduced Waterpark at Westhill, and the dining-room would have been congested with rosy-cheeked English footmen. I myself, eighty years later, with a succession of erratic and ill-natured 'cook-generals' still make desperate efforts to create here the atmosphere of an English country house, and for the benefit of young relatives who probably think the whole thing ridiculous. We all try to recreate the conditions under which we have been happiest. I have been happiest in English country houses, so wherever I am I try to make that particular kind of snail's shell. Alice, although she enjoyed every kind of cultured living, had been happiest in Australia, and so when there, was content with the Australian country 'way of life,' even Cousin Sarah's version of it.

In the spring, when the hunting was over, she was determined at last to have some compensation for her separation from her children and for the patience with which she had endured the winter. Austin grudgingly took her to Paris. For him foreign travel was only associated with two wretched journeys, one taking his dying father to Rome, the other bringing his bereaved mother back.

Even in London he complained that nobody knew who he was. In Paris his anonymity was worse, whereas in Melbourne more than half the people he passed in the street were aware of his identity. He was a member of the Upper House of Parliament and of the best club, and he dined at Government House. These things may have been slight compared with membership of the House of Lords and the Athenaeum, and with dining at Buckingham Palace, but they put him on top of his own world. The only place in England where his self-importance was sufficiently gratified was at Waterpark. It may not have been such a wide recognition as he had in Australia, but it was more subtle. In Melbourne he knew that he was regarded slightly as a buffoon, and he played up to his reputation. At Waterpark the respect given him by the villagers extended to something beyond his personal character, so that he had a greater sense of security there. He was one of 'the family' connected with this soil for six centuries, and neighbours of far higher standing than the most important people in Melbourne received him as one of their own kind.

After a fortnight in Paris, Alice with wifely duty followed him back to spend the summer at Waterpark. She often went up to London. At this time there are hints in her diary, very slight and not even strong enough to need concealment in French, that she was not very contented, and that owing to his selfishness there was not complete harmony between herself and Austin.

At the end of August they were both in London, at the rooms in King Street, St James's, where they always stayed. Austin had half promised Alice to travel on the Continent in the early autumn, but now that the partridge shooting was soon to begin he was sulky about fulfilling his promise, though he would have kept it. Alice, however, had met two Misses Urquhart from Melbourne who were just off to France. She thought it would be better if she went with them, and let Austin return alone to Waterpark. He was obviously relieved when she suggested this.

On the morning when he had arranged to go down to Frome by a midday train, they were sitting together at breakfast. The retired butler who ran the house brought in their letters. Alice, seeing that she had some with Australian stamps, took them eagerly.

That evening she wrote again in her diary one of those entries in tiny French, which are like the scars on the record of her life:

'Cette journée est la plus terrible, la plus épouvantable de ma vie. Je ne peux pas croire que je continuerai à vivre. Tout s'est effoudré. Tout est ruiné. Je désespère d'avoir jamais une vie heureuse, même honnête et paisible. Ce n'est pas seulement l'avenir qui est sans espoir, mais les années passées sont devenues fausses et un rêve fol. C'est ça qui est le plus grand supplice. Je n'ai même plus de passé.'

She goes on to describe what happened at breakfast. She opened first the letter from Sarah as she knew that it would contain laborious but affectionate notes from the children. She read these and handed them across to Austin. She then turned to Sarah's letter, and read aloud anything that she thought would interest him—there had been heavy rains, the camelias had been very fine this year, Maisie had begun riding lessons. Then she read out:

'I suppose you have heard from Aunt Emma that Hetty has another boy.'

She felt Austin start and she looked up. He had dropped the children's letters. He appeared upset.

'That's impossible!' he declared.

'It can't be impossible, dear, if both Sarah and your mother tell us it is so,' said Alice, surprised.

'No one has mentioned it till now. We would have heard it was on the way,' he muttered, angry and confused. He pushed back his chair and wiped his forehead with his table-napkin.

He gave Alice a glance, shamefaced and suspicious and left the room.

She put down Sarah's letter unfinished, and sat for awhile, puzzled and apprehensive. She could not understand why he should be so disturbed. That curious glance he had given her before he left the room reminded her of something. It was when they were going for a picnic at Westhill and they came out and found him shouting at Arthur. He had given that same odd glance, questioning and ashamed. She distinctly remembered that afternoon—the damp aromatic gully, the bellbirds. She had asked Arthur why Austin was angry and he said it was because he had poked fun at the size of Hetty's children.

Hetty's children!

Alice felt as if the blood was draining away from her head. When two people have lived in the closest intimacy for over ten years, each little movement and glance may tell more than a volume of words. He had told her clearly in that glance before he left the room, that Hetty's children were his own.

The implications of this were too great for her to grasp all at once. The blow was too heavy. Her first impulse was to escape, not to see Austin again until her mind was clear. She had put on her bonnet as she had intended going shopping immediately after breakfast to make some last minute purchases for her trip on the Continent. She went quickly from the house, closing the door softly behind her. She hardly knew in which direction she was walking, but she found herself opposite one of the entrances to Hyde Park. She crossed the road and went in and walked for a long time across the grass. At last she felt tired, and coming to a bench she sat down to consider her position.

It must have begun, she thought, on the ship, when she was ill, in the first year of their marriage. When she realised this, that it had begun so soon, the tears streamed down her face. She tried to think how it had happened, even to find some excuse for it. She was ill. She knew Austin's strong appetites, what it would mean to him, after the first rapturous months of marriage, to find himself deprived of his young wife. And there at hand was Hetty, who had always wanted him, ever since she was a child in the schoolroom, and had snatched the cardboard crown.

Even so she could not understand how it had come about, and once or twice she thought it could not have happened, and that the whole thing was a trick of her imagination. She almost started up to return to King Street, to catch Austin before he left for Paddington and to conceal from him that she had held such grotesque suspicions. But she saw how it all fitted too well—his detour to Zurich when he should have been hurrying to Rome to help his mother. He would want to see his child, the baby which was supposed to be Percy Dell's and premature. Hetty had gone to Switzerland so that no one should see how large and robust their 'premature' child might be. And this of course was the reason for her sudden marriage to Dell. As Alice sat there she was struck by new details of the whole sordid sequence, and shaken by fresh bursts of contempt and grief.

The entry in her diary for this day is entirely in French and deals largely with her bewildered emotions. Arthur provided a more detailed account of the affair, as I sat on his mother's needlework chairs at another of those intimate dinners I had with him in the early 1920s, at his house in East St Kilda. I do not know why he told me, unless he thought that I was the most interested, and that family history should be passed on. It may have been simply that in his old age his love of gossip had grown stronger, his desire to startle more imperative, and having less contemporary rumour to draw on, he plunged recklessly into the past. Or, and perhaps this is the real reason, he thought that gradually this story might leak through to me, and he wanted me to know, if I was to be the repository of family history, that his brother had not been wilfully cruel and deceptive to his wife. When the story had leaked through to the older generation, their condemnation of Austin had been savage, and linked with ridicule of his eccentricities, the bells on his harness, his noises on trumpets and shawms, his often outrageous wit, so that one might easily gather the impression that he was an immoral buffoon. Arthur wanted me to know that this was not a true impression. He may also have thought that I might hear malicious tales about himself, about Damaris and her money, and so see his generation as altogether discreditable.

He began by 'throwing Hetty and Sarah to the wolves'. It is not quite accurate to say that he disliked them. He had had so much fun mimicking them that he had quite an affection for them; as if they were a literary creation of his own. He spoke to them kindly when he met them, and in his later years as we have seen, often met Hetty for luncheon. It was not conscious hypocrisy. He did like them when he saw them. When he did not the idea of them filled him either with hilarious ridicule or scorching indignation.

'The thing about the Mayhews,' he said, 'was that they had no taste—at least the women hadn't. The boys were nice gentle creatures and should have been girls, and Hetty and Sarah the men. In that family the natural order was inverted.'

Arthur was speaking at a time when ignorances were assumed which made this kind of remark possible.

'The trouble was that though Hetty should have been a man, she could never have been a gentleman. But even if Hetty wasn't a gentleman, Austin was, and I don't know how they could have gone on like that. They say that being at sea has a certain effect, I must say it wasn't my experience. I felt deathly. Of course . . .' he looked at me sideways, and again asked: 'D'you know about this?' Again trying to make my voice sound indifferent I said: 'No.'

We were back where we had been a few months earlier, when his disclosure had been interrupted by my answering the telephone to Cousin Hetty. Arthur had drunk most of a bottle of claret and now gazed meditatively at his glass of port. He was thinking more of past events than of me, and was not particularly aware of my identity.

'I don't believe that Austin would ever have done it off his own bat,' he said. 'People don't realise what Hetty was like. She may be an intimidating old woman, but as a girl she was terrifying. If you danced with her you felt that you were being dragged into the womb of the eternal mother. And that was if she didn't care a fig for you. If she was determined to have you she must have been irresistible, not because of her charm but because of some super female magnet with which the Almighty had fitted her. Austin hadn't a hope. How the devil they managed it on that little sailing ship I can't imagine. They may have got into a lifeboat of course,' he said pensively. Here Arthur forgot that he was describing events which had cost him life-long unhappiness, and gave himself up to speculating as to how the actual seduction might have been performed. Some of his conjectures were funny but not printable. Suddenly his indignation overcame him.

'And all the time,' he exclaimed, 'Alice was lying sick in her cabin, a bride of six months, carrying her first child. And that beast . . .' He stopped with a slight gasp. 'If Alice had discovered it then I think it would have killed her. I believe that she did find out, many years later, and she was never quite the same again. I only hope that she didn't discover all the details, how soon it had begun. I never knew how much she knew. I could only admire the way she behaved when she did find out. Your grandmother was practically faultless, and yet she never condemned anyone. It may have been because of her own mother. I don't know—but she was so kind . . .'

Again Arthur stopped and caught his breath. Whenever he heard of innocent suffering, or of any injustice he was powerless to remedy, he found it difficult not to cry, and he had to stop speaking for a moment. This is a characteristic of many Langtons. They could not bear to think of people suffering. In Dominic this trait, fortified by Byngham vigour and Teba passion, became a searing anguish. Sir William could only bring himself to sentence a man to death by concentrating his thoughts on the murderer's victim. Arthur himself used to perform quixotic acts of charity in wretched poverty-stricken homes. To the astonishment of his relatives there turned up at the funeral of this witty, malicious and self-indulgent aesthete, a crowd of indigent working-class people whom he had from time to time befriended.

'Well,' he went on, 'one may understand Austin's succumbing on the ship because of the sea air and Hetty's snatching him into a lifeboat every night after dinner, but I'm jiggered if I know how he could keep it up all those years. He must have been afraid of her. In fact he told me he was. Then she found that she was going to have a child. That was a couple of weeks before they reached Plymouth. She set to work rapidly in another direction and grabbed Percy Dell as a form of insurance. You'd think that would sicken Austin for ever, as he was naturally as straightforward as it's possible to be. In spite of Percy Dell, she still wanted to get Austin, wanted him to clear out with her. She made several attempts before she finally married Dell. She persuaded her uncle Mayhew to take her up to London to a lecture by Thackeray. She then pretended to be unwell and went to bed in the hotel. The Mayhews went off to hear Thackeray and she sent a message to Austin, who she knew would be in London on that night, to come round to her. She tried like blazes to make him clear off with her then and there, and threatened to tell everybody and force Alice to divorce him. He said that he'd tell Alice everything himself, and that she wouldn't divorce him. She couldn't anyhow unless he abandoned her. That was the only thing that held Hetty back. She wasn't sure that Alice wouldn't forgive him. She contented herself for the time being with raping him in the hotel bedroom. You see, he didn't really like her, but he couldn't resist her vile body.'

I had tried to lead Arthur back to the point he was at on that evening when Cousin Hetty telephoned, but I was hearing more than I had bargained for. I was half fascinated, but really thought it would be better if the knowledge of these ancient scandals were to die with the last of the generation to which they belonged. But Arthur was in his stride. It was evident that he knew much more than he had originally admitted. When he first spoke to me on this subject, he pretended that various fictions were true, that

Percy Dell for example, was the father of all Hetty's sons. Bit by bit he had revealed a little more, like an Oriental dancer discarding her numerous veils, until this evening I was to see truth uncovered.

'It's a pity,' he said, 'that Austin didn't go back to Waterpark the next morning and make a clean breast of it to Alice. If he had all the horrible business of the next ten years would not have happened. Those so-called Dells would never have been born.' He paused, and twisted his wineglass. 'It's odd, you know,' he reflected, 'that though their origin is scandalous, those boys have done very well. One can hardly say it would have been a good thing if they hadn't been born.'

It was true that if the Dells had not existed the importance of our clan would have been diminished. Except for Arthur's brother Walter who became a High Court judge, they were our most prominent, wealthy and successful relatives. Hetty, never forgetting that she was the daughter of a dean, sent two of them into the Church. One became Bishop of Yackandandah, and the other an archdeacon. Her third son made a fortune on the Stock Exchange and had a fashionable wife and a mansion in Toorak. The fourth became a General in the 1914 War, was knighted and actually killed in battle. His statue stands in the St Kilda Road. It is annoying when we pass this only to be able to say: 'That is our cousin'—when he was really our uncle, but like Sir Launcelot's, our honour rooted in dishonour stands. Arthur seemed puzzled by these considerations and reluctant to continue, but then he said:

'Even if good does come out of evil, it doesn't justify the evil.' Having reassured himself, he again took up his story.

'The next shot Hetty made at him was ten minutes before her wedding. Austin had to give her away as Papa was ill. He tried to get out of it, as it was too appropriate to be decent, though there was no-one he would have more gladly given away, to the devil himself, if necessary. In fact he would rather have given her to the devil. To bestow someone on a piece of protoplasm doesn't guarantee that you're rid of her. He and Hetty were the last to leave the vicarage at Datchet for the church. She had arranged that. She came downstairs all orange blossom and white lace and again asked him to go off with her at that very moment. Her clothes were packed for going away. It wouldn't take her a minute to change her dress. They only had to drive to the train instead of to the church, where her miserable piece of jelly was already waiting at the altar. Austin must have felt like death, but he wouldn't go. She flung her arms round his neck and crushed all her white satin. When he told her she was ruining her wedding dress she moaned: "I am only a bride for you." She had a deep moaning voice when she was young, but it was by no means weak.

'Austin got her to the church and gave her away, a bit crumpled in body and soul. When she drove off after the wedding reception, I bet he mopped his forehead. A few days later, at Waterpark, he heard that they'd gone to Switzerland to live, and he thought a squalid incident was closed, but he mistook Hetty, and what was worse, he mistook himself.

'At that time Papa was very ill, and in the spring he died in Rome. Mama was there alone and Austin had to go out there and settle things up and bring her home to England. If you're in Rome you might go and look at Papa's grave in the Protestant Cemetery and see whether it's kept decently.

It's just on the left as you go in, up towards Shelley's.'

'I've seen it,' I said, 'when we went to Italy before the war. One of the Tunstalls is buried quite close to it. It's rather a coincidence, two people from Frome, buried so close together.'

'I know,' said Arthur crossly, 'it's Aubrey Tunstall, my brother-in-law.'

I thought I had made some kind of gaffe, but was not sure what. Was Arthur annoyed at my referring even so indirectly to his unfortunate marriage? Or was he cross because I affected to know more than he did about his grand connections, his honour again like Sir Launcelot's? Or were his feelings identical with mine when Julian spoke with detachment about my grandparents? I remember thinking old people were difficult, and now probably Julian thinks just the same of me.

'Anyhow,' said Arthur, 'it was not much out of Austin's way to stop at Zurich where Hetty and Dell were living, and where she was nursing her baby, and Austin's of course, a few weeks old. Austin was only about twenty-two, the age at which people are most apt to get into scrapes. They have the judgment of a boy and the feelings of a man. He wanted to see his other child. He was proud that he had achieved two extensions of his personality in such a short time. I don't know why. Any idiot can reproduce himself.'

Arthur paused again. This was probably the first time that he had related this story in full to anyone, and as he did so new aspects of it occured to him, and he found that now in his old age he did not quite hold the views he had thought he held.

'And yet,' he went on more thoughtfully, 'it is perhaps right to be proud of fulfilling the natural law, to be a healthy part of the design of nature. However . . .', his inborn levity returned, 'you don't want to overdo it. Austin had some of the instincts of a sultan. At Zurich he found Hetty looking the picture of animal health, the eternal lioness with her young, a bouncing boy who could no more have been premature than Henry VIII. Austin's pride was a good deal damped by Percy Dell, who though I had always called him the protoplasm, wasn't even that, poor wretch. He was bursting with sniggering paternal pride. He nudged Austin in a sort of "we fathers" manner. The worst thing Austin had to endure in his life was to hear his own children talked about, criticised, laughed at, or even praised as if they were another man's—and such a man! All the family made jokes about the weakling Percy and his enormous boys. I dropped the biggest brick of all just after I came back from England. I went on about Hetty and the protoplasm when Austin suddenly turned on me in a blazing rage. I had never known him do such a thing, and I was staggered. In the evening when we were alone in that room full of bassoons which he had at Westhill he apologised and then he told me the whole story.

'He was ashamed of it. He hated the endless deceptions, especially of Alice, and yet he couldn't help being proud and fond of Hetty's sons. Poor old boy,' Arthur added reflectively, 'from twenty-two till the end of his life, there was no escape. Whenever he was in Australia which he felt was his home, much more than Waterpark, he was afraid that a bomb might explode under him at any moment, that his life and all his affections might be wrecked. By nature he was the most straightforward man alive, yet he was always forced to acquiesce in deceit, and for ten years to practise it even against his wife. It soured his open and generous nature. He became suspicious, wondering who might know about the scandal. He blew himself up into greater importance than he had, and as a kind of defence compiled a book of all the people in Melbourne who had convict ancestors, but he didn't keep it in Melbourne. It was in the library at Waterpark. D'you know what happened to it?'

'I never saw it,' I said. 'It was probably sold with the house.'

'Good God!' exclaimed Arthur. This possibility distracted him further from the thread of his story, but not for long. He was determined now to tell me everything, and though occasionally he might be drawn aside by some irrelevant association, or be seized by some ribald conceit, he was more serious in manner than usual. He was justifying Austin to his descendants, and he went on:

'Well, after Papa's death they all came back to Melbourne. Mama bought this house and Alice took a house opposite Kilawly where those red-brick flats are now. Austin, with ten thousand miles between himself and Hetty, thought no more about her. He got a devil of a jolt when he heard that she was on the way out to Australia, bringing Dell and the baby, and a worse one when she settled only a couple of hundred yards away. Even then he didn't think it would be anything worse than an uncomfortable reminder of what he'd rather forget. But Hetty didn't want to forget. She hadn't been in the house a fortnight, when she sent over a message by the milk-boy, asking if Austin would come over and fix some broken thing in the house, a tap or a door handle or something. It was a natural enough request for someone who had just moved in. Dell was in town for the day. When Austin arrived Hetty didn't bother about the door handle. She had sent out their servant and nurse or whatever they had, and they were alone in the house. She took him into her bedroom to show him the sleeping baby, and she said: "Our son" and stood close against Austin. He was very emotional and though he didn't *like* Hetty, she excited him. Almost before he knew what he'd done, it had happened again. He went home in a funk, disgusted with himself and furious with Hetty, determined not to let it go on. He did everything he could to avoid seeing her alone, but she kept sending over about the door handles.'

Although Arthur's face was solemn and almost tearful as he told me this, he could not resist his instinct to put it in a ridiculous light. He loved to fix on some commonplace article like a door handle, and turn it into an obscene symbol.

'He said he wouldn't go over and mend her bloody door handles, but Alice actually forced him to, saying it would be unkind to refuse. He half-felt that this gave him a kind of excuse, and off he went again. He was probably feeling like it at that moment, and people aren't consistent in their feelings, especially about that sort of thing. Then she told him that she was going to have another child by him, and he felt trapped, especially when the baby was born and it was the spitting image of Austin. There is no Langton blood in the Mayhews, and Austin is a pure Langton—he doesn't take after Mama, but the fact that they were cousins was used to explain the likeness of Hetty's boys to Austin. What I can't understand is how Hetty managed to have children only by Austin all the time he was in Australia. I suppose she played some gynaecological trick on Dell which the ordinary man doesn't know about. The poor devil didn't even deserve to be called a protoplasm. Even after this second child was born Austin tried to break with her. It was like trying to break from the clutch of a gorilla. That is the real reason why he persuaded Alice to buy Westhill and move into the country. If they hadn't done that Mama wouldn't have agreed to go to England again, so Hetty has had far-reaching effects.' Arthur paused, thinking of his own marriage, perhaps wondering what he would have done if he had not married Damaris Tunstall and inherited her money. As he told me this story it became evident how much our misfortune and our good luck were dependent one on the other.

'The move to Westhill nearly blew up the whole show. Hetty was furious and said, what she was always halfthreatening to do, that she would declare the true father of her children. She imagined that the result of this would be a double divorce and that Austin would have to marry her. Austin was not so sure that Alice would now forgive him if she knew of it. He was no longer guilty of a single uncontrolled impulse. She was as likely to be governed by justice as by mercy. Hetty couldn't be certain, either, what Alice would do. She might forgive Austin, while Dell might divorce herself and she'd be left in the lurch. It was only because he emphasised this probability that Austin managed the move to Westhill without an explosion. But that wasn't the end of the business.

'I think that Austin, having got away with it for so long, had almost persuaded himself that other people knew about it, and condoned it—even Alice. He couldn't realise that when she persuaded him to stay the night with the Dells, as a convenience when he went to town, she had no inkling of his relationship with Hetty. Alice wasn't used to dealing with moral thugs and that's what Hetty was. She used to invite herself to Westhill for weeks and squat there with the insolence of a brigand. There are far more near-criminals in the world than we imagine. Alice was indignant and wretched about it, but she didn't know how to cope with anyone who ignored all the rules of decent behaviour. Your Uncle Reggie Byngham said the other day: "One can't argue with a dishonest bookie on a racecourse." Alice probably felt the same about Hetty, squatting in her drawing-room as if she owned it—almost deliberately provocative and not minding if there was a bust-up.

'This state of affairs lasted up to the time Mama and I came out from England. Austin must have known that I didn't know about it, and yet on that afternoon at Westhill when I laughed at the size of Hetty's sons, he couldn't believe that I wasn't pulling his leg, though he also knew perfectly well that if I had known it was the last subject on which I'd pull his leg. It's that sort of confusion that puts people in a rage. To get rid of the confusion he told me the whole story that evening. A few weeks later he and Alice left for England. I don't know how he got away from Hetty, whether there was a final bust-up or what. I think there must have been, as when they came back, although they had a house in Melbourne, they never went near the Dells. The boys used to go up to Westhill, but I don't think Hetty ever went there again—or not for years. I think that Alice discovered the whole thing when they were in England. She looked different when she came back and of course when once Alice knew Austin was free to break with Hetty.

'There was one thing which was very funny. When Austin had been away a year, Hetty had another boy— Harold. This time it was the protoplasm's. There was no mistaking it either, apart from Austin's being away. You only had to look at the poor little devil. Beside his brothers he was like a white mouse beside a lot of prize stallions. Austin must have laughed when he saw him, but of course we never referred to the subject again, after that night at Westhill.'

Arthur chuckled and sipped his port, proud to think his stock had proved so immensely superior to lesser breeds within the law. Then he suddenly switched back to his sylphides and pioneers mood.

'What I want you to understand,' he said, 'is that your grandfather was one of the kindest and most honourable men of his time. He never did a cruel thing, except this that I have told you, and he did not do that willingly.'

Arthur in the last minute or two had unconsciously revealed his own attitude to women. They meant so little to him that he thought that Austin would be amused at a woman, whom he must have regarded as a kind of wife, producing a child by another man. Also he put every bit of the blame on Hetty. He may have been justified in doing this, but can a man of Austin's physical and moral development be held to have no responsibility for his actions? It is unlikely that he would have claimed such immunity.

Arthur pushed back his chair and we went into the drawing room. He walked with his head a little on one side, looking like a man whose private life is disreputable, but who is reverently performing some ecclesiastical function. He lighted the tiny lamp behind the glass miniature of Alice, and then sat down and played the Chopin prelude in G. As I listened to him I no longer had that feeling of old-world tranquillity which I generally had in this room when Arthur played the piano after dinner. I thought that it was rather shocking of him to tell me all this about my grandfather, and yet Austin had died when I was six years old. He is the dimmest memory—not anyone in whose eyes I had recognised a fellow human being. He is only that portrait in the lobby which I discussed with Julian, and a ghostly giant with a hunting crop. Also when people are as old as Arthur was when he told me these things, and when they are as intelligent, and have drunk a little wine, they are apt to see humanity *sub specie aeternitatis*. He was relating to me history and human behaviour, and was hardly aware that he was talking of a man on whose moral nakedness it was not seemly that I should look. Because of Arthur's lack of self-consciousness, I was not embarrassed, and now I thought that perhaps the only thing I should not have heard was his subdued exclamation: 'Poor old boy!' I felt that in those words he revealed the sadness of his own life, and his affection for the brother with whom he had played all the games of childhood in those early days which to him, even more than to myself, must have seemed the sunlit morning of the world. It was a sadness I could not share, and therefore I thought which I should not see.

Since that dinner with Arthur, thirty years ago, I have had access to other sources of information, and now I have the diaries, from which it is clear that the birth of Cousin Harold, which he thought must have amused Austin, really shocked and shattered him, not merely because it was the occasion of Alice's discovering the situation. It revealed to him fully the immorality of his own relationship with Hetty. He had believed in his simple fashion that Percy Dell really was some kind of eunuch. It was easy, looking at him, to think that he was not properly a man. When he had to face honestly the fact that he had been sharing Hetty with this miserable specimen, he was revolted. He saw her as an adulteress not because of her relations with himself, but with her husband. On that morning when he caught the train to Frome, he must have been in a wretched and anxious state of mind. Alice had not come in before he left. He was almost certain that she knew, and yet he dared not do anything which might reveal the facts, if she did not know. At the last minute he scribbled a note: 'I have to go to catch the train. I hope you have a good holiday.' He sent for a hansom and drove off to Paddington.

It was all these events related by Arthur which Alice must have reviewed as she sat in misery in the park. She had never forgotten the details of that first voyage to England, and she recalled those oddities in Austin's manner during its later weeks, which had caused her to write the first of those tiny French entries in her diary. She went on through all the events of the last ten years—the time when they lived near the Dells in East St Kilda and later at Westhill. She lived again through those long visits from Hetty, when she had squatted there as if she owned the place, and no doubt she felt she did own it as she owned Austin. Alice's indignation when she realised the full meaning of those visits, their vile impudence, was so great that she felt she could not bear to see either of them again. Then there was Austin's burst of anger against Arthur, who had been poking fun at the Dell boys. The meaning of the whole thing was clear. It all fitted, right up to this morning, when she had read out Sarah's letter. She stayed in the park till the late afternoon, her reason convincing her that it must be true, her imagination repudiating the convictions of her reason.

7

'Il y a déjà trois semaines depuis que j'ai quitté Austin et je ne sais encore que faire. Je me sens le coeur déchiré, que ma vie est tombée en ruines, mais il me semble sage d'oublier et de tout pardonner. Il faut aussi penser aux enfants.'

This is a sample of the entries in Alice's diaries during her three weeks tour with the Misses Urquhart. Until they parted there is hardly any reference to those two ladies except that one of them made herself tiresome complaining about the poor quality of the tea. They visited the towns immediately to the south and east of Paris. This was Alice's first experience of mediaeval France, and one to which she had been looking forward all her life, but she was so numbed by her own wretchedness that she could not respond to it. This inability was an added injury—to be given what she had longed for at the very moment she was unable to enjoy it. She remembered Lady Langton's words about periods of an adverse fate. She felt that her fate was not merely adverse, but malignant. Occasionally she made an attempt to appreciate what she saw. She wrote:

'The little city of Troyes is like a jewel with its many beautiful churches.' Of Chatillon: 'When I went into that dark narrow church on the hill I almost felt the ghosts of Charlemagne's knights emerge from the walls.' Each of these entries is followed by others in which she returned bewildered to her own problems. At Vézelay she escaped from the Misses Urquhart and sat for a whole afternoon on the ramparts, looking down on the summer hills and fields, but thinking of nothing but herself and Austin.

At last they were back in Paris. They had arranged to return to England together, but Alice felt too undecided to face Austin yet. She believed that if she were to join him at Waterpark, it would mean that she had accepted the situation. She told the Misses Urquhart that she would stay in Paris a little longer.

'But wouldn't it be very marked, dear Mrs Langton,' said the elder sister, 'for you to stay alone in Paris?'

The Misses Urquhart were both over forty and Alice was not yet thirty, so that although she was married they were more in the position of chaperone. Alice said that she wanted to do a little shopping and to see Paris more thoroughly.

'I hope that Mr Langton will not be vexed at our coming home without you.' These mild words were uttered in such a vicious tone that Alice realised her conduct was thought exceedingly unconventional. With a curious mixture of reticence and impertinence the two ladies managed to convey to her that she of all people should be careful, as her elopement was not forgotten, while her mother's behaviour in Sydney could not be forgotten, as it was perennial. These references and the disapproval which they emitted as they said goodbye left Alice in greater depression then ever. She took it as a foretaste of what would happen if there were any break between herself and Austin. She would lose not only her husband but the complete trust of her friends. She nearly changed her mind and followed them by the next train. She felt intolerably lonely and prepared to forgive anything if she could return to the security of affectionate family life. But that sense of justice which was so strongly developed in her, would not allow her to do it. She could not return to something which she now thought had never existed, except in her own imagination. She had been cheated and she could not acquiesce in that. There would have to be some adjustment, and half of her wretchedness came from her inability to see how this could possibly come about. She could not help being aware of the benefits the Langtons had from her. Austin had a marriage settlement of £1,000 a year. She had lent Lady Langton money to furnish her house in London, and again to return to Australia after the death of Damaris. She had lent money to Mrs Mayhew when the dean died, and even to Owen Dell when he was in difficulty. Some of these loans turned out to be gifts. She did not think that she had done anything excessive, but when she found that in return she had not even the fidelity of her husband, the channel through which these benefits flowed, she felt that she had been exploited. This suggests that she was confusing her finances with the feelings of her heart, but it was not so. She simply believed that it was only honourable to accept gifts from those for whom one had completely loyal affections. She felt that she had been a party to dishonourable transactions. I do not want to pretend that Alice had no faults. She had to deal so much with money, and was responsible for the security of so many people that she may have treated it with more respect than most women. If she had not done so, she would soon have had none.

She stayed for two or three days alone in Paris. She went sightseeing to the Louvre, to Versailles, but found that after staring at some of the most famous pictures in the world, she had then turned away without the faintest idea of what she had been looking at. Suddenly she decided to go to Italy. She did not expect to enjoy it, but she had always wanted to go there and she thought she might as well snatch this one ambition from the wreckage of her world. Also it would provide a non-commital excuse for not returning at once to Waterpark. She wrote to Mrs Thomas Langton and said that as her time in Europe was short, she was taking this opportunity of visiting Rome. She still did not write to Austin.

I have now come to the entries in Alice's diaries which I discovered on the night when I discussed with Julian the possibilities of this book, when we had examined the portraits of Alice and Austin in the lobby. They are the entries which decided me to write it. I already knew about Austin and Hetty, but it had never occurred to me as the subject of a novel, partly because I first heard of it from Arthur at a time when it would have been impossible to write about it. Hetty herself was then living. Now thirty years have removed the survivors of one, and the whole of the succeeding generation, and only the ghosts can be grieved at my disclosures.

Alice had intended to go first to Florence, but on the afternoon of the second day, as the train was approaching Pisa, she caught sight of the leaning tower. To come unexpectedly on a world-famous curiosity was exciting, especially to an Australian who had seen few of them. She left the train at Pisa station, drove to an hotel, and then, glad to be free of the train, walked briskly along to the Campo Santo. As she passed along the river bank, with the solid line of renaissance palaces on her right, for the first time since she left London she felt a faint gleam of pleasure and of hope. It may have been largely due to her physical relief from the cramped space of the train. She puts it down to a liberation of the spirit brought about by her first glimpse of the Renaissance, but she wrote all this in the evening before going to bed, and this feeling may not have awakened until she reached the cathedral and may have been due to something quite different. The marble of the three lovely buildings, the cathedral, the baptistery and the tower, mellowed with age to a golden tint, was bathed in the evening sunlight. Beyond the walls of the Campo Santo was a line of distant purple hills, which might easily have been the background of a cinquecento painting. Within sight there was nothing of the modern world. She writes that she had the feeling that the centuries between herself and Giorgione and Perugino had been swept away.

She walked slowly across the grass to see the buildings from the other side. As she turned the corner of the cathedral she came upon a man who was standing looking at the baptistery, which was behind her, so that for a moment he glanced straight into her eyes. He immediately looked away, and with a kind of impersonal courtesy, moved out of her path. She thought he must be an Englishman, but his face and manner were more sensitive than those of the fox-hunting neighbours at Waterpark. He disappeared round the building, the way she had come, but for the rest of the time she was in the Campo Santo, she was aware of this slight encounter and pleased by it.

In her hotel when she came down to dinner, she saw this man seated at a table near her own. She felt that he was aware of her, but he made no sign of recognition. He finished his dinner before she did, and he had to pass her table to leave the room. She was prepared to bow to him, as she was sure that he was English, but he did not look in her direction. She was disappointed as she was longing to talk to almost anybody.

The next morning at the railway station, she was having some difficulty with the porter about her luggage, when this man again appeared. He came along the platform and asked if he could be of any help. She explained which things she wanted with her in the carriage. He addressed the porter in fluent Italian and there was no further trouble. She noticed that he scrutinised her luggage with particular interest, and she thought it strange in a man who otherwise appeared so well bred. Then he said that he could not help noticing that, on her trunks were some labels: 'Langton, Frome, G.W.R.' and added:

'Surely you must be one of the Langtons of Waterpark?'

'My husband is a cousin of Mr Thomas Langton's,' said Alice. 'We are Australians.'

'Are you Mrs Austin Langton?' he asked.

'Yes,' said Alice, 'but how do you know my name?'

'I am Aubrey Tunstall. My sister Damaris married your brother-in-law.'

'Oh!' Alice paused, a brief acknowledgment of the tragic aspect of the connection between them. 'How extraordinary that we should meet here!'

'It's more natural for us to meet here than at Dilton, I'm afraid,' he said smilingly. 'I'm hardly ever in England.'

Alice had an idea that the Tunstalls might hold the Langtons to be in some way responsible for the death of Damaris, but there was no suggestion of this in his reference to it. He asked if he might travel to Florence with her, if that was her destination. She said that she intended to spend a few days there on her way to Rome. She told him that Austin was hunting at Waterpark, that she did not hunt, and that she was taking advantage of this to see what she could of Italy. She said that she had not very long as they probably would soon have to return to Australia.

'When you see Arthur Langton, give him my kindest regards,' he said. 'I feel that we might have been very great friends if he had stayed in Europe.' He said that he had a little painting that Arthur had given him. She was surprised, as Arthur had never mentioned his friendship with Aubrey Tunstall. From the way he spoke it was clear that he regarded Arthur as quite free from any share of responsibility for the tragedy. He even remarked that Damaris had a very difficult temperament.

He asked her where she intended to stay in Florence, and when she said that she did not know, he recommended an hotel. He said that he was going to stay a few days with his sister, Ariadne Dane, who had a villa up towards Fiesole. He also lived in Italy and had an apartment in Rome.

'Yes, I know that,' said Alice. She told him of the strong impression made on her by the three beautiful buildings in the Campo Santo and that she had not really meant to stop at Pisa, but had been unable to resist the glimpse of the leaning tower. He seemed very pleased by her enthusiasm, especially when she said that she would prefer the leaning tower if it were straight.

'It is such an exquisite thing in itself,' she said, 'that it ought to be admired for its beauty, rather than its oddity.' He gave her a glance of warm approval, and she felt that there was already a basis of friendship between them.

At the station in Florence, he saw to her luggage and engaged a cab for her, which he directed to the hotel he had named. His own things were put into a carriage which had been sent to meet him. He gave a hint of surprise that Alice was travelling without a maid, and she told him that Australians were self-reliant. When her cab stopped at the hotel, his carriage drew up behind it. He alighted and came into the hotel with her. He spoke to the manager, who treated him with deference, and evidently told him that Alice was someone who must be shown great consideration. Alice thanked him for what he had done and he said:

'It is the least I could do for a neighbour who is almost a relative. I am much more indebted to you for making what might have been a tiresome journey delightful.' He shook hands and said goodbye.

The rest of the day was very dull to Alice. All her problems which she had forgotten while she was talking to him in the train, returned to distress her. She thought the English were strange and unfriendly, judging as people are apt to do, a whole nation by one man. She was sure that an Australian, after all the pleasant intercourse of the journey, would not say goodbye in that final manner. In the evening she wrote in her diary, after the long description of her encounter with Aubrey Tunstall:

'I should remember what Lady Langton says about periods of misfortune—that it is foolish at these times to attempt to seek any pleasure or happiness. I should not have come on to Italy, but have returned with Miss Urquhart. Tonight I feel dreadfully lonely. I wish I were at Westhill with my darling children. How lovely it would be to stand on the hill looking across the bay, and to smell the gum leaves, and to hear the children shout in the evening air.'

The next afternoon, Mrs Dane left a card and a note for her. The note invited her to luncheon on the following day and apologised for the short notice but the writer understood that Alice was only in Florence for a limited time. If Alice was able to come a carriage would be sent for her. Mrs Dane excused herself for writing by mentioning that their families were neighbours in Somerset, but she did not refer to Arthur or Damaris. Alice was excited by this invitation, as she had heard at Waterpark that Mrs Dane was both beautiful and cultivated, though not entirely approved of by her relatives. Also she was longing for some human contact.

In the afternoon she went to the Uffizi and she deliberately noted certain pictures so that she could discuss them with Mr Tunstall.

Mrs Dane's villa had none of the associations of that word in Alice's mind, which were purely suburban. It was a villa in the Vergilian or Renaissance sense of the word. She had been in some fine country houses near Waterpark but never in anything comparable with the magnificence of this. She was led down a colonnade which made her think of a Fra Angelico *Annunciation*, into a very large drawing-room. On the yellow brocade walls were paintings which appeared to be by those masters whose works she had seen yesterday in the Uffizi, and on the domed ceiling were painted gods and amorini revelling in sunset splendour. There were about a dozen other guests and Alice was the last to arrive, not by her own arrangement as she could not come before the carriage was sent for her. Amongst these people were a young Italian tenor, a Roman principessa, a Royal Academician, a French duke and duchess and an English lady novelist, festive with orchids and jewelry, whom, it was said later, Mrs Dane had horsewhipped for stealing her lover. Alice thought Mrs Dane extremely distinguished in appearance and like her mother whose portrait she had seen at Dilton. Caroline O'Hara, Lord Dilton's second wife and as I have mentioned the grand-daughter of the duque de Teba, was the mother of Aubrey, Damaris and Ariadne Tunstall. She was a famous beauty, a poetess and amateur actress in whom the Regency tradition lingered well into the Victorian era. I also have seen this portrait. It shows her to have had one of those passionate chiselled faces, and an immensely emotional mouth. I also when a boy saw Mrs Dane, then very old. I shall not describe her here, except to say that she terrified me. Even when Alice saw her, I think her beauty must have been more of bones than of flesh. Alice wrote:

'She is very animated in conversation and has fine eyes. When I was announced she gave me a second's scrutiny, but then seemed satisfied with my appearance. I think she may have arranged for me to arrive last, so that she could warn the others that an Australian was coming. When she introduced me she said that I was almost a relative, though she had made no reference to this in her note.'

They went into a long dining-room, even more splendid than the room they had left. There was a footman in blue livery behind every chair. There was also a vaulted ceiling and it was rather like having luncheon in a luxurious church.

As I had said to Julian, the Langtons were witty, quick-minded but rather shallow in their perceptions. They had to see the funny side of everything, which did not make for any great depth of culture, but they were by far the most cultivated people whom Alice had known hitherto. With this limited experience perhaps she was unduly impressed by Mrs Dane and her circle. She writes that she had never heard such brilliant conversation as at this luncheon. There was hardly any subject which Mrs Dane could not discuss with apparent competence, though she spoke mostly of art and music. She gave Alice interested and almost affectionate glances down the table. Much of the conversation was in French and occasionally in Italian. Alice could understand the Italian, but did not attempt to speak it because of her accent. She spoke in French however to the Duc de C., who was on her left. When Mrs Dane saw that she was talking quite fluently and intelligently her eyes lighted with pleasure. Back in the drawing-room she fastened on her and asked her how long she was staying in Florence. Mr Tunstall came and stood beside them.

'Only a few days,' said Alice.

'But you can't stay *only a few days* in Florence!' cried Mrs Dane. She made a despairing gesture with her long thin hand. 'Listen. Why don't you come here? It's absurd for you to be staying at that hotel when you're really a relative. I'll show you all Florence—everything that's worth seeing—even Mr Browning.'

'Mrs Langton only has a very little time in Italy,' said Mr Tunstall, 'and she must go to Rome.'

'Now Aubrey, don't be tiresome,' said his sister, and she gave him a quite vicious glance from her dark emotional eyes.

Alice was very flattered by this invitation. It opened up to her a world she had never dreamed of entering, where people with charming manners, whose names, like those of the duc and the principessa, are read in St Simon or Roman history, were absorbed above all things in art and literature and the cultivation of the spirit. At luncheon, Mrs Dane did not hesitate to quote with eyes magnificently aflame those lines of poetry which most stirred her heart and mind. This appeared to Alice the very highest level of civilisation and she would have liked to remain on it forever. Their standards of reference dazzled her, but they were not altogether beyond her understanding. She thought it would be well worth sacrificing a few weeks in Rome as a sightseer, to stay in Florence in this society. It would also, she thought, dispel a little her terrible feeling of insecurity. To stay here would be considered quite normal by the people at Waterpark, whereas every day that she spent wandering alone and aimless on the Continent widened the breach between herself and Austin, which she longed to heal.

Mr Tunstall looked irritated. She felt that he did not want her to accept his sister's invitation, and as it was through him that she had come to the villa, she thought that it would be in bad taste to do so. She explained that she had such a short time in Italy, and Mrs Dane did not press her further.

'It's a great shame,' she said rather petulantly. 'It's all Aubrey's fault.' She drifted off to talk to the young tenor.

'I really think that you ought to see Rome,' said Mr Tunstall quietly, as if he admitted the responsibility for her refusing Mrs Dane. 'Before you go, perhaps you would let me show you some of my favourite parts of Florence.' Alice said she would like it very much, and they arranged to meet the next afternoon.

Mrs Dane announced that the young tenor was going to sing. They moved into another yet more palatial room, where in addition to a grand piano there was a harp, at which she seated herself. Alice felt a little uncomfortable as she watched her hostess's long thin hands plucking almost convulsively at the wires, accompanying the throbbing passion of the young tenor's song. When Alice left she said:

'You won't like Rome at all. It is dark and full of enormous marble popes that loom up at one everywhere. Rome has always been a pure expression of megalomania. You will soon sigh for our light and golden Tuscany, our beloved flower town, and don't forget that when you do, you must stay here. Aubrey has been very tiresome indeed.'

Alice enjoyed very much her afternoon's sightseeing with Aubrey Tunstall. He did not take her to large and obvious things like the Bargello, but into some small out-of-the-way place to see a Mino da Fiesole altarpiece or an iron well-head in a cloister. In the late afternoon they drove up to San Miniato, and stood at the edge of the terrace, looking down to where Giotto's tower rose through the strata of golden mist. She told him that he had taught her how to see a city.

'May I teach you how to see Rome?' he said.

She hesitated and asked if he were going to Rome soon. He said he was going there in two days time. Alice still hesitated and he said:

'You should allow me to perform the duties of a relative.'

'It would be very kind of you to spare me some of your time in Rome,' Alice replied. 'It would certainly make a great difference to my appreciation of it.'

'It is a great pleasure to show the things one loves to someone who can enjoy them,' he said. 'Ariadne is an enthusiast for Florence. I am a Roman. She was annoyed at the victory of the rival city.'

'Is her husband alive?' Alice enquired.

'Yes. He lives in Meath. I'm afraid the Tunstalls are not good at happy marriages.'

'Are you not married?' asked Alice diffidently.

When he said no she was a little relieved. She thought that somehow it made it slightly more conventional for her to go about with him if he were unmarried. He asked if he might accompany her on the journey to Rome. She thought it would be foolish to refuse this, and they arranged to meet at the railway station, two days ahead. In spite of this he turned up at her hotel early on the following afternoon, and asked if she would care to drive with him to the Certosa.

The journey to Rome was as pleasant as that from Pisa. There was a carriage waiting for him at the railway station, and he drove Alice to a hotel nearby, and again gave instructions for her comfort. He said that he expected she would want to rest after her journey, but that on the following afternoon he would call if he might, and begin to teach her to see Rome.

Alice felt a little flat, but she was beginning to see that these postponements and formal arrangements were part of his style of living and did not mean to show any unfriendliness. She thought they were very English. An Australian would say: 'Well, I'll just take my bags along, and then I'll come back and see how you are.' Mr Tunstall's way was a little chilling, but when their friendly meetings were separated by this external frame of formality, it gave them a special value. In the morning she did not go far from her hotel, partly because she did not want to go to see anything which he might be intending to show her. She began on this day to adjust her plans to suit his movements.

Up to this point Alice's diary from the time of her meeting with Aubrey Tunstall is written with a good deal of telegraphic abbreviation, so I have transposed it into narrative form, though without any embroidery. I was able to give an idea of Mrs Dane's villa from my own memory. But as Alice is the only authority I have for what happened while she was in Rome, and as she wrote about it at much greater length than she gave to her other entries, it seems best to let the account stand in her own words. It has been rather difficult to join it all up in its right order, as she wrote far more than would go into the space allotted by the printer for each day, and so continued her entries on back pages which she had not filled, turning the book upside down and writing from the bottom of the page.

On the first afternoon when she had arranged to meet Aubrey, he took her for a drive to give her a general idea of the city, before showing her individual sights. In the evening, after writing some of her impressions of Rome, she added: 'He is certainly a very cultivated man and I am most fortunate to have met him.' Then, as throughout all the diaries there comes the sign that her emotions are affected, either painfully or otherwise. She writes in French: 'Il m'a fait oublier un peu ma grande peine.'

In a few days she begins to write almost entirely in French, which I am translating, except for a few short passages, written with evident intensity of feeling but in a kind of flowery language which might sound ridiculous in English. It is only decent to allow Alice this slight amount of concealment. For some reason it seems permissible to me to reveal her grief but not her joy. On 3 October she wrote:

'This morning I did a little shopping. It would be foolish to go sightseeing by myself when it is so much more interesting with Mr Tunstall. I bought some pictures of Rome and posted them to Sarah to give to the children, the Spanish Steps for Steven, the Temple of Vesta for Mildred, and some pretty little *putti* for the others. I think they should be made aware of Europe from the beginning. I do not want them to suffer any disadvantage from being Australians, and to grow up unfit to mix with people like Mr Tunstall or with those whom I met at Mrs Dane's villa. They should be able to enter the best society that is open to them. If Austin inherits Waterpark, there is no reason why they should not have a wide choice of friends of the best kind. The problem of Austin tonight seems less urgent to me. I am becoming averse to the idea of an open break. It would be a purely negative action and harmful to everyone, especially the children. I feel that already Rome has given me a wider and more generous outlook—perhaps even a more worldly view.

'After luncheon Mr Tunstall called for me and drove me out beyond the Porta Ostiense to S. Paolo. On the way, he asked me about Australia, but I do not think that he is really interested in any country but Italy, not even in the beautiful countryside around Dilton. It was strange to tell him about our little Westhill when I thought of Dilton, even more in comparison with Mrs Dane's wonderful villa near Fiesole. It made me feel rather sad and protective towards the children, and determined that they should not be deprived of any good thing if I could help it. By good things I do not mean what can be bought. He asked me about our friends in Melbourne and I mentioned the Bynghams. He said he believed that he had some relatives of that name, but did not know them personally. This struck me as an odd coincidence, that he and therefore Damaris should be a connection of the Bynghams. I do not think Arthur knew that.

'4 October. Today I lunched with Mr Tunstall at his apartment. M. and Mme de C., whom I met in Florence, were there. Mr Tunstall introducing me said: "You remember ma belle-soeur whom you met at Ariadne's." I had the feeling that he had asked French people, as they were unlikely to know how slender is our relationship. I expect it is very unconventional of me to be so much in his company. It certainly would be very marked in Melbourne. His apartment is in a sixteenth-century palace, and the rooms, if anything are even more splendid than in Mrs Dane's villa. The conversation was in French, which I could follow easily and join in without too much discredit. It was pleasant, but quite simple, and did not seem to me to have the brilliance and culture which impressed me so much at Mrs Dane's. I think Mr Tunstall is simpler than his sister. I like him for that. After luncheon he took us into a small room, a kind of study, in which he keeps his more personal possessions. Over the writing table in an old gilded frame is the painting Arthur gave him. It is quite small, of a winged boy, naked in a fig-tree. An unusual subject, but it struck me as being very well done, much better than anything I have seen of Arthur's. I was surprised and pleased that Mr Tunstall thought it good enough to hang in an apartment where there are some fine old masters. He drew Madame de C.'s attention to it, partly I think to draw her attention as well to our "relationship" mentioning that the painting was by my brother-in-law. We had not planned to make any excursion this afternoon, and as soon as the duchess rose to leave I followed her example, so that she would not think that I was staying with Mr Tunstall. I was quite contented for the rest of the afternoon to stroll alone to the Spanish Steps and mount up into the sunshine where I sat for an hour. This evening I wrote to Lady

Langton and told her I had seen Sir William's grave, which we visited yesterday on the way back from S. Paolo. I did not hint at any rift between Austin and me, though I fear she will think it peculiar for me to be travelling alone.

'7 *October.* Mr Tunstall is really a wonderful courier. He never crowds too many things into one day, and he alternates some major visit, as to the Vatican, with a country excursion. If we go to see something that is not tiring, we may go out both in the morning and the afternoon. He never lets me see more than two churches, and a limited number of pictures in one day so my appetite is always keen. It is exceedingly kind of him to give me so much time, but he says that my appreciation revives his own, and I can understand this. I enjoy best the drives and little excursions outside the walls. In this rich autumnal season, I am seeing Italy at its best. The vines are hung with ripening purple grapes. In places I have seen them trailing over the olive trees making a beautiful combination of colours, and it is like a dream to stand on Monti Pincio and look over the domes of this noble city. I said to Mr Tunstall that I had no conception of what beautiful places there were in the world until I came to Italy. I have read of them and seen pictures but they did not convey the reality. Of course there is very striking scenery in Australia, and the view even from Westhill is magnificent, but it has not the same connection with humanity. If on a fine day, I can see a tiny ship in the far distance, moving down the bay, and know that it is setting out for Europe, that association in some way enriches the scene. Mr Tunstall said: "You love Italy because Italy is humanity. It provides the pattern of life for the whole Western world." I told him of the feeling I had as soon as I came into the Campo Santo at Pisa, that it was the scene of some life I had known before, and I said I had this feeling even more strongly in Rome. He looked at me with great understanding and kindness and said: "Then you feel as I do."

'*12 October*. I have not written in my diary for the last few days because as soon as I took up my pen I did not know what to write. I have not dared to write what I felt. We have been for some beautiful drives, and I must keep a record of what we have done as I do not want to forget such remarkable experiences. We went for a whole wonderful day to Tivoli. The day was still and full of sunlight, but down amongst those fountains and waterfalls it was a mysterious fairyland. Driving back through the golden evening we passed some blue carts laden with grapes, and some singing peasants who had been gathering the vintage. I thought one or two of them were tipsy, but Mr Tunstall said this was not so. They were only a very happy people. Of course they could not become intoxicated with fresh grapes. This was two days ago. Yesterday we did not go out in the afternoon as we were going to the Opera in the evening. The opera was *Figaro* and Mr Tunstall sent me a beautiful bouquet of yellow roses. The Opera House was crowded with distinguished looking people, the women with magnificent jewels. Mr Tunstall pointed out to me the Colonnas, a Russian grand duke who is in Rome, some Sforzas, and others with famous names. I have been to Covent Garden when the Prince and Princess of Wales were there, but the audience did not seem as brilliant to me as last night's. There is so much vitality in the Italians. *Figaro* has always been one of my favourite operas, for the music, but last night I became fully aware of the plot. I really hated it for its treatment of love as if it were only a matter for silly and sordid intrigue. I felt dreadfully confused and unhappy. It made me think of A. and H. and I felt myself mixed up in it too. In the interval Mr Tunstall introduced me to a number of people, always saying that I was his sister-in-law, Mrs Langton of Waterpark, as if Waterpark were a kind of title. I think that he did this so that my position should not be in any way equivocal. Normally, I should have enjoyed this exceedingly, but I felt wretched, and in this splendid scene, amongst all those grand people, I only longed to be back at Westhill. In anyone else such an exhibition of poor spirit would have angered me, and I only hope that I did not show it.

'After the opera, Mr Tunstall asked if I would go to supper with him at his apartment. I did not know whether it was to be a party, or whether we would be alone together, but whichever it was I did not feel that I could refuse without vulgarity, seeing that he has always behaved towards me with absolute courtesy. The supper was laid in his huge dining-room and we were waited on by two Italian footmen, in addition to the butler; this absence of any attempt to create an intimate atmosphere again showed his respect for me. At the end of supper the servants went out, but we sat on over the table. He asked me in a friendly but disinterested voice, so that it did not sound impertinent, if I was happy. I said that there had been times in this past week when I thought I had not been so happy for years. He said: "Yes, but I mean generally happy in your life." I could not answer for a while. I did not know what to say, as before I came to Italy I had been almost in despair, but I could not tell him that. Then

I thought that he was so kind and honourable that I could trust him entirely, and I said: "I have not been happy." He said: "If you don't want to tell me, of course you mustn't speak of it, but I thought it might be a relief to you to tell me, as you seem very much alone." So then I told him about A. and H. how it had begun long ago, and how I had discovered it. When I had finished he was silent for awhile. At last he said: "I was hoping it was something in which I could help you, but in this matter I don't see how I can. All the same, I hope you won't mind having told me." I said that I was glad I had told him, that it was a relief. Then I rose to leave, as I was upset, and did not want to embarrass him. I think that all his actions are very considered. When he left me at the hotel he kissed my hand. That is usual here but it is the first time he has done it. When I saw him kissing the hands of the Italian ladies at the opera, I was a little jealous. Je crois que je l'aime. Je l'aime. Je l'aime.'

Between the leaves of Alice's diary for this day are some silky brown petals, pressed for three quarters of a century, which may have been those of yellow roses. The next entry is in tiny writing, which I had to read with a magnifying glass, and which I have not the heart to translate.

Je sais que je l'aime. Je ne sais pas s'il m'aime. Depuis le soir de *Figaro* il m'a envoyé tant de belles fleurs. Ma chambre est comme un jardin, mais dans ce jardin je suis une prisonnière, ne sachant pas que faire. Je ne sais pas si je suis mauvaise, si je suis folle. Quand je pense à mes enfants à Westhill, je pourrais le croire, mais quand je pense à lui je ne me sens qu'heureuse. Et pourtant je doute encore. Malgré les fleurs, il ne se comporte que comme un frère aîné et bien gentil. Dois-je l'encourager? Peut-être est-il trop délicat pour me parler d'amour si le signe ne vient pas de moi. Je me tourmente parce-que je ne sais pas ce que je veux. Quelquefois il me semble que la porte du paradis est ouverte, rester toujours dans cette ville merveilleuse avec cet homme le plus sympathique, le plus spirituel que j'ai jamais connu. Si je peux obtenir de divorcer avec A. et ensuite m'épouser avec M. Tunstall, je crois que les enfants seraient encore à moi. Mais à Rome, dans son palais magnifique, ce n'est pas une chose que je peux envisager. Ma chambre aux fleurs est devenue une chambre de torture. Je dois être deux femmes, pouvante habiter deux mondes.'

The next entry is also in French but in her ordinary handwriting. Apparently it was only at times of intense feeling that she wrote in that minute style.

'*16 October.* Last night I dined at his apartment. He did not say whether it was to be a party, but that is his manner, not to be very communicative about his arrangements. I made a rather grande toilette, in case it was a party, but there were only the two of us. The same three men waited on us as on the night after the opera. All his appointments are beautiful, gold filigree Venetian glass, and gold or silver-gilt candlesticks, salt cellars, etc. I imagine he dines like this every night, even when alone, as there was a sort of simple routine about it. It gave me an odd feeling of unreality to dine in such state when I was so emotionally disturbed. The ceiling is high with heavy rafters, painted in rich designs. The walls are covered with a soft blue velvet, which looks darkish in the candlelight. It is faded unevenly so that it looked as if the great room beyond the little golden island of our table was enclosed by mysterious clouds from the sea. It is far more splendid than anything I am used to. Waterpark is a cottage to it, and even the few great houses I have been to in England still have a feeling of domesticity about them. But Mr Tunstall's apartment is full of the ghosts of cardinals and princes. At dinner he was very friendly and natural, and yet I felt that this grandeur of Roman life, which at first fascinated me, and still does, was something separating us rather than bringing us together. One could not imagine there the children coming in for dessert. It seemed to me that he made his life a picture rather than a natural growth, or that he had created for himself a setting so perfect that it restricted the fullness of his life. Or was this setting for himself? Wasn't it for some long dead cardinal? This did not lessen my regard for him. It may even have increased it by making me aware that he was not entirely contented with the circumstances to which he had been born. He is perhaps in something the same position in Italy as I am in England. We may both be said to be living outside the countries where we were born a little "above our station in life". For just as Waterpark is above Westhill, so is Mr Tunstall's palace in the princely style of life which it suggests, above Dilton. This makes for a sense of artificiality in his life, though he himself is in no way artificial.

'After dinner we went into the drawing-room. He sat down at the piano and asked me if I would sing. I do sing a little, but I was nervous of doing so before him and I refused. I had a feeling that he would be impatient of anything not of the very finest quality. At the opera he made subtle criticisms which would have escaped me. I too like the best that can be had, in music, in art, in society, but I think this can be a danger to one's love of one's friends, which is the most valuable of all things. When I said I would not sing, he played a Chopin prelude, while I stood looking down from the window. It was a beautiful warm night and I could almost have read by the moonlight. The buildings were very distinct but softened. The statue of the Virgin in a niche opposite looked almost alive against the darkness behind it. One cannot move in Rome without seeing on every corner, through every archway, some evidence of the genius and the faith of the people. After a while Mr Tunstall left the piano and stood beside me. I asked him what he had been playing, as it condensed for me all the beauty of this wonderful night. He said it was a Chopin prelude and he wrote down the number for me on a piece of paper.'

In this page of Alice's diary is a slip of paper on which is written 'Chopin—Prelude in G. Op. 28'. The handwriting is curious and at first glance suggests that it is not in European characters, but though decorative, it is easy to read. She continues:

'I must learn to play it when I get back. I see that I have unconsciously written "when I get back". Mr T. then said that we should pay a visit to the Fountain of Trevi, for me to throw in the coin which brings one back to Rome, and which must be thrown in by moonlight. It is only a short distance from his apartment, and as I had brought a simple dark cloak, we agreed to walk. When we came to the fountain we sat on the rough-hewn stones at the side. Behind us giant statues loomed staringly white from the black shadows made by the high moon. The perpetual noise of that silver sheet of falling water made it easier to talk. At times, since I have been in his company, I have felt that our minds are absolutely in accord, that we see everything in the same light. This gives me a sense of security of a kind I have not known before. It was very strong last night. I could not bear the idea of leaving Rome, and in one way Mr T. is Rome to me. I was silent, thinking about this. He must have thought I wanted to return to the hotel, as he stood up and said: "Well, now you must throw in the coin." I did not move, but said: "Even if I don't want to leave Rome?" There must have been something in my voice which contained not more than I felt, but more than I wanted to reveal. He started and turning towards me, took both my hands, and exclaimed softly: "Alice!" It is the first time he has called me Alice. At that moment I knew that his feelings for me were the same as mine for him. His voice was so *kind*. I thought that he was going to make some further gesture, to say something which showed his feelings, but when he had raised me to my feet a kind of diffidence came over him, as if he was not certain how I would receive any declaration. "In any case," he said, "you had better throw in the coin, to be on the safe side." He handed me a lire which I tried to throw into the centre basin, but it only fell into the wide pool below, and made a tiny silver splash in the moonlight. We walked back together to the hotel where he left me. When he said goodbye he again kissed my hand, and he gave me a long look into my eyes. I am certain now that I have the choice. He would have spoken tonight but he was taken by surprise. At the next opportunity he will speak. I do not think that I have the power to refuse him. I cannot turn away from a region which, the moment I entered it, I knew was the home of my spirit. This opening to a new world has come at a moment when my old world has utterly failed me, when I found that it had never been mine. I cannot feel that I owe any duty to Austin when he has ignored his to me from the very beginning. The children will be mine. That will have to be arranged. They will be better off here. They will have more opportunities, they will be free from the shameful association with the Dells, and they will not have that restlessness which comes of having two countries, which has been so bad for all of us. I have to deny a whole side of my nature and my life, to end some of my closest friendships if I stay in Europe, but I have to deny my life itself if I leave Rome.'

And then in tiny writing, not perhaps so that it would be illegible, but to minimise its importance, she wrote:

'Je ne suis pas toute contente.'

'*17 October*. This morning a letter from Mr Tunstall came up with my breakfast. I knew it was from him because of his writing down for me the number of the Chopin Prelude, and no one else knows that I am here. I thought that he had written what he had hesitated to say by the fountain and my heart beat violently as I opened it. I destroyed it because I could not bear to keep such a souvenir. But I remember every word. He wrote: "I must go away for a while. Do not think it is because my regard for you is any less. It is because it is greater. Rome, my Rome at any rate, would be a drug to you. You are worthy of more nourishing food. I am immune to the drug, or perhaps it is all I can thrive on. Do not stay in Rome, but come back to it. Please forgive me for everything and remember what I told you about the Tunstalls. Do not blame Arthur for Damaris. With all the love of which I am capable, which is great enough to care most for your good, Aubrey." I have not been out all day. I cannot think.'

There is a gap of a fortnight before the next entry, which is as follows:

'2 *November.* We are back at Waterpark. I shall never forget the last two weeks, but I shall write down what happened in case in years to come my memory distorts it. I stayed two days in the hotel in Rome. I could not bear to go out as every street and stone made me think of A. T. Nor could my mind turn in any direction. It was like the suffocation of my spirit, as bad as the day when I discovered about Austin and Hetty. I tried to think of Westhill and the children to heal myself, but my heart was numbed. On the third morning I was in my room, which was still full of the flowers that A. T. had given me. They were wilting but I could not bring myself to throw them away. A waiter came to tell me that a signore was downstairs, asking to see me. I was sure that it was A. T. returned. I did not see how it could be anyone else, as only he knew I was here, excepting a few people like M. de C. who would hardly be likely to call on me without his wife, and in the morning. I was filled with the greatest joy I have ever known, not the deepest or most enduring, but the most sudden and excessive. I went to the looking-glass to see that I was tidy before going down, and I was astonished at the expression of my eyes.

'When I came into the hall I saw not A. T. but Austin. I nearly fainted, but I have never actually fainted. I began to tremble and held onto the bannister of the stairs. He came over to me. He looked dreadfully concerned and ashamed, like a clumsy schoolboy who has broken a very valuable piece of china. The first thought I had that emerged clearly from the tumult in my mind was that all that Austin had done did not matter. It was only a broken vase in a house which remained standing. He did not say anything, or move close to greet me. He was waiting to see how I would receive him. When I had recovered control of my voice and my limbs I led him to a little sitting-room on the right of the hall, which was empty. I asked him how he knew I was here and he said: "He told me." We talked a little in a formal way, but we both knew that everything was right between us. I asked a few questions about Waterpark, but he said that he had not been there. I was surprised as he had been looking forward so much to the hunting. "Where have you been?" I asked. "In London," he said. "I've been reading for the bar." When he said this I felt that even the vase was not broken, and at last I burst into tears.

'We left the same day for London, and all the way back I felt as if I were awakening from an extraordinary dream. I could not understand myself—I can not yet—how I could turn round in a few hours from a desperate longing for A. T. to feeling all my old love for Austin as strong as ever. I wonder if there is a looseness in my character which can only be controlled if I cling firmly to my husband, whatever he does. If any other woman had behaved as I have, I should certainly have condemned her. I have not forgotten the dream. How could I? There was an unusual affinity between myself and A. T. We should have recognised it anywhere, but Rome produced the perfect conditions for its acknowledgment, just as a plant will grow in any part of the garden, but there is one particular corner, beneath a sunlit wall, where it will blossom on every branch.'

They left the following week for Australia, and were back at Westhill in time for Christmas.

There were certain things which Alice did not explain in her Rome entries, and about which one can only make conjectures. Austin, when she asked him how he knew of her whereabouts, said: 'He told me.' Who was 'he'? Austin arrived in Rome only three days after Aubrey had left, therefore the latter may have written to him before the night by the Fountain of Trevi, probably after Alice had told him of her troubles and he said he could not help her, which suggests that he realised that her only enduring happiness lay in her return to her husband. It is pathetically clear that his feeling for her was not as great as hers for him. She had identified him with the splendour of Rome itself. All the same, when on the night by the fountain he saw that Alice was ready to live with him, or marry him if possible, he wanted to take her, but as he had already written to Austin, saying he should come for her, there was no course open to him but to check his impulse and go away.

This explanation fits. It is most likely the true one, but there is another. It is possible that Austin's 'he' was not Aubrey, but the hall porter or the concierge, that Austin had learnt Alice's whereabouts from her bank, and on enquiring at the hotel if she were still there, had been told so by a servant, to whom he referred indifferently as 'he'. Again, why did Aubrey in his farewell note mention Damaris and Arthur? May his flight have had nothing to do with Austin's coming, but have been due to his consciousness that 'the Tunstalls were not good at happy marriages', at least those three who were the children of Caroline O'Hara? Did he feel in his blood some taint of Teba perversity or Renaissance wickedness which made him unfit to be the lover or husband of anyone as innocent as Alice?

And yet, when one reads his farewell letter it is impossible to deny that it is slightly nonconformist in tone—so much anxiety for her good, when he was probably just as anxious not to have half-a-dozen Australian children sliding on the marble floors of his palace. Could Renaissance wickedness have a nonconformist tinge, like 'poetry touched with decency,' the conception of a Cambridge don?

I wish that I had asked Arthur what Aubrey was like, but when the former was alive I was hardly aware of the latter's existence. The Tunstall boys whom I knew at Dilton, were grandsons of Aubrey's elder half-brother, a very different type, and there seems still to have been a taboo on the subject of the spectacular and scandalous children of Caroline O'Hara. But I had heard a reference to Aubrey which stuck in my mind. I was about sixteen, when a contemporary of his, a rather crusty old neighbour called Colonel Rodgers, was calling on my mother at Waterpark. They were discussing the Tunstalls.

'That Irishwoman's children were bad hats,' he said, pretending with the rudeness of old people who exploit their own bad memories, that he had forgotten that my mother was Irish, that one of them was her husband's aunt, and that they were all her second cousins. 'What chance had they with those names—Damaris, Aubrey, Ariadne?' He snorted with contempt. 'It's a good thing Aubrey had no children— bringing art into the county. He lived and died in Italy, and we all know that an Englishman Italianate is a devil incarnate!'

I remembered this so well, because I thought that Damaris, Aubrey and Ariadne were the loveliest names I had ever heard. I thought it would be glorious to bring art into the county, and I immediately conceived the ambition to be an Italianate Englishman.

8

Alice's joy on being reunited to her children at Westhill, according to her diary, exceeded any of the sufficiently strong emotions she experienced in London and Rome, but she makes two adverse comments, one: 'The house seems very small and overcrowded. Sarah has got the furniture all cluttered in the wrong places.' The other: 'Mildred has developed a dreadful voice, whining and nasal. I asked Sarah why she had not corrected it, and she said an Australian little girl should speak like an Australian. I was very angry at such nonsense. The other children speak nicely. Sarah seems to have made a particular pet of Mildred and calls her Mildy.' There are other hints that in spite of her pleasure at being back with her family she was depressed by her surroundings and suffered from dreadful bouts of nostalgia for Europe. Westhill, compared with the palaces of Rome and even the ordered dignity of Waterpark, must have struck her as a dingy place to call her home, especially after it had been subjected for eighteen months to Cousin Sarah's genius for creating a drab and impoverished atmosphere. In those days, too, the surroundings of the house were more wild. The oak trees in the long avenue were little more than two rows of twigs, and made no impression on the landscape, and the European trees round the house were the same size. Only the thin drooping leaves of the gum trees, designed by the Almighty more to let the light through than to provide shade, were a scanty protection from the scorching January sun. Also at that time the furniture of the house must have been undistinguished. It had been bought when they moved in, and when they had not much money and were worried with the whole business of the move, complicated by the approaching birth of Mildred. Lady Langton retained any really good furniture and prints which Sir William had owned, and the eighteenth-century portraits and old chests from Waterpark which are here now, were not brought out till about thirty years later. It is even possible that there were not yet any wire blinds on the doors and windows, to keep out the flies, without which life here in the summer would be a nightmare.

Apparently it was more than Alice could stand, and they had not been there a week before she set about finding another house in Melbourne. Again she took one in East St Kilda, but in Alma Road, further away from the little colony formed by the Bynghams, Lady Langton and the Dells.

Neither Austin nor Alice wanted to be too close to Hetty. They could not avoid meeting her occasionally, and so it was not possible to make a complete break. Alice was fond of the little 'Dell' boys. They had always been welcome at Westhill, and she could not suddenly deny her affection to children, and as they were Austin's she had a vague feeling that she was responsible for them. They continued to come and play with their half-brothers in the house in Alma Road. This arrangement illustrates the way in which so many of the family escaped or ignored the influences of the nineteenth century. It would have been quite usual a hundred years earlier, though then everyone would have been aware of the relationship.

We are now coming into the period of the lives of many people whom I knew well, and so I have more information about it, though I cannot remember exactly who gave it to me. But again, it is largely superficial information, as I only knew them as a child knows an adult. Unless one has access to a find like the diaries, or acquaintance with a reckless old gossip like Arthur, the preceding generation must always appear uniformly respectable. Their idiocies were all committed before one was born, and in the sedateness of middle-age they are not going to give each other away. Who is going to tell a boy that when his father was in his early twenties he got into financial difficulties and gave worthless cheques, or that he only married his mother because her father 'asked his intentions,' or even that his uncle was found in bed with a laundress a little older than himself? We have to assume that our parents were always as upright and respectable as when we knew them, and though all the world knows otherwise, no one is going to tell us. And this is quite right, as the sins of the fathers should not be allowed to destroy their authority, or there would be no civilisation left.

Arthur told me something about Hetty at this time, but not what I would most like to have heard—an account of the first meeting between her and Austin and Alice. It must have been a strain on their *savoir faire*. Perhaps he was not present, or perhaps the situation was too sensitive, and too full of deep unhappiness for him to be funny about it. He was never ribald about anything which touched Alice immediately, but having once let the cat out of the bag with regard to Austin and Hetty, he could not resist talking about them whenever he had me alone. It had been bottled up in him for so long. He went on about them at the last dinner I had with him in about 1920, before I went to England, and did not come back to Australia for nearly thirty years, until on the death of Dominic I inherited the wreckage of Westhill.

'I felt quite sorry for Hetty at that time,' said Arthur. 'It is always uncomfortable when someone who has been outrageously bumptious crumples up. Sometimes one has a devastating retort to make to some pompous ass, but doesn't make it as one couldn't bear the indecent spectacle of his collapse—so the brute goes on being pompous. Hetty collapsed. She seemed to have shrunk. Of course with her it could not last for very long, but she was like that for nearly two years. Her clothes looked as if they didn't fit, and her spirit was so broken that when she and the protoplasm, who it turned out after all really was one, went out in their jinker, she actually let him drive, while in her arms was that horrible little badge of her shame, your cousin Horace.'

'But he was legitimate,' I protested.

'You talk like a grocer,' said Arthur impatiently. 'If she met Alice and Austin in a friend's house, she would give them furtive guilty glances, and there were some damned awkward moments when that fool Dell boasted about his splendid sons. Before this Hetty had had a confident, rapacious vitality, which made her clothes unimportant. Now people began to notice how dreadful they really were. What in a way made it worse was that Alice looked better than ever. When she went away she was a very pretty young woman, but when she returned she was beautiful, with the air of someone who knows the world. She had a look in her eye which you don't see in provincial people. You don't see it either in the eyes of people who are just worldly. Their eyes are merely shallow and hard. The expression I mean comes from a mixture of knowledge and tolerance, but tolerance with very clear limits, and kindness where it is possible to be kind. You can tell gentle people more by their eyes than anything else. Then Alice's clothes were always in perfect taste, so that when you saw her beside Hetty in her black alpaca and her cairngorms, or whatever those pebbles are she hangs round her neck, you would not have thought that they could possibly be connected, and if you had been told that Alice's husband had been unfaithful to her with Hetty, you would have said he was blind and mad. I must say that I was a bit bewildered by Austin's lack of taste. If one is going to do that sort of thing, it should be all mixed up with secret passages and scented notes, and flunkeys and gold beds. You shouldn't just sneak into the scullery while the servant's out, to do a bit of carpentering. Anyhow when they returned Hetty's game was up. Austin told her Alice knew, and she couldn't blackmail him any more. He never looked at her again, not in that way, though I believe it half amused him to meet her occasionally, especially in some place like Bishopscourt or at a dinner party at Mrs Hopkins's, who was president of the committee of the Home for Fallen Girls. Poor old Austin, he had some funny kinks in his nature. As a matter of fact it was damned funny. Hetty all through stuck grimly in the most respectable society, even in this shrunken and collapsed period. It wasn't only that she had lost Austin, you see, and that Alice knew— that was bad enough—but for the first time in her life she was ashamed of herself, the reason being of course that she had produced Horace. She had exactly the feelings of a great dane that finds a white dachshund in its litter. It was only Horace, nothing else, that made her look so furtive. I was quite sorry for her and saw her fairly often. Alice didn't mind.'

Arthur's close life-long friendship with Alice began at this period, or at least became intensified. It is hard to know exactly the time of developments of this sort and in my eagerness to 'get them across' I may place them too soon. In spite of Arthur's little lamp and the painting on glass, his friendship with Alice was not sentimental. It was founded on similarity of taste and interest, and particularly maybe on the fact that they had both had brief, intense, abortive attachments to the two Tunstalls. Alice may have hinted to him of the events in Rome. He knew that the prelude in G had powerful associations for her as he mentioned it to me. I may now say of Arthur 'poor old boy' for if he had known that one day I would have access to all the details of this affair, more than he knew himself, he would have exploded. His lighting the lamp every night may have been due as much to his love of ritual as to his affection for Alice, or it may have become so. When he was a young man in England he was very High Church, a 'Puseyite,' but after the death of Damaris he gave up all outward observance of religion. He believed that she had deliberately driven over the cliff and therefore according to the orthodox was a lost soul. He could not accept this and so felt that he could not consistently go to Church, a great sacrifice for him. He belonged to a generation that was very exact in its doctrine. Nowadays a young man in Arthur's place would say: 'Oh, no one could be hard on Damaris. God is too big for that' and continue to walk in processions with candles and incense.

It would be interesting to know whether Alice told Austin about Aubrey Tunstall. One feels it would have been only fair. She does not mention having told him, and yet there appears to have been greater confidence between them after her return from England, and a general atmosphere of greater happiness in their lives. She was like someone who has believed herself to be in perfect health, but puzzled by an occasional weariness and dull pain in her side, and who then after the climax of an operation, realises what true health can be. Although she must always have felt the attraction of Europe she settled down contentedly to her Melbourne life. She may have felt that Europe, however attractive, was a place from which it was safer for her to stay away as both of her visits there had had unfortunate and nearly disastrous accompaniments, though she did not know that this sequence was to be repeated more than once again in her life. Her interest was fully occupied with her new house in Melbourne, a much larger and better equipped one than she had had before, and in her growing children who were very lively and full of high spirits and 'Langton wit,' except Mildy who remained under Sarah's influence. A year after her return from England she had her last child, a girl who was christened Diana. This name was a departure from the Emmas and Hettys of Victorian tradition, and was considered by the relatives to be both pagan and affected. There can be no doubt that when Alice chose it she had in mind Damaris, Aubrey and Ariadne. She now had five children not counting a baby that died. They were in order of age, Steven who was my father, Margaret, who was called Maysie, Mildred, George and Diana. Steven, and George when he was old enough, went as day boys to the Melbourne Grammar School. Margaret and Mildred went to a school kept by a Madame Pfund, whose portrait by Longstaff hangs in the Melbourne National Gallery. They spent their holidays at Westhill, where they were nearly always joined by some of the Dells and the Bynghams.

I keep referring to the Bynghams, but I have given no account of them. Over the chimney piece in the little drawing-room at Westhill, where I began to write this book, there is a portrait 'attributed' to Kneller, which I have already mentioned, of a William Langton who was born in 1691. He wears a green velvet coat and riding breeches, while swathed around him, like 'ectoplasm' in a spiritualist photograph, is a gorgeous furbelow of cherry-coloured silk, which can hardly have been part of his costume as he went hunting round Waterpark. It was probably one of the artist's 'props' as it appears also in a portrait of William's wife. He wanted a patch of cherry-colour to contrast with the green coat but it was not essential to the portrait. In the same way the Bynghams appear in this story. They are a patch of colour, a broad influence rather than a clearly defined number of distinct individuals. I found it hard to distinguish between my many Byngham uncles. Except for John they come more to my mind as a species. They were important to us as they were the channel through which Teba blood might come in an unexpected spurt, to darken the nature of someone like Dominic or Julian. They were only transmitters, not containers, as the Bynghams were the most large round jovial horse-loving extroverts it is possible to imagine, although they were capable of scarlet rage when confronted with a dirty trick. This, combined with the fact that Captain Byngham would not for a moment tolerate any departure from the highest standard of courtesy and good manners gave them a reputation for chivalry. Amongst that horde of boys, my mother and her sister were the only girls.

They had not, as much as the Langtons, taken on the colour of Australia, partly because there were so many of them that they made a community of themselves, and because of their father's insistence on manners and their mother's naive conviction of her superiority. She had a definitely Spanish appearance, and apart from her ancestry, did not look the kind of person with whom one would be flippant. But she was very kind to us children, and whenever we went to Kilawly gave us presents on a scale she could not then afford.

The Bynghams were supposed to be rich, and perhaps in the early days they were. Captain Byngham owned a large station in the Riverina, but it became increasingly mortgaged.

To bring up eleven children, all with expensive tastes and a love of hospitality, must have put a strain on any reasonable income. Even if they had been paupers the young Bynghams would have been attractive to women, who could not resist their sanguine faces, their aplomb, their lively Irish eyes, their round noble voices, their excellent manners, the caressing charm which they turned on automatically for pretty girls, and the social position which they assumed so naturally that no one, least of all themselves, ever questioned it. Captain Byngham was intimate with governors like the Normanbys and the Hopetouns, and when in the eighties the Duke of York with his brother Clarence and one of the Battenbergs came out to Melbourne, my mother danced in the opening cotillon with the future king.

It was inevitable then that about half of the Bynghams should secure by their marriages financial lifebelts which kept them afloat in the deluge which followed their father's death, though they certainly had not married for money. They were far too impulsive children of nature for that. And yet as I write this chronicle I cannot help being a little startled at the number of my relatives who have lived on their wives. Even this shocking custom had its merits, for however greedy they may have been about money they did not regard it as sacred. They grabbed at the golden calf but they did not worship it, like the bourgeois who sees in cash the condensed holiness of his labour. They were possibly parasites, but not idolators. Austin did not merely live on his wife. He allowed half his children to be clothed, fed and educated at the expense of his mistress's husband, though he did give them holidays in the country. This was not so unjust as it appears, as in return

Percy Dell had the satisfaction of boasting about his sons, which he could never have done if himself had been their father.

To return to the Bynghams. I only just remember Kilawly, that is the interior, and not with any accuracy, but I imagine it as a place where there was always some form of hospitality in evidence, where on Sunday mornings after Church my grandfather sat on the Gothic verandah sampling sherry, where young people carrying tennis racquets and croquet mallets streamed in and out of the French windows, where at night the long dinner table, often with twenty-four guests, was like an illustration from Mrs Beeton, and where later in the drawing-room my grandmother dispensed tea from that colossal florid pot, while from the wall above her the full length portrait of the sinister duque de Teba, a little bewildered at finding himself in an Australian colony, stared gloomily down on the festive scene, and possibly with envy of the apple cheeks of his great-great-grandsons. That portrait came to my mother and was at Westhill, but once when we were in England, a lamp fell over beneath it, and the flames blistered it out of recognition. Cousin Sarah was in charge of the house, and no one believed it was an accident. It was the frame of this picture that I found in the stables, and used for Dominic's 'Crucifixion'.

When my grandfather Byngham died, those of his sons who had not secured lifebelts in marriage, found themselves with no means of keeping afloat in the society of which they had been unconsciously brought up to regard themselves as the cream. I remember some elderly relative, perhaps Arthur, warning Dominic that when a gentleman sank socially he did not just stop comfortably at a middle-class level, but went plumb to the bottom. It might be said that we belonged absolutely to the middle-class. I also remember hearing a duke's daughter who had married a baronet say 'we middle-class people.' This of course was a silly affectation, but she meant that she was not, like her mother, Mistress of the Robes, and did not, like her father, own four castles. All the same I do not think it is accurate to call the landed gentry middle-class, even if they have small incomes, as the middle-classes are essentially of the towns, burgesses, bourgeois. Recently some Left critic described Jane Austen as the great novelist of the middle-classes in her period. It is doubtful if she ever heard that label, and it is a quite inaccurate description of the people with entailed estates of whom she writes. The idea is to blot out the memory of these people, and to make the far less admirable bourgeois capitalist the opponent of the Communist revolution. It is an intentional falsification of history, and as a certain amount of social history, and possibly its falsification, is inevitable in this story, these remarks are not irrelevant.

The fact that the Bynghams did not come at all from the middle-class—the Langtons were much more mixed up with them—explains, I think, why those of them who had no money did not just descend a little way. It was as if they were in a runaway lift which would not release them until they reached the bottom and walked out amongst the tobacconists and fishermen. I am sure that even Arthur, if he had not had a lifebelt from Damaris, would have sold hyacinths and narcissi at the street corner, before he would have gone into a bank.

I do not think this tendency when sinking socially to by-pass the middle-classes is peculiar to my relatives. One finds very few of the aristocracy in middle-class professions. Peers' daughters may keep shops, but one seldom if ever hears of them as Newnham dons. They cannot either become that refined upper-middle-class which is met in the pages of E. M. Forster and Virginia Woolf. These people are distilled from several generations of Quaker merchants. At first they seem far nicer, far more interesting and intelligent than the landed gentry as they sparkle round Cambridge and Bloomsbury, but then one finds that they are all suffering from spiritual pernicious anaemia. The aristocracy lives from the land, the peasant lives from the land—they are akin. Their blood is nourished red from nature, and the flesh and the spirit are one.

The above may be largely quartz, but it contains enough golden truth to explain why my uncle John, finding himself at twenty-two cast on the world with three thousand pounds, and having no envy of the social position he would have had in a bank (and anyhow he could not add up) went straight off to Mallacoota and bought a fishing boat, and there he lived all his life, healthy and happy and free, sailing and selling fish. We loved going down to see him, and he always gave us half-a-crown each, with a most endearing shame-faced gesture because it was not a guinea. We were very proud of our uncle who was a fisherman. We were also very amused though not so proud at the idea of our uncle Algernon Byngham who also had gone down the social lift, bump to the bottom. He went as a jackeroo in Queensland, but he was thrown from a buckjumper and broke his leg in a way that made it impossible for him to ride again, so he spent some of his three thousand pounds in buying a tobacconist's shop in the local town. He married a very kind barmaid who put on his trousers for him every morning because of his gammy leg, but mercifully, from the snob point of view, they had no children. The only person of that generation who deplored these occupations was Horace Dell, who after he had passed through Mallacoota said: 'I saw John Byngham but thought it wiser not to speak to him in case he should claim relationship.' The others, the Bynghams and Langtons were like myself and my brothers rather amused, and the former referred almost more than was necessary to 'my brother the fisherman at Mallacoota' and 'my brother the tobacconist at Bungaroo.' This was a sign that Australia had already begun to affect them. English people are more reticent about relatives in humble positions, as also are Australians on the upgrade. It is only English gentry in Australia who, at first secure in their position, imagine that they need take no precautions to sustain it. The Langtons possessed by an endemic levity, threw away their advantages almost with hilarity. They could not resist provoking the shocked expression of a parvenue when they told her about Uncle John. They would not have done this in England, because there they took the social hierarchy quite seriously.

This was all far ahead of the period I am treating, that following Alice's second return from Europe. Then there was no sign of the Byngham decline. It is hard to imagine these nine uncles of mine as boys, perhaps because they were always boys, little different at sixteen from what they were at sixty. Their vitality must have been overpowering. Their boyishness made them choose occupations like a tobacconist's and a fisherman's. If their parents had returned to Ireland they would like most of their relatives have been sent automatically into the army, which is above all things a boy's profession. At home was the machinery, apart from matrimonial lifebelts, to keep them afloat. Their cousins in Co. Sligo still miraculously go to Eton and have commissions in the Irish Guards. Again their boyishness was what made them so attractive to women, who love the idea of mothering a boyish husband, not boyish in physique but in simplicity of mind. How Aunt Mildy would have loved one! There they were, only a mile away, nine of them, the closest friends of her brothers, always in and out of the house, but she could not secure one even, as Arthur said, for ready money. Badly as they were in need of lifebelts, they would not use her girdle of chastity.

The lives of these young people were probably much the same as our own a generation later. At Westhill in the holidays they went for picnics, they ate a great deal of fruit, they killed an occasional snake, they bathed in the dam, they twice fought small local bushfires, the girls bringing buckets of cold tea to the sweating, blinded boys who were beating out the flames, and they spent half their waking days on horseback. A being arriving at Westhill from another planet would not have known which species owned the place, the humans or the horses. There is a long passage which leads from the lobby where now hang the portraits of Alice and Austin, round a corner to the entrance hall. When the cavalcade of carriages, carts and assorted escort arrived back from a picnic, the younger children rode their ponies in at the front door and down, out through the lobby, into the stable yard. There were domestic protests against this custom, but it was amusing, and no Langton could resist anything that made him laugh. Ultimately it made them weep, and if it had not been allowed the fate of our family might have been very different.

Austin was always surrounded by half-a-dozen young people, either Bynghams or his own children, Langtons and so-called Dells. They helped him harness horses in odd formations. Sometimes he put the boys up as postillions and they drove round the countryside, blowing the coaching-horn. He had a hobby of learning to play odd musical instruments, and in that room at Westhill, where Aunt Mildy was born amongst the blowflies, and which is now the chapel, he kept an assortment of bassoons and shawms. One day the boys concealed a number of brass instruments under the seats of the drag. When they set out with six horses and Austin blew his coaching-horn, they produced these trumpets and responded with hideous groans and blasts, and the horses bolted. Happenings of this kind seem to have been frequent and to have added considerably to the gaiety of their lives.

From Arthur I only heard justifications of Austin, and Alice's diaries only mention his activities and not his character. He was a very simple man and a very unhappy one, though he gave the appearance of being neither of these things. His simplicity led him into his relationship with Hetty—the mere gratification of an appetite. It also prevented him from extricating himself. In fact it was the whole basis of his character. It made him long for the happiness which he would readily have found in an uncomplicated married life. It made him prefer the society of children and seek that happiness in playing horses with the boys. He found a good deal of it there, but when they played their occasional tricks on him, like blowing trumpets in the drag, although he cursed them in outrageous language, he was nearly on the verge of tears. He was always wondering who knew about himself and Hetty. He thought he must have many enemies, and so became suspicious. If he thought anyone was an enemy the things he said to and about him were appalling.

A self-important woman was brought by a neighbour to luncheon at Westhill, where life, owing to outdoor pre-occupations and Cousin Sarah's management was always something of a picnic. However on this occasion Alice had bestirred herself to see that there was very good food with civilised accessories. The guest thought she would indulge *le plaisir aristocratique de déplaire*, and ignoring the flounder cooked in cream and the quail, she said: 'What delicious bread you have!' Austin told the servant to take away her plate and to give her bread, and for the rest of the meal would not allow her to be offered anything else. The rude lady had tried to play the game with an expert. Austin understood much better *le plaisir aristocratique* which consists not as his guest had imagined in rudeness to someone whom it is safe to snub, but in a confidence so complete in one's own values that one affirms them clearly, indifferent to the fact that they are incompatible with the ideas of a bourgeois society, and the pleasure consists in seeing the bewilderment of a conventional mind, when faced with an idea too generous, or a taste too eclectic or even an honesty too obvious for its comprehension. The Bynghams felt this pleasure when they talked about their brother the fisherman at Mallacoota. It is the pleasure of the *enfant terrible* raised to the highest level, not that Austin's level was always very high, especially when he was displeasing Cousin Sarah.

The above incident seems to indicate that eccentricity had already slightly debased the Langton currency, that this woman dared to be impertinent to Alice. Recently a young man in Melbourne said to me: 'The one crime here is to be eccentric.' He went on to explain that towns with names like Melbourne all have the same ethos, a kind of heavy Sunday luncheon atmosphere, and gave as examples Bournemouth, Eastbourne, Malvern and some others which I have forgotten. It could hardly be expected that the Langtons would flourish there. The repeating pattern, becoming more distinct as the years went on, seems to have been Waterpark, hunting, European travel, and then financial or some other crisis, and back to the bolt-hole, Westhill for some hard-up, easygoing fun. In these last years I myself have repeated it, probably for the last time, with the design grown very faint and wobbly.

Austin disliked Sarah, not only because of an instinctive temperamental opposition, but because he suspected that she knew the parentage of Hetty's children. His suspicions were justified. She did know, but how I have not discovered. I have been told that women are able to divine instinctively any sexual relationship between people in their proximity. But if Alice could not divine it, why should Sarah? Alice was unsuspicious and satisfied in her life, while Sarah had all her frustrated senses alert, all her evil antennae extended to contact sin. It is even possible that Hetty was unable to resist boasting to her sister that she had achieved her ambition of the deanery schoolroom, as success loses half its savour if no one knows of it. However she acquired it, the knowledge created in Sarah's mind a terrible malicious confusion. She had to hold her tongue, because if she had ruined her sister it would have reflected on herself, also she would have had to leave Westhill and experience real poverty instead of that grey film which she tried to spread over the Langton's prosperity. When she had to sit at the Westhill dinner table and listen to Austin's Rabelaisian quips, she sometimes felt that she was in the presence of the devil himself, the personification of lust, the man who had ruined her sister—which was how she saw it—and could not even bridle his indecent tongue. Often with glinting, angry eyes she pushed back her chair and left the room, once exclaiming in muddled disgust: 'Vulgarity I like, wit I detest!'

This situation produced what was in a way a tragedy. Arthur told me of it, but I shall not give it in his words, as there was something coarse in the way he told it. I do not mean his references to behinds and door handles, but the absence of sympathy he showed for what must have been great mental suffering in a young girl. Again I come to the falsification of history which can come from putting events in the wrong sequence. It has always been assumed that Mildy's unfortunate characteristics were born with her, and that her nasal voice with its humble note was inculcated at the age of four by Sarah. This may not be true at all, and the injury which produced the traits we laughed at, calling her behind her back 'Aunt Mildew,' may have resulted from an incident which happened in her seventeenth year.

There is no doubt that Sarah, by a thousand ingenious allusions, had made her believe that there was nothing in the world more degraded, more absolutely bestial than irregular sexual love, or even regular. One Christmas holidays when there was a large family party at Westhill, including Byng-hams and Dells, they had all gone for a picnic down to the dam. The tea was spread out on a cloth on the ground, but Mildy instead of helping Sarah arrange it, went over to watch one of the Dell boys, who was trying out a fishing-rod he had made. When Sarah called them to tea, having carefully kept a space beside herself for Mildy, the latter ignored it and sat beside Tom Dell. Worse than this, Mildy did not, walking back to the house, take one handle of Sarah's basket, but dawdled behind with Tom.

Sarah, savage with jealousy, at once sniffed the most vile immorality, a boy with his half-sister. But with her anger was a gleam of triumph. She now had every right to disclose her secret. Mildy must know, to save her from sin. There was no one to whom she would have greater delight in revealing it. Before bedtime she called her into her room, that horrid little room which I myself remember, with its smell of vinegar and cough drops, and its little black religious books, from which Cousin Sarah tried to teach us a religion which bore no resemblance to Christianity. There was no mention of con-sidering the lilies, of turning water into wine, of breaking boxes of spikenard, of forgiving harlots, of beautiful seamless garments and dining with the publicans, but only of Jezebel flung down for the dogs to lick up the blood. When I told Julian to paint the Assumption of the Virgin in the chapel, I think my motive as much as anything was to send the black ghost of Cousin Sarah and her hell-born Calvinism, shrieking out into the Australian bush. I can imagine the look in her eye as she drew Mildy into her room, probably the same expression she had when she carefully broke the lamp, with the fire extinguisher all ready, in exactly the position where it would destroy the Teba portrait and nothing else—a smile of dishonest, vicious righteousness.

Mildy had spent the evening in a simmer of quiet happiness, not as definite as the awakening of love, but all the air seemed soft and gentle and the petals of the flowers were like a caress. She came into Sarah's room with bright eyes and a vague, happy smile. It is not difficult to imagine Sarah drawing her to her side and holding her close in an affectionate alpaca embrace, while she poured the deathly disclosure into her ears, so that Mildy might realise, as her love for her father and her respect for her family, her trust in their security and decency died, that she had a friend who would never fail her, who was all her own. What Mildy said nobody knows, but Sarah may have found out as hissing with an indignation which she expected the girl to share, she told the shameful story, that the effect was very different from what she had intended. It is likely that Mildy, too terribly shocked, too deeply wounded, said nothing, but, leaving Sarah just a little uneasy, went in a daze from the room.

She must have been uneasy when Maysie's voice was heard early in the morning, crying out in the passage: 'Where is Mildy? She hasn't slept in her bed.' In a few minutes everyone was awake. Byngham boys, Dell boys, Steven and George, streamed into the passage looking like choristers in their nightshirts, saying: 'What's up?' 'What's all the row?' Alice and Austin came out of their room, Alice anxious, Austin puffy but with a kind of furious look. 'Mildy's disappeared,' Maysie repeated. 'She hasn't slept in her bed.'

'She's probably in Sarah's room,' said Alice crossly. She imagined that with a tiresome sentimentality, as she thought of it, Sarah had persuaded Mildy to spend the night with her. Determined at last to put her foot down firmly, she went along to Sarah's room and rapped sharply on the door. Sarah, who had heard the noise and Mildy's name called several times had been too frightened to come out. She would be quite ignorant of whatever had happened.

'Come in,' she said, putting on a sleepy voice which Alice realised at once was not genuine.

'Is Mildy with you?' asked Alice opening the door, and seeing she was not added: 'D'you know where she is?' All the young people crowded behind her staring in at Cousin Sarah in bed as if they expected to see some remarkable sight. Arthur's description of this was extremely funny, but again quite unprintable.

'I haven't seen her since she said goodnight,' replied Sarah.

'Isn't she here? Oh dear, oh dear! Please shut the door.' Alice turned back into the passage as Austin said:

'All you boys dress. Tom, you and Steven go to the dam. The rest of you spread out all over the place and see if you can find her.' To Alice he said: 'Get that infernal jinx out of bed, and find out where she's likely to be. She's always with her.'

He dressed himself and saddled a horse and went riding about the road, in search of some trace of her. At eleven o'clock everyone was back at the house, hungry, exhausted and depressed, but no longer so anxious, as Maysie had discovered that Mildy had taken with her a small basket with some of her clothes. After a hurried breakfast Austin drove off to Dandenong, where the station master told him that Mildy had gone to Melbourne early in the morning by the milk train. He sent the dogcart back with the groom, and went on to Melbourne. He went first to the house in Alma Road but she was not there, then to his mother's house and to the Dells, but none of them had seen her. From St Kilda he went into police headquarters to ask for a search. As he was not only a member of The Legislative Council but at that time Minister for Home Affairs, he could arrange that Mildy's disappearance was kept secret.

At Westhill they passed the most gloomy day the house has ever known, except one other, some fourteen years later, when it was darkened by an irrevocable tragedy. The boys stood about in a serious grown-up way, and discussed what could have happened to her. They decided that 'she had got some idea into her head' and that 'girls were silly'.

It may have been due to her own manner, but as the day progressed a feeling grew up that Sarah was in some way responsible. Her nose and eyes were red with weeping, which made her look more shifty than ever. In every discussion she was on the defensive. At tea time one of the Dell boys who combined Hetty's pig-headedness with Austin's directness of speech, the one whose statue is now in the St Kilda Road, said to his aunt:

'I bet you drove her away.'

'Me!' cried Sarah. 'I love her!' and with a horrible throaty sob, which had a family resemblance to Hetty's roar of pain when Austin brought Alice in to the dinner party at Bishopscourt, she rushed from the room. After that everyone, including Alice, was convinced that Sarah was at the bottom of it, but they could not think how.

The next evening Austin, looking haggard, returned from Melbourne. Mildy had disappeared into thin air. Alice did not tell him of her suspicions of Sarah as she was afraid that he might do something freakish and frightful. The next day the party, unable to enjoy its usual pastimes, broke up, and they all went back to East St Kilda, to be nearer the region of the search. Sarah still red-eyed was left at Westhill in case Mildy should return there.

In five days Alice had a letter from Brighton, from a Mrs Hale with whom she was unacquainted. This lady wrote that five days earlier she had engaged a housemaid from the registry office in Melbourne, a very young and pretty girl called Mildred Verso. She was quite unused to the work and seemed to be in a very troubled state and could give no information about her family. As Mrs Hale knew that Alice's maiden name was Verso she thought this girl was probably a relative, and that Alice might be glad to know where she was.

Alice at once ordered the brougham and drove off to Brighton. She rang the bell at Mrs Hale's house and the door was opened by Mildy, in a cap and apron.

'Is Mrs Hale at home?' said Alice, whose first emotional relief at learning of Mildy's whereabouts, had given way, during the drive down, to anger at the needless anxiety they had been caused. 'If she is, say I would like to see her. Then go and take off that ridiculous cap and pack your things. We've been worried to death about you.'

She saw Mrs Hale, told her who Mildred was, said she

was unable to explain her conduct, and begged her not to mention it to anyone, to which that lady agreed. Mildred and her basket were packed into the closed carriage and they drove home.

She would not give any explanation of why she had run away, except that she thought she should earn her own living. Long afterwards she told Maysie, who told Arthur. She could never then have given the real reason. Its obscenity appalled her, though later in life she enjoyed talking of such things in an arch and allusive way. Until now she had been full of family affection and pride. Perhaps it was the strongest feeling she had, and it had been profoundly injured. As she stumbled through the night along the nine miles of stony road from Westhill to Dandenong, carrying her few pathetic possessions in a basket, she must have been engulfed by that sense of complete disaster which can attack a young person with no perspective. She saw her whole life as degraded and false. Alice might have been more sympathetic with her if she had known that Mildred on that night walk had something of the same sensations that herself had had in Hyde Park, on the day that Austin had reacted so strangely to the news of the birth of Horace, and from the same cause. She was sympathetic, but irritated by Mildred's absolute refusal of any explanation.

Mildred, partly owing to Sarah's training, had confused social position with sexual morality, a mistake which the duque de Teba could have corrected for her. On learning of her father's conduct she thought that the way they lived, the carriages, the crested silver, the general air, Australian and haphazard though it was, of being in the top drawer, was a mockery of the Almighty. She felt even the name of Langton to be a badge of shame. In a sort of expiation she went to the registry office where she knew that Cousin Sarah engaged the servants, and offered herself as a housemaid. When on her return, she would not look Austin in the face, Alice thought it was because she was ashamed of what she, not of what he had done. As I have indicated, later in life Mildy's attitude changed round. She accepted her shame and took all this as an endorsement of her own frustrated desires. But for the time, she was overwhelmed. By this one disclosure Sarah had done more to twist her nature than by her years of poisonous pious talks.

The effect of this incident was to send Alice to England again. Steven was overdue to go to Cambridge, and had spent a year at the Melbourne University, filling in time, until Austin and Alice could bestir themselves to take him to England. He could have gone alone but there was a kind of apathy about it. Now Alice said she would go with Steven and take Mildred as well for six months in Europe to give other people and Mildred herself a chance of forgetting that she had behaved in such an extraordinary fashion. So that if Sarah had not made this mischievous revelation to Mildred, my father might never have gone to Cambridge, which, particularly when he inherited Waterpark, he would have felt as a great deprivation, and again as I write this story I am struck by the close connection between evil and fortunate happenings.

9

Alice's diaries again give the only information about this short visit to Europe. Maysie had wanted to go with them. As she was older than Mildy she thought that she should be taken first, which Alice recognised as just, but Mildy had already begun to exercise the prerogative of neurotics, which is to skim the cream off other people's milk. Sarah also, another neurotic, was partly responsible for Maysie's not going, as Alice did not think it wise to leave her in charge of the household with no buffer between her and Austin. Sarah pretended to think that this was to protect her virtue from such a monster, though she was now over forty, and as brittle as old sticks. She was paid her usual wages and sent to live with

Hetty, where she was rude to all the boys except Horace.

Alice did not make any very interesting entries on this trip. At Waterpark she wrote: 'It is a little depressing here now, the house not in good repair. I think that Mr Langton must be short of money. He told me he had sold some of the land. He was apologetic about it, as if he were robbing Austin. They have very kindly asked Steven to spend his vacations here. There is the same damp patch on the wall of the main staircase. I met Lady Dilton today. She told me that Mr Aubrey Tunstall is still in Rome. I shall not go there, especially with Mildred.'

There are a good many hints that Mildred was unlikely to acquire much finish from her contact with European civilisation.

'Lady Dilton very kindly offered to present me at Court, and then I would be able to present Mildred. When I told M. this she made a great fuss, and said she could never go into the presence of the Queen. She became almost hysterical so I have had to give up the idea. I wish I knew what was the matter with M. She seems so *ashamed* of herself all the time. It dates from that night when she ran away. I cannot believe that any of the boys wronged her. It has something to do with Sarah, I feel, but again how could it? It is a most disagreeable mystery. I shall present Maysie and Diana when I bring them over.'

In Paris she wrote:

'This morning I took Mildred into a shop in the Rue St. Honoré to buy her some pearls for her birthday. She made a scene and said she could not wear anything costing so much. She chose a brooch in not very good taste. I bought the pearls and shall give them to Diana when she's old enough.'

A few days later still in Paris there is this entry:

'Mildred is exceedingly shocked by the statues in the Louvre, and yet she stared at them very intently. Quand on voyage avec M. tout le monde devient plein des indécences.'

It appears that Alice was glad to be back in Melbourne from this voyage. Although it had not been very lively with Mildred as her sole companion, after she had left Steven at Cambridge, at least it had been free from the major disturbances associated with her two earlier trips to Europe. She was however faced with one disappointment when she arrived home. Maysie was practically engaged and only awaiting her return and approval before making the announcement. The disappointment lay in the fact that no one had ever heard of the young man before. When Alice thought about husbands for her daughters she had always imagined they would be young men of their own sort, Bynghams, or the sons of one of the better clergy or the legal lights of Melbourne, several of whom came from very good Irish county families. Next to these she would have preferred the son of a Western District squatter of good origins. For Diana she had different dreams, unconnected with Australia. But Maysie's young man came into no category. He had a square solid kind of face, a reserved manner, unnoticeable clothes, a quiet unnoticeable voice, at any rate in Australia, and unlike any of the clan except the despised Percy Dell, he went to the city every morning. His name was Bert Craig. There was nothing one could reasonably object to about him, and nothing one could much admire. Whatever he did in the city—I never knew but think it was something to do with stock and station agents—brought him in a bigger income than was possessed by any young Mayhews or Bynghams. Even so to Alice, fresh from Waterpark, Dilton, Cambridge and Paris, he appeared grim. She was in a dilemma, as she did not want to hurt Maysie, who was deeply in love. If she did so everyone would think she was unreasonable and arrogant. From the Australian point of view there was no objection to him, but in England one simply would not come across a young man like that in the houses which the Langtons frequented. She could not put that forward as a reason to forbid the engagement. He had been to the Melbourne Grammar School with Steven, which was how he had become acquainted with Maysie. Austin did not like him and grumbled that he had no family, and yet here there was nothing discreditable. His father was a Presbyterian minister at Wangaratta. His mother died when he was a baby and there were no other children. He had an uncle a doctor in Bairnsdale.

They could not oppose him as they had no point of contact with him, and so the marriage was reluctantly agreed to, as it were in a vacuum. Maysie proved to be the exception to the rule I have referred to, and in her social descent did not race to the bottom, but stuck in the middle-classes. We may thank Heaven she did, as Uncle Bert made more and more money in his city activities. He gave financial advice to Alice, my father and to all the family which kept us from the workhouse, he steered them through the rocks of the boom and its collapse, and in her old age Aunt Maysie in a Toorak mansion is the only impressive relative we have left. If her grandchildren were to see Julian Byngham arrive in the middle of one of their smart parties, they would die of shame.

At the time of the marriage however, no one saw any reason for congratulations. It appeared to Alice that her chances of desirable sons-in-law had shrunk from three to one. She did not imagine that any sensible young man would marry Mildy and this reduction had all happened, without warning, in one year. It made her the more determined to safeguard Diana, a beautiful child, for whom she had always cherished particular ambitions. In these years the tide of prosperity was rising to the boom, the Italianate mansions were being built in Toorak and Malvern, and Alice's income was comfortably into five figures, but as she sat in the ballrooms of the mansions, watching Mildy ogling her partners, or listening to Maysie praising people whom she could not imagine in a London drawing-room, simply because they had a great deal of money, she must have already begun to feel a touch of the disappointment that lies hidden in success.

Arthur's description of Mildy at this time, though cruel, was probably fairly true. 'She was very proud of her blue eyes,' he said, 'which she inherited from Austin, but in him they were like the fierce noonday sea, in her like a dewpond in a fog. When a young man was introduced to her at a ball or a lawn party, she opened them wide in a stare of gentle reproach, and pursed her lips in the sweetest smile, so that she looked like some kind of puritan whore soliciting at a Band of Hope meeting. The young man at once became acutely embarrassed and thought he must have already met her and forgotten her, or else that he had seen her leaving the lavatory. He escaped as quickly as possible, and she was left, the expanding flower which could only repel the pollen-bearing bee. Alice tried to instill into her some ideas of sense and dignity, but she was impervious to them. She was convinced that men were attracted by supine imbecility. You never saw anything more indecent than her affectation of female modesty. When at the age of fifty-three she discovered that she had been following the wrong tactics, her intended prey was even more alert to avoid this tigress dressed in blue chiffon.'

In three years Steven returned from Cambridge and very soon became engaged to Laura Byngham, whom he married with the full approval of both families. Kilawly excelled itself in flowers and champagne, and the duque de Teba had the satisfaction of looking down on what may have been the last uncontaminated full-strength parade of the best families of early Melbourne. I think we grew up rather smug in the knowledge that our mother was the only one of the in-laws of whom our Langton grandparents approved, though this smugness was qualified as we became older, by respect for Uncle Bert's increasing riches.

Last year, as soon as Westhill was reasonably in order, I gave a party here, to which moved by snobbery, or piety or a sense of history, I invited only those, or the descendants of those, who would have been present at this wedding. Some were very old, some poor, some still fashionable with fine jewellery, but all were gentle and courteous and pleased, perhaps because seeing so many whom they had imagined long dead, they thought that they were in paradise. One, thanking me as she left, said: 'I had not seen Emily for sixty years. We had quite a lot to talk about.' Mrs Briar evidently thought that I did not know people in 'society' and was unaware that the list of names which appeared in the newspaper the next day was almost identical with those which were printed sixty years ago, and that the house had been filled, as it were, with the Faubourg St. Germain of Melbourne. It is still possible to hear in some secluded drawing-room in Toorak, one old lady say to another: 'When we are gone there will be no one.' Unfortunately Lady Gugglesberg and Mrs Mainprice have no idea that they do not exist, and there is only too much evidence to support them in their misconception. I was the only one conscious of the distinction of the party, as to the guests themselves it seemed merely like the Resurrection Morning with sherry.

My parents were given Westhill and a good allowance, but the lively harum-scarum existence had come to an end. My mother has often told me how lonely she was here in the first two years of her marriage, after the teeming entertainment at Kilawly. They had no sooner settled in than news came from England of the death of Thomas Langton. His wife had died the previous year, and Austin at last became the Langton of Waterpark, such as it was. He was very impatient to take over his inheritance. It was assumed that the whole family would go back to live in England. This would mean prolonged preparations for departure, packing up and selling the Alma Road house, but not Westhill which had already acquired sentimental associations. Austin could not wait for all this. He left with Alice in a fortnight, the idea being that they should come back in a few months to settle up. Sarah was again installed in charge of Mildred and Diana. George had just reached the age for Cambridge and went with his parents.

Again we are faced with one of those inexplicable stupidities of history, like Hetty's being allowed to travel in the same ship with Austin. Alice may have thought that Mildy had reached saturation point and could suffer no further mischief from Cousin Sarah, while the beautiful intelligent apple-of-her-eye Diana was much too sensible to be affected by a silly old maid. Also they did not intend to stay away for so long. But when they arrived they found that not only had the acres shrunk, but that the farm buildings and Waterpark House itself were dilapidated. The pioneering spirit which made Austin blaze roads into the Dandenongs, came upon him in Somerset. They stayed at an inn in Frome while the house was repaired and redecorated, and the damp attacked but never conquered on the staircase wall. Then they moved in and supervised the repair of the remaining farm houses and buildings. Alice paid for it all in spirit as well as in money, as she was longing to get back to Melbourne to collect Diana. She was delayed for a month longer by Austin's waiting to see unveiled a window which he had put in our chapel in Waterpark Church in memory of Cousin Thomas. This window was full of coats-of-arms and in the three lights were our illustrious collateral, Archbishop Stephen Langton, St. Austin and St. Thomas. It was one of the things which, like the duque de Teba and Uncle Wolfie's symphony, made us conceited when we were young.

At last Alice returned to Melbourne to one of the greatest disappointments of her life. Diana, her pride and her hope, who was to compensate her by the brilliance of her life for Mildred's idiocy and Maysie's terre-à-terre pre-occupations, for whom she had dreams which she half recognised as fantastic, of launching her in the drawing-rooms of London and the palaces of Rome, and whom, the most secret, absurd, and precious hope of all, she planned to marry to one of the three Tunstall boys who were of a suitable age, had fallen in love with a music teacher called Wolfgang von Flugel. Arthur told me about this. He did not really dislike Wolfie, but he did not mind 'throwing him to the wolves.' None of the family disliked Wolfie. They thought it outrageous and unspeakable of him to marry Diana, but he made them laugh, and they could not dislike anyone who made them laugh.

'It was madness,' said Arthur, 'to engage Flugel as a piano tuner with two unmarried girls in the house.'

'Was he a piano tuner?' I asked, surprised.

'Well, music teacher then,' Arthur growled. 'I believe that Sarah disliked your grandmother. People often dislike their benefactors and the Mayhews were always envious of the Langtons. She certainly hated Austin. With her curious love of the anaemic, her passion for economy, it was a form of torture for her to live in a household like theirs. She did everything she could to make them drink their champagne out of kitchen cups, but she didn't always succeed. I think she brought Flugel there deliberately, hoping he'd marry Diana. She knew that it would be a bitter blow to Alice and then she would be revenged for all the kindness she'd received from her.'

'But even Cousin Sarah couldn't have been as wicked and silly as that,' I protested. 'To feel resentment for kindness. It's mad! It's devilish!'

'I'm glad you think so, my boy,' said Arthur. 'It may not

have been conscious, but people do a lot of evil that is both unconscious and intentional. It was really your uncle Algernon Byngham who precipitated the affair. The Bynghams, you must understand, were very chivalrous. On another occasion Algernon stood a porter on his head on Windsor railway station for speaking impertinently to your mother. Anyhow, Wolfie was engaged for Diana, but Mildred insisted on having singing lessons from him. One day she was having a lesson when Algernon came in. Mildred, as must have been fairly frequent, sang a false note, and Wolfie turned on her with the vicious rudeness of a neurotic musician whose ears have been tickled the wrong way. If he hadn't been a musician he would have been a very decent chap, but his manners were at the mercy of his ears. He had disintegrated his guts with music. His mind, you see, was full of meaningless patterns of sound, or if they had meaning it was nebulous, not like the forms and ideas in the mind of a painter or writer. So the man who is purely a musician and nothing else is just an empty sponge when he isn't playing something. But Wolfie was so soaked in music he was like a full sponge all the time, like one of those cakes soaked in rum. You touch them and out squelches some liquid. You touched Wolfie and out squelched a tune. Anyhow he called Mildy a fool and Algernon told him to apologise. He said: "It is my good right to call her so." Algernon led him out by the ear and pushed him down the front steps, where he fell over and grazed his invaluable hands.

'That started it. Diana was furious. She never forgave Algernon and was very glad when he became a tobacconist. She brought Wolfie in and bathed his hands, and bandaged them, and invited him to stay to dinner, and afterwards Sarah took Mildred along to see Mama, and they were left alone. In a fortnight they announced that they were engaged. A week after that Alice arrived from England. She was always very quiet and patient, whatever happened, and tried to reason with anyone she thought was behaving badly, but this time she was really angry. She gave it properly to Sarah, who although she looked shifty and guilty, had a gleam in her eye that showed she was pleased to have got under Alice's skin. Alice said it was ridiculous, impossible, and she wouldn't hear of it, that Diana was too young to marry anyone, let alone a penniless German music teacher, but she made the fatal mistake of calming her anger and beginning to reason about it. Also Austin didn't mind him so much because he helped him play his bassoons, and he was a 'von'. He said his cousin was a baron with a castle somewhere or other. I looked him up in the Almanach de Gotha. I did find the name Flugel but I couldn't find Wolfie, but they don't give the whole crowd like Debrett.'

Again the Langtons' kind hearts or their Australian tolerance betrayed them. In England there would not have been a moment's hesitation. Wolfie would have been forbidden the house and Diana packed off to an aunt in Aberdeen or Penzance. But here, as Arthur said, they began their fatal discussion, while Austin was always inclined to look with favour on the waifs and strays of old families, as a man who is fond of antiques but has little money, will buy a worm-eaten Chippendale chair.

While all the furious argument was going on, mostly between Alice and Diana behind the scenes, Wolfie still frequented the house with the perfect self-assurance of an accepted suitor. Nearly every evening he played to the family after dinner, if there was no other engagement. He had round child-like eyes, soft mouse-coloured hair, rather like a baby's, and a round full face which quivered when he played with emotion. When I was first aware of him he had coarsened, but he must have been quite attractive in the early twenties when Diana fell in love with him. He was very sensitive, but only about his own feelings. Arthur said that Diana was not in love with him at all, but only with the Moonlight Sonata and the other music which he squelched out for her. Arthur himself was very musical, but he attacked Wolfie for being too musical as he was envious of his greater ability.

Then the family made the even greater mistake of beginning to be amused by him. Alice sent up to Westhill for Steven to come and support her in her stand against the engagement. Steven came into the drawing-room at Alma Road and found Wolfie whom he was supposed more or less to kick out of the house. Wolfie rose, clicked his heels, bowed very politely, and with a beaming smile called Steven his brother, and Steven laughed. All the rows went on behind Wolfie's back. Alice writes:

'This afternoon I had another talk with Diana. She was quite irrational and obstinate. She said that we were a dull provincial family and that Mr von F. was an artist and came from the great world of European culture. I was astonished as, apart from the fact that he has no money and I think would be very selfish, the very reason I don't want her to marry him is because I want to introduce her to that world. I said something of the kind. Diana was rude and said I didn't understand the artistic temperament. It was useless to continue the discussion. Diana is either rude or else she cries. I am afraid that it is a mistake to bring up children in Australia if later one wants to take them into the world. Now that we have Waterpark and adequate money, she would have exceptional opportunities in Europe. It is bitterly disappointing.'

But still Alice held out. Austin was inclined to give in. He was not ambitious for his daughters, was not concerned about money, and was grateful if they managed to find husbands from what he called 'real' families. He said that they could let them have an allowance to live on decently, though of course Wolfie would have to give up teaching music, except the bassoon to himself.

Alice did not mind using her money to benefit the family, or for such things as the restoration of Waterpark, but she had no wish to reduce her income to enable her daughters to make unsatisfactory marriages. Also she was certain that if Diana who was only eighteen, could recover from this infatuation, she would make a happier marriage under other conditions, and have a much wider and more interesting life in every way than in a suburban villa with Wolfie.

Suddenly Alice gave in. Nobody knew why, and I only discovered the reason a few weeks ago, when I was reading her diary for that year. One evening Alice, Austin and Diana were sitting listening to Wolfie playing the piano. Sarah and Mildy had gone to a lantern lecture on Chinese missions. Diana's eyes were dark with weeping and fixed on Wolfie, who himself did not show any signs of anxiety or wastage. At the height of the crisis he said: 'I eat and sleep well.' He had paused at the end of a piece of music, and then he began to play the Chopin Prelude in G Alice wrote:

'I could hardly bear it. I felt as if my nerves were the strings of a violin which was being played. I nearly cried out to him to stop. When he had finished I signed to Diana to follow me to my room, and I told her that I would no longer oppose her marriage to Mr von Flugel. Her face was so wonderfully radiant that I had my reward. She embraced me and we both wept. I do not know whether I deserve my reward. I gave way to the feeling that all love is good and must not be opposed, and that is not sensible. I then sent Diana for Austin and told him that I would agree to the marriage. We all went back to the drawing-room, and Austin said in that gruff way he speaks when he is shy: "It's all right. You can take her." Mr von F. stood up and bowed very low and said: "Then I understand that Miss Diana is now my affianced."'

After this Alice began to call him Wolfie. He was completely accepted into the family, perhaps rather like a favourite dog, in a way that Uncle Bert never was. Although the latter was our financial salvation Alice always called him Albert. I think it was because they recognised, though quite unconsciously, that Wolfie was on the right of the *pale*. On the other hand it may simply have been that the name 'Wolfie' amused her, while plain Bert suggested a Cockney.

Austin was impatient to get back to England. Cousin Thomas was ninety when he died. If only he had been obliging enough to have died five years earlier, the lives of my aunts might have been entirely different. Mildy would not have received her psychological shock, while Diana might have married anybody, possibly Dilton himself, and to the horror of Colonel Rodgers have filled the county with singing birds, with art and poetry and music. It is hard to imagine Aunt Maysie married to anyone but a rich business man, but it might have been a Bristol wine merchant. As it was, Cousin Sarah made cheap, nasty and hurried arrangements for Diana's marriage to Wolfie, about which Alice was increasingly unhappy. She could not take any interest in the preparations, and left them entirely to Sarah, who had a punitive attitude towards the wedding. Sarah, from the muddle of her mind, always picked out the malicious and the righteous by which to direct her actions, even if they were incompatible, but here she could reconcile them. She liked to humiliate the Langtons, and she thought that Diana did not deserve a grand wedding as she was opposing her mother's wishes, so her malice and her conscience combined to help her to provide a wedding breakfast like a Sunday School treat. The whole thing was such a disappointment to Alice that she could not give any heart to buying Diana's trousseau, and even the wedding dress was rather poor.

Alice was thought to have behaved rather meanly about it, and years afterwards Diana rather sadly confided to me that she had felt humiliated as a bride. Perhaps Alice was tired of being onion woman to the Langtons, who hung so heavily onto her skirts and did not even want to ascend into loftier regions, and decided to shake one off, though it was strange that she should choose her favourite child. But we always turn with the greatest bitterness against those whom we love when they fail us. Even so, she did allow Diana five hundred a year, which in those days was a comfortable middle-class income, and no one gave her any credit for that.

This marriage caused a sort of general post or mad tea-party in the family. Alice could not bear the thought of returning to England with only Mildy, when she had expected to have Diana. After a great deal of impatient discussion, it was decided to uproot my parents and take them back to Waterpark. My oldest brother Bobby had been born here at Westhill. It was thought that he should be educated in England and brought up in his future inheritance. My mother was only too glad to go to England, which she had never seen, and to escape the loneliness of Westhill. The family, as much of it as could be saved, was in the process of being re-Anglicised. And yet they were stretched across the world. Alice could not have contemplated separating herself for good from the two daughters to whom she was most attached.

Wolfie, of course, was ordered to give up music-teaching. He and Diana were sent to Westhill in place of my parents, and he was told that he could earn his living farming the place. Perhaps Alice's conscience pricked her before she left, as she sent them up a concert grand piano to replace the upright walnut instrument with a ruched-silk and fretwork front, which was all my mother had. As against this she sent up Cousin Sarah, and here we are faced with another of these incomprehensible facts of history. To send up Sarah to keep house for a honeymoon couple is an action one can only think of as conceived in the heart of the foul fiend. It was presumably because the house in Alma Road was being given up and there was nowhere else for her to go. Austin, perhaps more confident now that he held property in his own right, flatly refused to have her at Waterpark. Again, though I emphasise the black, dismal character of Cousin Sarah, it does not necessarily mean that she was as I describe her. I only state how she appeared to me. Undoubtedly to many people Cousin Sarah was a self-sacrificing Christian gentlewoman. Whatever she was they imposed her on Diana, while Mildy, whining and reluctant, was led aboard the P&O liner, and a horde of relatives, whose names I have not yet mentioned, waved from the Port Melbourne pier.

10

Alice began to be aware of the germ of evil fortune inevitably concealed within the good, at any rate in her own life. Times which she had thought were entirely happy, like the first months of her marriage, or the night by the Fountain of Trevi, turned out to be fools' paradises. Now she could not free her mind from anxiety for Diana, living with Wolfie and Sarah at Westhill. She wrote:

'We should never let a subsequent evil spoil the memory of a good we have known. If we have loved someone who later proves indifferent to us, we should remember the time of that love in all its freshness, and not let the mistrust which followed impair that memory. When we see the autumn rose trees, with a few discoloured and frost-bitten blooms, we do not say that because of these the summer roses were worthless. As we grow older we become to some extent different people. I must separate the memory of the children at Westhill from whatever they may become later.'

Yet it must have appeared to everyone that at this time Alice was at the height of good fortune. Her large income was still increasing with the land boom, which enhanced her position as Mrs Langton of Waterpark. It may appear that Alice was too much concerned with social position, but it is humbug to pretend that most people are indifferent to their status in the world. Alice may appear socially ambitious, because the social ambitions of today are different. In another fifty years people may angle to be seen in the society of commissars, and boast that their grandparents had been presented to Stalin, while the commissars will most likely have coronets or some equivalent on their motor cars, and their footmen's buttons. After the slaughter, the purges and the concentration camps, the eternal patterns repeat themselves. Alice only wanted to fill properly the position in which circumstances had placed her, and to see that her children had and used all the opportunities available to people of their kind. She was not primarily concerned with importance, but she wanted to be in the society where she thought she would find the better qualities of mind and manners.

She could not put away from her the thought of Diana living with Wolfie and Sarah at Westhill. There are repeated references to it, and when she had taken Mildy somewhere, to a lawn-party at Dilton or to an opera in London, she often writes: 'I wish I could have had Diana with me.' This was not simply that she would have liked to appear with a presentable daughter. The thought that Diana might be unhappy was with her like an incessant dull pain. She visualised Westhill looking its worst, and Diana shut up there with Wolfie surly and selfish, and with Sarah's dingy housekeeping. It seemed to her that she was now for the first time experiencing an old person's sorrow, which so often lies in seeing the failure of those whom we love, rather than in our own personal griefs.

Fortunately Alice got on very well with my mother, who was no discredit to her. She had the Byngham aplomb, and good connections in England and Ireland. She was also of course a second cousin of Damaris, Aubrey and Ariadne, and though these were not viewed with great favour in the neighbourhood, they were far from being a bourgeois association. Even so my mother did not give Alice the same satisfaction as if she had been her own flesh and blood. Mildy, the only daughter she could produce, was frankly not presentable, either at Court or in the Waterpark Vicarage. Her silliness and her twang were appalling, and she often gave voice to those improprieties which are uttered by old maids in their innocence of double meanings. At the same time one was not quite sure that she really was unaware of what she was saying.

Alice sent her to an elocutionist in London to be cured of her flat vowels. She came back with an extraordinary articulation, which was neither Australian nor English, nor any known variety of speech. Whenever she had to say 'cow' or 'house,' she went through contortions of refinement, and she produced sounds like 'caoo' and 'haoose'. Also the elocutionist taught her text book idioms which were not used by gentlepeople. Fortunately when she returned to Australia she abandoned these efforts, though on special occasions she would revive them. We used to mimic 'Aunt Mildew's English voice.'

During these years at Waterpark they appear, until towards the end, to have led a quiet country life. Two of my brothers were born there, Dominic, a few months after they arrived, and Brian two years later. Bobby, the eldest, was Alice's favourite, and she frequently tells little anecdotes about him. Mr Dunn, a neighbour, came to ask if he might fish in the garden stream. Bobby said:

'You mustn't catch Charlie.'

'Who's Charlie?' asked Mr Dunn.

'He is our private trout. He comes and talks to us.'

'What does he say?'

'He says: "I don't know how you can stand about up there with a dry skin. It would set my teeth on edge."' Alice adds: 'Bobby enunciates his words beautifully.'

In the summer they drove about the country side in the wagonette, or in that landau, which now, entwined with brambles, is rotting in the shed below the stables. Sometimes they went to lawn-parties, or to Henley or to Cambridge in May Week to see George. They were unlike ordinary English country people in that they were always ready to go anywhere to see any new or any very old thing. In the ancient home of their family they remained sightseers. In the winter the men hunted and the women often drove to the meet. Once or twice my father was thrown through his horse swerving at a jump, and once 'Austin came home with the tights, a form of cramp.' Sometimes they went shopping in Bath, or up to London to see a play or Mr Whistler's pictures, but all through this pleasant *andante* existence, came at regular intervals the upsetting discord of Sarah's letters from Westhill. Pages of thin angular writing told of Wolfie's misdoings. When he found that the cows had to be milked twice a day, he sent them down to Burns the farmer, and either Sarah or the maid-of-all-work had to go down to fetch the milk, very heavy two-gallon cans so that there would be some to set for cream. Wolfie said: 'There must be cream. It is nice.' He did not do any work on the place. He paid one of the young Burns to mow the lawn, otherwise the garden was a wilderness. Sarah was doing her best to keep the weeds down, but she had enough to do indoors. The bottom paddock was full of thistles. Rabbits were everywhere. One could hardly gather apples in the orchard because of the brambles that tore one's skirt. It sounded as if the place were reverting to a wilderness, to much the same condition it was in when I took it over last year. There were also hints that Wolfie was filling the house with drunken and immoral friends. The final authentic touch of squalor was when Sarah wrote: 'Yesterday he did not even go for the mail, so I did not know that the parcel from the Mutual Store was at the station, and I was relying on some tinned herrings for tea.'

Diana in her letters made no mention of this. All she said about Wolfie was that he was busy composing. Alice tried to find signs of unhappiness or loneliness in her letters, could not do so, and then thought that perhaps Diana was concealing her wretchedness because she was too proud to admit that her marriage was a mistake. Alice discussed it with Austin, and asked what they were to do about the apparent wreckage of Westhill, but as all the information they had came from

Sarah, Austin was prejudiced against it, and said: 'That damned jinx is making it up.'

After Christmas 1890 Austin was not very well. He said he did not want to hunt any more that winter, so early in January they all went off to Biarritz. Here Bobby made two interesting contacts. He spoke to an aged groom, who had held the Duke of Wellington's horse in the Peninsular war. He also attracted the attention of a Princess Frederica, presumably royal, as she had with her a lady-in-waiting called Countess Braemar, whom she sent to ask Bobby and Dominic, the latter aged three, to an entertainment of performing dogs, at which Dominic was sick. The next day Princess Frederica herself called to ask how he was, and she showed herself very friendly to Alice, who thus, for the six weeks they were at Biarritz, found herself in exalted company. Alice very much enjoyed this society, and she gave a grand dinner party in a private room at the hotel, which she considered a great success, but again the perpetual fly was in her ointment, and at the end of the long description of her party she writes: 'If only Diana could have been here!' For the whole evening she was haunted by the thought of her beautiful daughter having 'high tea' with tinned herrings in a ruined house.

The next day she heard that Diana had given birth to a baby daughter at Westhill. She was filled with a dreadful pity. She remembered the birth of Mildy, the blowflies, the heat, the lack of proper conveniences. It was intolerable to think that Diana had gone through the same thing. The contrast between that room at Westhill and the parties with princesses at Biarritz was too painful to contemplate. Alice went to

Austin and said that she was going across to Marseille to catch the next ship to Melbourne. The rest of the family went on into Spain on a somewhat morbid pilgrimage to the Castle of Teba. Bobby and Dominic were taken into the sinister crypts of the chapel, but not on that occasion told of the idiosyncracies of their ancestor. It was I think during this trip, but as Alice had left the party I am unable to verify it by the diaries, that the Empress Eugénie saw my mother, asked who she was, and finding she was some kind of kinswoman invited or commanded her to luncheon, so that in those early months of 1891, the family soared to the highest social levels, not alas to remain for long. On the other side of the world Uncle John had already bought his fishing boat. Our family appeared to live on a social see-saw, up in Europe, down in Australia. Noticing this I have spent most of my life in England, but with me it did not seem to work properly. I did not even have the satisfaction of sinking to the bottom, with matey contacts with tobacconists and fishermen.

Alice had not let anyone in Melbourne know that she was on her way, as the letters would only have travelled in the same ship. She arrived in the morning, drove out to luncheon with Lady Langton and Arthur, and immediately afterwards took the train from Malvern railway station to Dandenong, where she hired a wagonette and drove up to Westhill. As they turned into the drive her sensations must have been much the same as my own when I arrived back here. She saw neglect on every side, broken fences, fallen trees, blackberries and thistles. But these things did not disturb her so much as her fear of what she would discover at the house. Would she find Diana in the same condition as the land, like one of those 'cocky-farmers'' wives who struggled bravely against drought and possibly drunkenness, with rough hands, bowed shoulders and bright but anxious eyes? The wagonette turned into the garden before the house. The flower beds were as Sarah had said, and the big lawn was so dry after the summer that it was hard to say whether it had been mown or not. The windows of the house were clean, but of course Sarah would see to that. It needed painting.

The door was answered by a cowed but clean-looking girl of about eighteen, who had a slight resemblance to Mildy, and Alice was reminded of the morning she had called to retrieve her from Mrs Hale's. She felt the memory was a bad omen and she had a momentary feeling of despair about her daughters. It vanished as soon as she entered the drawing-room. Diana and Wolfie were so astonished and apparently equally delighted to see her that it was some minutes before she could take in what they or their surroundings were like, or recall the apprehensions with which she had driven up the hill. As far as she could see her fears had no foundation at all. Diana, far from appearing anxious and haggard, was blooming and beautiful, much better-looking than Alice had ever seen her. Wolfie too looked very well, a little fatter, a little emotional with fatherhood, kind and not at all drunk.

'Where's the baby?' asked Alice, and was told it was asleep.

'Who is it like?' she asked.

'Oh everybody,' said Diana, airily. 'It's charming—like a doll.'

Alice enquired after Sarah.

'I expect she's gone for the milk. She's always going for

the milk,' said Diana laughing. 'But never mind Sarah. You must hear some of Wolfie's symphony. He only finished it the day before the baby was born. Wasn't it amazing? All creation reached its climax at the same moment.'

Alice was not sure of the good taste of Diana's remark, but she was so immensely relieved that she would not have minded what she said. Expecting some awful grey scene of disintegration she was delighted by their well-being and their cheerfulness. Then she noticed the drawing-room. Most of the heavy furniture had been removed, and there seemed to be a lot of blue plates, bamboo and peacocks' feathers. The room was rather untidy, with sheets of music manuscript everywhere but it was not dingy. Diana had brought the aesthetic movement to Westhill. Alice commented on this but Diana could talk of nothing but the symphony. Professor Handley who was staying with them but was out for a walk at the moment with a Mr Pickering, said that it was equal to the work of the greatest modern composers. 'Yes, it is very good,' said Wolfie. 'It will make me famous.' Professor Handley and Mr. Pickering came in from their walk, the latter a young man with musical tastes, and after their introduction, immediately began to talk about the symphony. Mr Pickering in a low earnest voice told Alice it was equal to the best of Wagner, and Professor Handley in a loud voice said the same thing. Wolfie sat down at the piano, and, as much as he could on that instrument tried to give her some idea of it.

The evening meal was very peculiar. Sarah might try to make one of Alice's Alma Road dinner parties like a Sunday School treat, but she could do nothing with Diana and Wolfie. They followed no pattern for her to wreck. If she wanted tea with her dinner they did not mind. Wolfie had his beer, so teapots, beer bottles, ham and honey were all on the table together. The conversation when it was not about Wolfie's symphony was about Aubrey Beardsley and the Yellow Book. Westhill was far more *fin de siècle* than Waterpark. Sarah sat through this bearing in her own mind the burden of all its wickedness. Wolfie and Diana were much too absorbed in themselves to care about Sarah's private world. When for example, at the end of the meal, Wolfie said suddenly: 'Now it would be nice to have a jam omelette' Diana without looking at her said: 'Sarah, darling' and she went off, like a hypnotised Caliban to produce it. There was little wonder that she released her resentment in letters to Alice, though she hardly conveyed an accurate picture of their lives.

Alice went to bed in the small room they had allotted her, a great deal relieved and more than a little amused. She was even amused at their giving her this room, while they occupied her own. If they had wrecked Westhill they had not wrecked themselves, and that had been her main anxiety. She did not admire poverty of spirit, the sort of thing one noticed in the declining Mayhews. She was sorry for Sarah, but she could not help laughing at the way they were quite unconscious of her malice. Everything was far, far better than she expected.

The chief cause of her satisfaction was the discovery of Wolfie's creative ability. There was nothing she admired more. She would have been more genuinely proud of a son-in-law who was a good painter or writer or musician, than of one of the highest rank. She was naively pleased to meet duchesses, but she mentions in her diary with much greater pride the few meetings she had with creative artists of any eminence. In the morning she had a long talk about Wolfie with Professor Handley and he was quite serious in his assertion that Wolfie was a first-rate composer. In the afternoon she offered to take the Flugels back to England with her, and they both exclaimed: 'Then the symphony can be performed in London.' They were delighted with the invitation but not over-grateful. The same day Alice arranged with Burns, the farmer, to rent the land at Westhill, and then went down to Melbourne and installed herself at Menzies Hotel. Pleased as she was with Wolfie and Diana, she could not face another of those meals with beer and tea.

A married couple was engaged for Westhill, but Sarah stayed there, and it was used as a holiday home by various Dells and Craigs. Alice sailed with the Flugels, the baby and a nurse three weeks after she had arrived. They left the ship at Marseille and stopped in Paris to buy Diana clothes. They stayed a day in London and Alice bought her pearl and diamond earrings, and bracelets to go with the pearl necklace which Mildred had refused, and which she gave her as soon as they arrived at Waterpark. Alice was compensating herself, or satisfying her conscience for the meanness she had shown Diana at her wedding and for the austerity of the past three years. She also had to give Wolfie some money to buy suitable clothes for the English country. He looked a little fat and Teutonic, but that was not a social disability, and in Somerset a German accent was preferable to an Australian one. Again in the northern hemisphere the standards were changed.

Alice at last thought she was happy. She no longer had that dull ache and anxiety about what was happening at Westhill, and she had someone of her own whom she could exhibit with pride in the county, or in a box at Covent Garden or at Biarritz. Her illusion did not last long. The only permanent Flugel resident at Waterpark was the baby. Diana and Wolfie were always dashing off to London or Germany in search of music. They would announce their return on a certain train, generally one most inconvenient to meet. A carriage was sent to Frome for them and they were not there. They turned up the following day in the station fly, explaining there was a concert the previous night which they simply had to hear. Alice would not have minded so much if they had sometimes suggested that she should accompany them, as she liked music and she liked travelling *en famille*, but the only thing she shared of their travels was the expense. Wolfie had probably been impressed by the Langtons with the dignity of their ancient seat, but he was frankly disappointed in Waterpark.

'My cousin has a castle in Württemberg,' he said. 'It is very noble.'

Austin had the irritating sensation of a man whose financial position is being assessed by a pauper, who having nothing himself is able to stand aside and compare him detrimentally with a millionaire. Some relatives of ours in Melbourne were once asked to be kind to one of their cousins, a titled young Englishman who was coming out on a battleship. When he had left they exclaimed: 'Be kind! It was all we could do to get him to be civil to us.' At the end of this 1891 summer Alice must have felt much the same about

Diana and Wolfie. The symphony had not yet been performed and one evening Diana said to Alice:

'Don't you know any important people, mama?'

'I know the Diltons,' said Alice, taken aback, and she mentioned one or two other landed families in the neighbourhood.

'But I mean really important people,' said Diana impatiently, 'someone who could get Wolfie's symphony performed.'

'I am afraid not,' said Alice with dignity. 'In one way our position here is better than it is in Melbourne. It has a more solid basis. It is one that no amount of wealth could buy if you were not born to it, but it is not a particularly high position. There are strata above us. In Melbourne there are none. It's the old choice between being king of your village and serving in Rome.'

Diana looked bewildered and disgusted. She had a slight affectation of manner which reminded Alice of Mrs Dane, a faint air of drama. Alice preferred this to Mildred's complete absence of any kind of distinction, but that night she wrote in her diary: 'If one could take hold of the ends of the threads of evil and misfortune which are woven into the good to make our lives, and draw them out, would the rest fall to pieces?'

As Wolfie did not hunt she rented a little house in Knightsbridge for the Flugels for the winter. She thought she could stay there when she went up for a few days. She went once and they were quite pleased to see her, but when she left they did not suggest she should come again, and the ménage was so uncomfortable that after this visit she went back to the rooms in St James's.

At last we come to the entry which Alice made on the 25th January 1892, the one which attracted my attention on that night when with Julian, I brought in her diaries from the harness room:

'George rode with Steven to Boyton Manor. Austin had his horse taken by the groom and drove with Laura, Bobby and me. A lovely day, rather too fine and frosty for hunting, but the sun melted it by twelve o'clock, about the time they started. We saw Mr Phipps, Mrs Martin, the Duke of Somerset, Lords Percy and Algernon St. Maur, Mr and Miss Knight, and many others. Mr A. Tunstall was driving with his sister-in-law Lady Dilton. When he saw me he at once came over to us. He said that he was only in England for a few days to see his trustees. He was charming to Bobby, who wins all hearts, and he brought us refreshments. Boyton a beautiful house and grounds with a large pond. The meet very picturesque, but not many in pink owing to the death of the Duke of Clarence. We drove home when they started. I bought some plants at Boreham, white hyacinths, all flowering.' She continues in French. 'A. T. said to me that if I was in Italy I must certainly come to Rome. He gave me his address, but I had not forgotten it, even in twenty years. He has not changed very much. I was exceedingly pleased to see him, and I felt very happy for the rest of the day. He laughed into my eyes when he said that I had not changed either. It seemed only yesterday that I was in Rome.'

A few days later the Flugels made one of their sporadic descents on Waterpark, and Alice took Diana over to call at Dilton. She writes: 'Only Lord Dilton and Miss Tunstall were at home. They told us that Lady Dilton had gone up to

London that morning with Mr A. Tunstall, who was returning to Italy. I was very disappointed.' It was not likely that Alice was disappointed at missing Lady Dilton, whom she often saw. She wanted to show Diana to Aubrey, perhaps rather pathetically to let him see, that even if she no longer was beautiful she had a beautiful daughter. But she may only have thought that he would know the kind of people who could arrange for Wolfie's symphony to be performed. She does not mention Aubrey again for over eighteen months. During the following summer she was concerned about George. The engagements and marriages of her children seemed fated to bring her trouble.

It is not very clear what George did after he left Cambridge. There is still talk of examinations and of a cousin at the War Office who was doing something for him, so presumably he was trying to enter the army. He failed in some examination by two points, and when next mentioned he is at Carrickfergus in Ireland with a regiment of militia. While there he met a Miss Dorothea Potts, the daughter of a Major Potts, a widower, who lived at a small country house called Rathain somewhere in the neighbourhood. He mentioned her frequently in his letters and at the end of June he arrived at Waterpark and asked Austin's permission to become engaged to Dolly Potts, a complete reversal of the procedure at Austin's own engagement. Austin agreed but Major Potts would not give his consent unless what he called a 'proper settlement' was made on Dolly, and the amount he asked for was half as much again as his own income. He did not expect to get it, but he was determined to stop his daughter from marrying, as he wanted her to be a comfort to his old age. He did not imagine that anyone would pay £1,500 a year for Dolly, and certainly Alice was not very willing to do so. She had a large income, but like club members she had 'calls' on it. Austin had a settlement of £1,000 a year, which went entirely on his own pleasures. My parents were allowed £1,000 a year, and they also had no household expenses. George, Maysie and Diana had £500 each and Mildred £250. Out of what was left Alice had to keep up Waterpark and Westhill, pay P. & O. fares and all hotel bills when they were on the Continent. She also gave her children on their birthdays a present of a pound for each year of their age, which ranged in this year from about £30 for my father to £20 for Diana. She also had 'calls' from other relatives in restricted circumstances. If she had frightened fits of so-called meanness it is hardly to be wondered at. The onion woman did not want her skirts to be altogether torn away.

The wrangling about the settlement went on between the respective lawyers for over a month. Aunt Mildy went about saying in her piercing voice, or possibly with the elocutionist's overlay: 'I don't know how anyone can ask for money with my brother. How can people mix money and love! I never should.' At last a compromise of £1,000 a year was reached, and Dolly Potts came to stay at Waterpark. On the same day Alice had a letter from her lawyer in Melbourne saying that Maclean, the tenant of a building in Bourke Street, which provided a large part of her income, was unable to pay the rent. Dolly Potts on that first night must have thought that she had arrived in an extraordinary household. Mildred and Wolfie were sufficiently unusual, but Austin hardly said a word, except at intervals to give a little cynical chuckle and mutter: 'So the boom has bust!'

This did not cause them immediate embarrassment, as Alice had three or four banking accounts, all with good balances. The summer life at Waterpark went on as usual, made more cheerful by the presence of Dolly, but punctuated by letters from Uncle Albert Craig, full of caution and foreboding. They made their habitual excursions to Bath, to Longleat, to the ruins of Farleigh Castle. At home the men shot clay pigeons or they played tennis, or 'had some archery' at which Dolly Potts excelled. I cannot give much account of the love affair of George and Dolly. I only know its sorrows which did not lie within themselves. Her name was a symbol of romance for us in our childhood. I once saw a photograph of her which Uncle George kept in a drawer, as Aunt Baba would not have cared to see it on his writing table. She had a round, fair English face, with a rather large mouth and very straight eyes. Everyone liked her and years afterwards, ten thousand miles away, her sad sweet name would be mentioned with affection. I like to think that for two or three months she and Uncle George were intensely happy, driving together along the steep and shadowed lanes to sit among the ruins of Farleigh or pick wild flowers along the road to Longleat. In the evening they must often have walked out after dinner, and crossed the lawn to the stream and murmured there together in quiet voices which blended with the sounds of the twilight, the mourning of the small gnats, the splash of a trout rising, or the last twitter of a bird, while all around them was the drowsy beauty of the English summer meadows, the scenes and scents of home. They were not yet disturbed by the fact that Alice did not think it right to sign the marriage settlement until the financial situation in Melbourne was more clear. I think this must have been so, as Waterpark always meant far more to George than to any others of his generation. He had in his study a print of the house, and a painting by my father, who was not a bad amateur artist, of the three oak trees on the lawn. Whenever it was mentioned a faraway look came into his eyes. He had probably enjoyed there the only months of perfect happiness in his life.

At the beginning of September Alice writes: 'There is still no satisfactory news of Maclean.' Then suddenly without any explanation, the whole household packed up and fled like swallows to the south. My mother often spoke to me of things that happened on this trek, but she never told me the reason for it. I always assumed that it had something to do with the financial crisis, but it may have begun with the simple wish to spend a few weeks in Brittany. The party consisted of Austin and Alice, my father and mother, my three brothers, Wolfie and Diana, their little girl, two nurses, some English cousins who joined them in Dinan, and George and Dolly Potts. The marriage settlement was still unsigned. Major Potts had not forbidden his daughter to join the party, but he said: 'If you go I shall not write to you.' He seems to have been a horrible old blackmailer with a strong sense of other people's duty. Alice makes some references to financial transactions between her different banks, but does not at first appear to be short of money. They were only concerned with amusing themselves, making excursions to Mont St. Michel and going in boats on the Rance. She bought old furniture to be sent back to Waterpark, and in the lobby here there is an oak cupboard, on the back of which is still tacked a faded card, addressed in foreign handwriting: 'Mrs Langton, Waterpark House, near Frome, Angleterre.' They must have intended to return in October, when the English cousins went home, but perhaps the crisis became worse, and it was cheap in Brittany. Dolly Potts stayed with them. She would not go home until her father wrote to her. Her married sister let her know that he would not do so until the engagement was broken off, his real aim.

Then everything seemed to go to pieces. Alice went off to stay with a friend near Bruges, where she had to sit through gargantuan meals. She describes one: 'Soup, cauliflower with melted butter and shrimps, roast beef and potatoes, fowl and french beans, a cake, pears, apples and grapes, claret, burgundy, beer, coffee, liqueurs.' It was probably this diet that brought on a violent attack of rheumatism which began in Paris, where George met her, not to take her to Waterpark, but back to Brittany, and to Roscoff of all places, in the middle of December, to where the family had moved. Again we have the madness of history. It may have been because they were Australians and they liked to see European things at their most characteristic, the rugged Brittany coast battered by winter storms.

Alice had a dreadful journey. On the day she left Paris she wrote: 'Could hardly get dressed, my arms and hands were so painful. Went for a good long walk with George past the Opéra. After dinner we drove to Montparnasse and left at about eight. My knees began to pain very much. The carriage warm and comfortable but I had to keep waking George to help me to move.'

The next day, 12 December: 'At Morlaix a gentleman helped George lift me down from the train. Arrived at Roscoff at about ten and met by Wolfie, who helped George lift me down. He was so gentle and kind that I was quite surprised. He said: "It is not good to suffer pain." The children very well. They made me up a sort of sofa, and I stayed there all day, my knees and hands paining a good deal. The view of beach, rocks and islands very open and fresh, but grey and sombre.'

Instead of returning to warmth and Waterpark for Christmas, they stayed a month on that grey and sombre coast, perhaps because Alice could not move, perhaps because of money. They had a letter from Arthur saying that Lady Langton was not well. Maclean still had not paid the rent and Austin decided to go out to see his mother and to look into their financial affairs on the spot.

I know a family of whom one, if he has to go on an errand, will say to a brother or sister: 'Will you chum me to the post office?' or wherever he may have to go. The whole clan decided to 'chum' Austin and Mildy, who elected to go with him, to Marseille to see him off at the ship. The journey was like a retreat from Moscow. The first stage from Roscoff was made under a sense of defeat, accentuated by the fact that Dolly Potts was leaving them at Rennes. She was going to stay with a school friend near Nantes, George accompanying her for a few days. Austin and Bobby tried to amuse the party by talking like Waterpark yokels. Bobby looked out of the window and said:

'This be martel bad weather for they wurzels, my sonnies.'

'Ay, that it be,' said Austin. 'Turrible bad.'

'Oh don't, papa,' said Mildy. 'You'll give him an accent.' Everybody laughed. Mildred looked as if she were going to cry and they were more dismal than before.

Wolfie told the children the fairy story of the mermaid who wanted to walk among humans. She was given feet but every step on land was as painful as the cut of a knife. Bobby said: 'She was like our trout Charlie,' but Alice thought this tale applied to themselves. They should have stayed in Australia, their natural element. When they came to Europe, every time their walking was painful. From Rennes they went to Tours, where her rheumatism again became bad. My mother put turpentine and a warm iron on her knees, but 'she had to use the fire shovel as Mildred had left the iron at Rennes, and her pretty Spanish shawl at Roscoff.' In spite of her pains Alice could not abandon her ruling passion, and the next morning, though the ice was floating down the river, she went to see the museum and the tomb of St. Martin. In the train to Mont Luçon, they had a meal of figs and cakes, to save money, except the children and nurses, who had a hot déjeuner before they left. Wolfie said: 'It is not good for me to be hungry.'

They arrived late and half-frozen at Mont Luçon, and went to an hotel with damp beds. They all sat about waiting for fires to be lighted and the beds aired with warming-pans, 'Austin swearing horribly.' Alice was afraid of the beds and lay down with rugs on a sofa. Diana's little girl was unwell and cried all night.

The next morning they left early. Austin on the railway station while they were waiting for the train, 'sat apart and laughed at his own thoughts.' He had an odd sense of humour. Diana was worried about her little girl. My mother was expecting another child—myself—and was feeling sick. Mildy was full of wailing prophecies of disaster, and said they would all be stranded penniless in the South of France. When they arrived at Lyons they thought it too cold to stay there as they had intended. They bought fowls, bread, fruit and milk, and ate it in their crowded carriage. Wolfie said: 'Hot food is better.' They arrived late at Marseille, and too tired to look for any other, went to a dirty hotel near the station. My father found that he had lost his notebook with the receipt for the luggage, so no one had any night clothes. They spent the next day in Marseille, one would have thought in bed, but no—Alice went to a picture gallery and to see the new, unfinished cathedral.

The following day they saw Austin and Mildy off on their ship. The next morning the depleted party left for Nice in an omnibus train, as the lines were blocked with snow and they did not know when the express would arrive. There were still twelve of them, eight adults and four children sitting up in their second class carriage. The express passed them at Toulon, and they took eleven hours for the journey, instead of five as they had expected. They had no proper meal all day. George, having come from Nantes and passed them in the express, met them at the railway station. He announced, barely restraining his tears, that his engagement to Dolly Potts was broken off . She could not stay for ever with her friend in Nantes. She could not indefinitely accompany the Langtons on their uncertain trek. She could only go home.

The frozen, hungry, unhappy, exhausted party descended on an hotel. That night Alice wrote in her diary this little song which du Maurier quotes, but rather badly translated, at the end of 'Trilby.'

> La vie est brève:
> Un peu d'amour,
> Un peu de rêve,
> Et puis—Bonjour!
>
> La vie est vaine:
> Un peu d'espoir,
> Un peu de peine
> Et puis—Bonsoir!

She did not know what was yet in store for her.

11

From the Sixteenth of January when they arrived in Nice, until the twenty-fourth of February there is no entry in Alice's diary, then this:

'Went to Monte Carlo this afternoon with Steven, George and Diana. A very beautiful drive along the Corniche Road. I won 36 louis on zero. George won quite a lot playing on pair and impair. Wolfie spent the afternoon practising on a piano I have hired for him. In the evening we all except Laura went to *Faust* at the theatre in the Casino. Jean de Reszke and Melba, de Reszke magnificent. Melba looked very nice. Wolfie shut his eyes and quivered a great deal during the final duet. George and Diana went to Lady

Learmouth's ball afterwards. Diana wore a flame-coloured dress and all her pearls and diamonds. She had pearls twisted in her hair and looked very striking. The masseuse has done me a great deal of good.'

Certainly something had done them a great deal of good. For months there is day after day of this kind of thing. It does not sound a probable life for people who have just been ruined and who only a few weeks earlier had to travel second class and go without proper food in mid-winter. If they could afford this life why did they not go back to Waterpark, at least in the spring, seeing that they had all these children with them, and that I was about to be born? It is where history again becomes irrational. Of course I may have stopped them. Perhaps my mother was not well enough for the journey. More likely they were amusing themselves, and no Langton could resist amusement. Being doubly uprooted people, they had not the same sense of responsibility as the average landowner, though when they were at Waterpark they were more generous than most squires to their villagers. In a hard winter they let tenants off their rent, and gave the sick and poor presents of food and wine, which their Australian money enabled them to do, and which the estate alone could not have afforded. Waterpark as a family seat would naturally have expired with Cousin Thomas. It no longer had within itself the means of survival. This Australian money was a kind of monkey-gland infusion, which kept it going for another two or three generations. It may be just as true to say that they were doubly rooted, and being equally drawn to two countries, were glad to escape the tension for a while in a third.

They stayed in Nice until the very end of the season. A few weeks before they left Wolfie achieved one of his main objects in coming to Europe. His symphony, conducted by himself, was played at a concert in the Casino. There was an appreciative notice of it next morning in the Nice newspaper, and that was the debut and climax of his European musical career. It has since been played occasionally in Melbourne and I have heard it. I believe that it is as good as Wolfie thought, but he was the victim of his own success. There is a story by Morley Roberts about a young writer who, inspired by the happiness of his first months of marriage, wrote a brilliant and moving tale. The editors were delighted with it, but they refused everything he wrote afterwards as it was not up to the same standard. He had ruined himself. Wolfie had written his symphony under the same inspiration. As he rose from the bed of his beautiful young wife and walked out under the scented gum trees, and heard the sounds of the morning, the magpies in the field, the clanking of milk pails and the shouts of the boys down at the farm, all liquid notes in the crystal air, his bursting heart sent harmonies up into his brain. The result was this symphony which, although it was not derivative had the same feeling as Wagner at his most lyrical, as the *Preislied*, the *Walkure* love music, and the *Journey to the Rhine*. Also the critics were reluctant to believe that an unheard of young man, who had produced nothing else, had composed a work of the first quality.

After this achievement the main body of the family moved slowly eastwards, while Alice, with a Mrs Blair-Gordon with whom she had become friendly in Nice, scouted round them, going off for a week or two to some capital city. Finally the time of my birth drew near and they all moved up into Switzerland, the only place where I could be born a British subject, and settled at Lucerne. Alice had bought her 1893 diary in France, and on 'Samedi, 10 Juin. S. Landry' she wrote:

'Laura not very well. I went for a walk and bought a bottle of eau-de-cologne, a chess-board, and three rakes for the children. Laura came down to déjeuner and had some fish that the Russian officer caught. Her baby born at twenty-five minutes past four in the afternoon. She has a *sage-femme* who speaks English, and a nurse who speaks German and French, and likes them very well. Everyone asked very kindly after her. Mrs Blair-Gordon came back from Brunnen today. Played bezique with her in the evening.'

At last I am born. All these people of whom I have been writing on this day became my relatives, ready-made, unchosen. If Alice had known while she was playing bezique with Mrs Blair-Gordon, that the not over-welcome pink baby upstairs (it would have been nicer for everyone, except perhaps myself, if I had been a girl) would one day not merely own all her private possessions, but reveal to the public the secrets of her heart, would she have thrown me into the lake to feed the kin of those fish which the Russian officer caught for my mother's luncheon?

But my dear Grandmama, which I am now entitled to call you, I have done you no wrong. You are fifty years before us on our journey, far advanced in Paradise, remote from us in spirit and in mind. So we must pray, or you would not be happy, seeing the condition of your descendants. Should we hope that you linger near Westhill with its broken trees, or hear the train rattle behind Waterpark and smell in the garden stream the seepage from the tanneries, which has killed Charlie the trout and all his descendants? Then, as you are so far from us, let us remember you, not by the banalities on a churchyard slab, not with hypocrisy, but as you really were, living and human and complete. Also, if you did not want your diaries to be read, why did you preserve them so carefully and leave them behind you?

A week after I was born Alice went off to Paris to buy clothes. I shall still call her Alice, behind her back as it were. She returned to see Laura and myself, then went to Munich and Nuremberg, taking Wolfie and Diana to hear music. She came back to Lucerne for my christening, and on her return notes: 'The baby smiles a great deal when spoken to.' On the day of the christening Alice 'went out in the morning and bought some striped silk Neapolitan fishing caps for the children. In the afternoon the baby was christened Guy de Teba. Diana was godmother and chose the names. Steven did not like 'de Teba' as it seems that the duque de Teba from whom Laura is descended (also A.T.) was not a very reputable man. Diana gave him a silver mug. He behaved very well and looked nice in his robe and the little Venetian lace cap I bought in the Piazza San Marco. Madame Miradoux de la Primaube gave him a bouquet. In the evening Diana, Wolfie, George and I went to the Casino. The inevitable rich young Russian woman gambling. Leave tomorrow with Mrs Blair-Gordon for Wiesbaden. Had a sad letter from Dolly Potts.'

The financial crisis was at its height, but there was still champagne for dinner 'to drink the Emperor of Austria's health.' One cannot account for the hideous economies of the trek from Roscoff. They may have been suffering from shock at the prospect of ruin, and then found that Alice's income, even when halved, left plenty to play with. Or it may simply have been that they failed to collect money sent to Roscoff or Rennes, which ran them short only for the journey. Throughout the whole summer Alice was writing business letters to Uncle Bert, and conducting negotiations with her banks. 'Paid £900 into the Commercial Bank,' she writes, and then, a few days later: 'Commercial Bank has ceased payment. Have £700 in the bank at Frome. Draft of £500 yesterday from Melbourne.' One must remember that the purchasing power of the pound was then four or five times what it is today. I was always told that I was born in the midst of ruin.

My parents, truants from both their houses, remained until the autumn in placid insecurity on the shores of Lucerne. The children bathed and fished in the lake, and they all rowed about in boats. My father painted in water colours, Uncle Wolfie played the piano, and every day there was an excursion to see some thing old or beautiful or curious.

The circumstances of my birth were under ancient and traditional auspices. Only the day before I was born my mother went to see the lion carved in the rock *fidei ac virtute Helvetiorum*, to the valour of the Swiss Guard, who died defending Louis XVI at Versailles, and a few days earlier she went with Alice to Mass, and to see the procession going into the Cathedral. 'It looked very nice. Hundreds of girls with white wreaths and veils, priests with banners, church properties of all kinds, images, hatless boys, acolytes, incense etc.' At home Alice was an ordinary Low Church Anglican, but abroad she and my mother frequently attended Mass. In Milan she writes: 'Heard a beautiful Mass at the Duomo.' In Florence: 'Laura, Bobby, Dominic and I went to Mass at Santa Croce.' In Brittany, Nice, Munich, Venice and Naples are similar entries. She does not give any reason, but I think it was because she had a strong sense of civilisation, and where the ancient liturgy of the Church was being celebrated in splendid and historic buildings, she felt that it would be ignoble, too much like Mildy and Sarah and Percy Dell, to go ferreting out a Protestant Chapel. This is an example of the double standard which she observed all her life, one for Europe, one for Australia. In Melbourne she would not have dreamed of attending a Roman Catholic church. Dominic was five when he last entered a Catholic church abroad, but it may have been some image then printed on his waxen mind that is responsible for the terrible painting on the wall at Westhill. And if prenatal influences count for anything, these acts of worship abroad by my mother may explain why I like to have a Catholic chapel in my house, even if it is seldom used, and why from the cradle I have been instinctively on the extreme right of the *pale*.

In the middle of September Alice was again in Munich with Mrs Blair-Gordon who left her there to return to England. On the day of her departure they 'went to see the statue of Bavaria. We went up into the head, three of us, and four other people came. Seven in the head. Herr W. dined with us and we went to the station to see Mrs B. G. off via Cologne and Bruxelles. At the station Herr W. introduced us to the artist Lembach and his wife, and the son of Bismark and his wife whom he met there.'

She came back alone to Lucerne. The autumn mists were gathering on the lake and the leaves were turning gold, but in her own mind were echoes of spring, and the coast was clear when on '24 Septembre, Dimanche, S. Izarn' she made this entry:

'Wrote to Honble. A. Tunstall telling him I would be in Rome on Thursday evening.'

12

In the first half of October, Alice's diaries are in French, but mostly not in very small writing. It has been a little difficult to disentangle as when she has filled the space allotted for the day she goes over onto the memorandum pages, or back to the days in February which she did not fill in, when presumably she was having the treatment by the masseuse. Where she uses some phrase which might sound too baldly sentimental in English, I have left it in French. She begins on:

'*28 Septembre*. Jeudi. S. Exupère: A. T. met me at the station. Although, except for the meet at Boyton, it is over twenty years since we have seen each other, there was no constraint. He appeared exceedingly pleased to see me, as I was to see him. I felt that it was as if we had both accumulated a great deal to share with each other. He had a carriage to drive me to the hotel, and on the way he said: "It is wonderful to have you here," and then he gave a curious little laugh and said: "I expect it was the Fountain of Trevi." I laughed too, and for the first time since that terrible morning when I was last in Rome, the pain it left, like a little dry stone in my heart, was completely dissolved. For long years I was not conscious of it, but by thinking I could always feel it. Now I knew I would never feel it again. What pleased me about our meeting was that it was so light-hearted. It might have been embarrassing with both of us trying to conceal that the feelings of twenty years ago were dead, or else if they were not, aware of their unsuitability today. He had engaged some rooms at the hotel, with a private sitting-room, rather expensive, but I don't suppose it will matter for a week or two. I am not going to think of money while I am here. I shall draw a cheque on Frome. My rooms were full of beautiful roses, a sort of tawny pink with a delicious scent. *The same kind that I left here withered!* When I was going up to change A. asked: "What do you want to do this evening? Are you tired after the journey? Perhaps you want to rest." He looked as if he would be disappointed if I wanted to rest, which I said I did not. He suggested we should dine together somewhere, not at his apartment as he had not ordered dinner there. I invited him to dine here. He was very pleased at my invitation. It is extraordinary, but we seem to know each other better now than we did before. Then there was the constraint between us, which comes with uncertainty as to another's feelings. Then he arranged things for me, very kindly, but without quite letting

226

me know what was going to happen. Now he is as simple and friendly as a schoolboy, asking me what I would like to do. After dinner we walked along to the Spanish Steps and up on to the Pincio. When we passed Keats's house he said: "He could have been saved if his trustees had sent him his money. Trustees are horrid people." We walked along the Pincio, and leaned against the balustrade, looking down over Rome. There was no moon, but the sky was full of brilliant stars, and the dark-leaved trees were mysterious in the starlight. Below us were the domes of those twin churches, but we could not see much beyond them. It reminded me of that evening at San Miniato, when we stood looking down over Florence, and he asked me if he might show me Rome. There are certain incidents in our lives, casual questions or remarks which sound unimportant at the time, but which we never forget. That was one of them. I don't think that I shall ever forget tonight either. He went on talking about Keats, and he said that a great civilisation resulted only when the aristocracy and the artist worked fruitfully together, that this co-operation had produced Rome. He said that was why he lived in Italy. That in England since the eighteenth century there had been none of this co-operation. I was very interested in what he said, and in the whole style of his conversation, which is far more cultivated than that I am used to. I thought this before, but now he is much more mature, as well as less reserved in his manner. He walked back with me to the hotel, and said: "What time shall I call for you tomorrow?" as if there was no doubt that I am going to spend my whole time in Rome in his company. So I asked him to come at half-past ten. He is very nice.

'*29 Septembre*. Vendredi. S. Michel. This morning I said that I would like to walk about and renew my impressions of Rome itself, rather than go to see any particular place. We went first to Trevi. The little square and the great fountain which I had last seen looming mysteriously in the moonlight, were now all clear in the morning sun. This seemed to me symbolic of my relationship to A.T. The sheet of falling water, then black and silver, was now all sparkling diamonds. How unhappy we make ourselves when we are young. I was going to throw in another coin, but A. said: "Not yet. You must do it by moonlight." I said there was no moon. Being with him makes me notice things so much more. If I had been with anyone else last night, I would not have remembered today that there was no moon. He said: "There will be before you leave." So we shall have to come to the fountain again one moonlight night before I go. From there we walked slowly up to the Quirinale, and sat on a marble seat in the piazza. There is something quite unique and delightful in walking about with him in this leisurely fashion, and sitting down in odd places in this wonderful city, where there is always some evidence of faith or genius before one's eyes. My other sight-seeing has been more conscientious, but never in the company of anyone with so much knowledge, though I never feel that A. is deliberately instructing me. It is simply that I feel the atmosphere of the place more when I am in his company. I said that he made sightseeing a pure pleasure. He said: "But what is it for if it is not for pleasure? It's not a duty. You don't feed the poor by looking at a picture. Not long ago a woman asked me what she ought to admire. There's no "ought" about it. One goes to look at Praxiteles's faun, because there one sees the spring-time of the world, all the unconscious careless impudence of the young male expressed in a single beautiful body. It makes one laugh with pleasure. One goes to see it to laugh with pleasure. One goes to see Michael Angelo's Pieta to weep. If you don't laugh or weep at these things there's no virtue in going to see them. But if you are filled with laughter and pleasure when you see the Praxiteles faun, you have increased your understanding, and that, as Blake says, brings you to Heaven. We shall go to see it this afternoon." I said: "I expect I shall laugh from nervousness." That amused him very much. After luncheon we went to the Capitoline Museum to see the faun. He would not let me look at anything else, but led me straight to it. It is very beautiful, but though it seems a shocking thing to admit, it reminded me of Austin when I first knew him, and I felt a curious emotion, and my eyes were a little moist. A.T. is very sensitive about other people, and when we walked away he said: "Well, I suppose any emotional response will do, as long as you're not academic." He talks a great deal like that, half-serious and half-amusing, and yet one never feels that he is really flippant about serious things. I can understand his being friendly with Arthur when they met, all those years ago, as they have much the same attitude, though A.T. has more knowledge than Arthur. I was looking forward to being with him in Rome, but had not anticipated this maturity of his mind, combined with his greater ease of manner. It is an added pleasure. Sometimes I feel he is chaffing me, as about the faun. I should have thought that I would have disliked this, but I rather enjoy it. He also assumes that my mind has developed along the same lines as his own. No man has ever spoken to me assuming such a high level of intelligence, and this is very flattering. When we returned I said that I was a little tired, which was true, and that I would write letters this evening and go to bed early. I don't want to make myself a nuisance to him. I don't know whether he was glad or sorry when I said this. He looked at me with a kind of quizzical expression. He certainly felt *something* about it. He was not just indifferent. Wrote to the lawyers agreeing to let Maclean off all debts and to let him have the Bourke Street property on a new lease at £3000 a year, as Austin recommends. Wrote to the Commercial Bank asking when my £900 would be available. Sent Steven a cheque for £105 on the Bank of Australasia. The £5 for the baby.

'*1 Octobre*. Dimanche. S. Rémy. Went to the High Mass at St Peter's. They all went in procession. There was a Cardinal in a beautiful cope of gold embroidery on petunia silk, but it clashed in colour with his scarlet train. Many Canons in purple with fur. Sistine choir singing Palestrina. The sunlight coming in misty shafts through high windows touched the whole atmosphere with gold and caught bits of gilded carving on the walls. The brilliant colour of the procession coming down the vast church was very impressive. When I came out I was astonished to see A.T. in the small crowd of people. I was also delighted and showed it perhaps too clearly. It is the only time I have met him unexpectedly, except at the meet at Boyton, and as then, I had a feeling of intense pleasure, which I cannot believe he did not share. He said that as I had told him I was going to St Peter's he had come to meet me. I told him how beautiful the Mass had been, and asked why he did not come. He said: "I thought you might prefer to be alone." I replied that he made everything in Rome more enjoyable. I thought it permissible to say this. He said: "But in church it is better to be alone." I thought this a strange remark, as I like to have my friends with me. It was a fine morning and the air had that soft clear quality which it seems only to have in southern countries. The piazza looked so light and spacious, with the little red-wheeled carriages and the sunlight on the fountains. I said it was like a Canaletto and he turned to me with the quick smile he gives when I say something he likes.

'In the afternoon we went to S. Maria in Aracoeli, I saw the first Christian altar in Rome, and a miraculous Bambino, and some huge marble popes. Afterwards we sat in the sun at the top of that great flight of steps. It was hot but I had my parasol, the one lined with Brussels lace. A. is more unconventional now than he used to be, which I like. He used not to sit about on steps or anywhere as he does now. Also he does not seem to care so much for society. He has not taken me anywhere to meet people, as he did before. Again this pleases me, as I would far rather talk with him than with Italian dukes. We did meet a contessa somebody in the Corso this afternoon and he introduced me, but not as his sister-in-law. He may think that at our age this sop to the conventions is no longer necessary. It became too hot on the steps and we went through the church again on to the shady steps on the other side. The view was very fine, over the arches and ruined temples and pine trees to the distant blue of the Alban Hills. I said how fortunate he was to live in the most beautiful city in the world. He said: "Yes, but then if one is depressed there is nowhere else to go." He sounded a little unhappy. Perhaps he is lonely. He has never married. I must not get ridiculous ideas into my head.

'2 *Octobre*. Lundi. S.S. *Anges Gard*. This morning we went to the Borghese palace. We sat in the gardens first as it was such a beautiful morning. We were so interested talking that we did not notice the passage of time, and when we stood up to go into the palace, we found it was time to return for luncheon. I did not mind as I really prefer talking to A. to anything. He shows everything in a more interesting and truer light. I don't only mean statues in Rome, but things like one's attitude to other people. We were very amused when we found that we had been so interested in our conversation that we had not noticed the time, also because we were quite satisfied that it should be so. We came back to the hotel. He has not asked me to a meal in his apartment. He says he has not a good cook, but I went there to tea this afternoon. It is not as magnificent as my memory of it, but I have seen so many palaces and fine houses since, and then I was new to Italy, and the grandeur of Rome. There were not so many servants. The only one I saw was a boy of sixteen in a footman's livery too big for him, who brought in the tea. The pictures also are not the masterpieces I had imagined. I liked them, but they are by unknown seventeenth century painters. I had thought they were by Titian and Veronese, though of course they couldn't have been, though Lady Dilton told me that A. had a large fortune from his uncle. All the same the rooms themselves are magnificent. I suppose the quality of his mind has improved and he feels less need for outward show. It makes us more at ease with each other. In the evening we went to a concert. The last piece was the *Siegfried Idyll*. After the concert, although it was very late, we went again on to the Pincio. A. said something like this: "There is a chord which continues all the time, the eternal music of humanity. Our lives break out of it and form different patterns of sound—they may be the motif of a single life, or the richer harmonies when two lives intermingle. Then they subside and are drawn into the eternal chord, as all the motives are drawn into the long chord at the end of the *Siegfried Idyll.*" The pine trees in the Medici Gardens filled the air with their scent. It is now after 2 a.m. but I find it hard to stop writing about these wonderful days. He is calling for me at 10.30 tomorrow morning.

'*3 Octobre*. Mardi. S. Trophima. I know it is foolish at my age, but I felt my heart beating rapidly this morning when I was expecting A. He was a few minutes late and I felt some apprehension. I shall have to stop this sort of thing or I shall become ridiculous. Perhaps it is worthwhile being ridiculous to be happy. One is only *not* ridiculous for the benefit of other people. The happiness one feels oneself. When he arrived he was preoccupied, almost impatient. He was quite polite of course and explained that he had to reply to an urgent letter from England. He said at once that I ought to see the Borghese palace and I felt that he was blaming me for yesterday morning, when we dawdled in the gardens. That was one of the happiest mornings I have spent for years, so it was particularly wounding to me to feel that he repudiated it. This may all be absurd, and I may be building up a situation out of nothing, but I do not think I imagined it. One is always more sensitive to a person's manner than to what he actually says. The palace was beautiful, particularly the entrance hall, and I saw some pictures I have long wanted to see, but I did not enjoy it. A. who so far has made me feel keenly the beauty of anything we have seen together, this morning seemed to blind me to it, and I might as well have been walking through Paddington railway station. He brought me back to the hotel and I thought he was going to leave me, but I asked him to stay to luncheon. He accepted, but in a faintly surprised way, as if I had thought of a nice idea, not as if it were a matter-of-course that we should lunch together, as we have done every day since I have been here. I ordered some rather expensive wine which he had recommended and he was pleased at this. His mood changed and he became as gentle and cheerful as I have always seen him. We walked a little way from the hotel and went into the cloister of a church, one of those odd, delightful corners of Rome, of which he knows so many. There were orange trees and a fountain in the middle. The line of columns was very dignified, and the sunlight was reflected up into the clean, simple vaulting. I said how pleasant it was to be able casually to stroll into places like that—that in Australia if there were just one such place people would travel a thousand miles to see it. He asked me for the first time with real interest if I liked living in Australia. I told him that for some things I liked it very much, for my friends there, and the climate and the scenery, which round Westhill is far more spectacular than round Waterpark, though the latter has more quiet charm. When I talked to him about these things I had that strange feeling one sometimes has that it had all happened before. We talked about the effect of all this classical art on one's mind, and he quoted a little poem about Greece and Rome, which began:

> Helen thy beauty is to me
> As those Nicean barks of yore . . .

'He went on to say that every good thing must have traces of past good things in it. "Arabs" he said "are the best coffee-makers. They leave the grounds of the last brew in the pot, and make the fresh coffee on top. In Europe we have all the grounds from the beginning, especially in Rome." He paused, and then he said: "Friendship is best when it contains the traces of early love."

'I felt that he meant this to apply to us, and also that it was exactly the right expression of our relationship. He so often hits on this true note, which makes it such a pleasure to listen to him. He said that it must be disintegrating to be drawn in two across the globe, and that I should integrate myself in Rome. On the way back to the hotel we passed a shop with some Russian wooden toys. There were some little figures that came in half, with a smaller one inside, and others inside that, six in all. I bought one for Diana's little girl. In the evening he had to dine with some people. He did not want to go, and said he would have put it off if he could. I had just come up from dinner when a waiter brought me a bouquet of yellow roses and an envelope from Aubrey. It contained only these verses:

> Alice, your beauty is to me
> As those strange Russian wooden toys
> Which come in half, and then we see
> A smaller size of painted boys.

For with my mind I can discern,
Beneath your stately woman's guise,
That other who my heart made burn
With light you kindled from your eyes.

And so I have two friends in one,
First love within the friend I see.
And no one knows, but I alone
How doubly dear you are to me.'

Between the leaves of Alice's diary for this day were some silky brown petals. There is no further entry until:

'6 *Octobre*. Vendredi. S. Bruno. I have neglected my diary for the last few days as there was nothing to write. I do not mean that I have been dull. I have been so happy that there was nothing to say except to state the fact. It seems to me that we have reached exactly the right degree of friendship. A.'s quaint little poem expresses it perfectly. We have gone about together with complete mutual understanding of the nature of our friendship. It is cool and sensible, and yet it is richer because of our former feelings. I am writing this tonight because I want to remember what A. said this afternoon. We were sitting in the Medici gardens at the end of one of those long box alleys. He was talking about limitation and freedom in love and friendship. He said first of all that love should not be labelled. He said it was right that we should love our husbands, parents, children, etc., but that modern society had laid down too exact rules as to the degree to which we should love them. It said that we should love most those most closely related to us. It might work like that, but it might not. If one's love of a friend enhanced the quality of one's life, that was enough justification. There was no need to label it. Too many things were labelled, especially in human relationships. He went on to speak of the proper physical expression for different kinds of affection. For some a handshake is sufficient, for others a linking of arms, and so on through varying degrees of demonstration to complete intimacy. I think that he was trying to reassure me about the propriety of our being together, and to emphasise that he would not destroy the balance of our relationship by pushing it too far. He certainly does enhance the quality of my life. I hope I do the same for him. I think I must or he would not want to spend so much time in my company.

'9 *Octobre*. Mercredi. S. Denis. We had arranged not to meet until luncheon today, but I went out to do some shopping and ran into him unexpectedly, coming out of the Bank of Rome. He was looking rather serious, but when he saw me ses yeux étaient pleins de joie, et pour moi les étoiles chantaient.' Here Alice's writing becomes much smaller. 'I don't know whether I have suddenly gone off my head. If I look in the glass it ought to restore me to sanity. I have five grandchildren. But I almost feel that the situation of twenty years ago still exists. It is natural that I should have the same feelings for him. He is nicer than ever—a little grey and lined, but with so much kindness and intelligence in his eyes. And yet I feel that he is sad. Could it be because of me that he has not married? Or am I crazy? These things do happen. Why did he come to meet me at St Peter's? Why does he fill my room with roses? Why does he talk so much about love and friendship? I know it is possible to mistake mere good nature for something more, but I must believe the evidence of my senses. I must also remember that there's no fool like an old fool. Whatever I feel I must behave with dignity. I feel as if I were in a wonderful dream. Had a letter from the secretary of the Commercial Bank saying my £900 would be available in November.

'*11 Octobre*. Lundi. S. Julien. Aubrey had to go to Florence today to see Mrs Dane, I think on some business matter. I was not dull, knowing he is coming back tomorrow. I went to the Baths of Caracalla to see if I could find the mosaic pattern which Lady Langton had copied and worked for her dining-room chairs, but could not find it.

'*12 Octobre*. Jeudi. S. Donatien. The situation *is* the same as it was twenty years ago. My reason tells me it is impossible, but my heart denies my reason. What can I do? Nothing of course. Imagine what all the family would say, with their strong sense of the ridiculous, if I were to elope again, thirty-three years later. I have no intention of doing so, yet I cannot deny that if A. asked me to, it would not be easy to refuse. I am sure I would refuse. I am not a fool. I am a fool in my mind. And yet how can I say I am a fool when, because of my feelings, every moment of the day brings me intense delight! Theosophists or some people of that kind, say that when two people are strongly attracted they have met in a previous existence and have been looking for each other ever since. It is like that with A. The moment I saw him, over twenty years ago in the Campo Santo in Pisa, I was *aware* of him, and again at the meet at Boyton immediately I saw him the day seemed brighter. How can I express properly sentiments which would only be decent in someone thirty years younger? What would

I think if I heard that, say, Hetty Dell had emotions like mine? I would recoil in contempt and derision. (Perhaps she may have!) I am sure that A. is very fond of me but his emotions are not stirred like mine, that is because he is still an attractive man and I am a middle-aged woman. It would not be natural for him to feel for me what I feel for him. Everything he says emphasises the proper degree for a friendship like ours. Even his quaint little poem, delightful as it was, was *cool* in tone. It spoke of past love. I have only a few days longer in Rome, during which I should be able to conceal my feelings, and at any rate they need not be labelled. Si je pleure dans ma chambre, personne le sait.

'*13 Octobre*. Vendredi. S. Géraud. Late this afternoon we were walking along the Via Babuini when we saw in an antique shop a little marble statuette of two cupids struggling over a heart, one trying to stamp on it, the other to prevent him. I admired it and A. went in and bought it for me. He said it was a farewell present as I leave on Monday. I am delighted with it. He told the man to send it at once, and it is standing on my table now. We went on up the Spanish Steps to Trinita dei Monti, where we sat on the balustrade, and looked down on the golden mists of the evening, rising round the domes. He likes sitting up on places like this. So do I. He recited a few lines of some poem which begins: "When the quiet-coloured end of evening smiles . . ." He asked why need I go so soon. Couldn't I stay another week? His tone was different from usual. I was sure that he was going to make some proposition. I wanted him to do it and at the same time was nervous lest he should. I said that I had many things to see to, and I mentioned for the first time that we had lost a great deal of money. He stared at me and then he laughed. I was very surprised and hurt. He immediately apologised and was very contrite. He said: "Please forgive me. I was not laughing at your loss. It was at something quite different that occurred to me at the same time. You know I would not dream of laughing at your misfortune. I would rather never laugh again." He was still smiling faintly, but he was so concerned that I forgave him. He came back to dine with me. At the hotel I found a telegram from Diana saying that Laura's baby was ill, and she wants me to return to Lucerne tomorrow, so I shall leave by the mid-day train. After that A. was très très gentil. At dinner he said quiet funny things to amuse me. It was very peaceful being with him, and yet I felt that something had happened, like a change of temperature. After dinner we went round to his apartment. He sat down at the piano and played a few things. He stopped for a moment. Then he looked at me with a smile of greater affection than I have ever seen, and he played the Chopin Prelude in G. I could not help the tears coming to my eyes, but I was very happy, as I knew that we had reached perfect understanding. We did not speak much after that. He walked back with me to the hotel and said: "Goodnight dear Alice. I'll collect you in the morning."

'*14 Octobre*. Samedi. S. Calixte. In the train. I was packing all the morning. Then Aubrey came and drove with me to the station. He gave me his last bunch of roses. When the train was about to leave he said: "You must come to Rome every year at this time." I said that I would if I could, but that Austin wanted us all to go out to Australia and I was not sure when we would be back. I see no reason why I should not go to Rome once a year. He said: "Come back before next October." Suddenly he said: "You haven't thrown a coin in the Fountain of Trevi." The train was beginning to move. I quickly took a coin out of my purse and gave it to him to throw for me. It happened to be a sovereign. I said: "Will that do?" He said: "It must. It must. Arrivederci!" I could only smile.

'*15 Octobre*. Dimanche. S. Thérèse. It seems very lifeless back here in Lucerne. The baby has recovered after all. It was only Diana wanted me back to buy some music for Wolfie. Wrote a cheque on Frome for our P&O fares, also to Commercial Bank telling them to transfer the £900 when available to Melbourne. It is only a fortnight since A. met me outside St Peter's. Wrote to Dolly Potts.'

13

The last chapter gives Alice's account of what happened in Rome, but is it necessarily a true one? I do not mean that she deliberately falsified it. She was incapable of telling an untruth and she would have had no object in doing so. She wrote in her diary to preserve her memories. But she was obviously in a highly emotional state and afraid of making a fool of herself. She was not likely to see others clearly, or to read Aubrey Tunstall's character accurately.

After all old Colonel Rogers did say that Aubrey, Damaris and Ariadne were bad hats. It is true that he called anyone a bad hat whose moral intelligence was above his own. But it was not only Colonel Rogers who spoke of them in this way. They were a sinister legend in our part of the country, though this may only have been because they lived in Italy and did not hunt. Beyond this I know no more than any other reader of the parts of Alice's diary which I have quoted, but I think that these show some internal evidence in support of Colonel Rogers's view.

It is fairly clear that Aubrey was short of money. When Alice met him at Boyton he had come over to see his trustees. When they passed Keats's house he said: 'Trustees are horrid people.' He did not entertain Alice lavishly as on her former visit to Rome. On the contrary he appears to have had a large number of meals at her expense. He did not go into society. This may have been due to the time of the year, but also to shortage of money, and it is even possible that his private life had damaged his reputation, though one does not know whether, or how much this would have affected his position in Rome at that time. Alice only saw a youth of sixteen when she went to his apartment, wearing the outsize livery of one of the footmen he could no longer afford. She thought that the pictures were not so good. Her memory was right. He had sold his Old Masters and also his gold plate, so he did not ask her to dine, only to tea. Certainly he did buy her the marble amorini, which are now on a table in the room where I am writing, and he did give her flowers, but she only mentions three occasions, not every day. He may have regarded these things as an investment. He went off in the middle of her stay to see his sister in Florence, probably to borrow money on his prospects of securing Alice, and to postpone a crash until he had done so. She had seen him looking serious as he came out of the bank on the previous day. This may sound shocking, but people of his kind who find their position slipping are apt to do that sort of thing.

Aubrey's sister-in-law Lady Dilton would have told him the previous year when he was in England, that Alice was now quite rich. He would not have heard of the boom bursting. Alice had been travelling about Europe for nearly a year without her husband who was in Australia. She had some of her family in Lucerne, but did not appear to be very much with them. He may have thought that she was far less attached than she was in fact, and that it would not be difficult to persuade her to throw in her lot with him, either just to share his apartment and restore his style of living, or even somehow to secure a divorce and marry him.

At the same time he wanted to be honest about it, and not to land himself in an intolerably false position. He was not physically attracted by women, and in those long talks he had with Alice, sitting about Rome on the sun-drenched October steps, he emphasised the validity of all love up to its proper degree. He was both justifying his own inclinations, and trying to explain to her that if they were to live together there were definite limits in his affections, and until she had grasped that he could not make his proposal. He did like her very much indeed. He had for her that affection which is the noblest part of love, but he had not the remaining part.

He must, on their last afternoon together, have thought that he had prepared the ground sufficiently to make his proposition. He had bought her, presumably with part of Mrs Dane's loan, those vaguely symbolic amorini, though whose was the heart to be stamped on? He asks her to stay longer in Rome and at that moment she reveals that she is no longer rich, and he laughs. He was laughing ironically at himself, perhaps with relief, as he could not have enjoyed the game he was playing. He was kind with the kindness which is possible to people without very strong feelings. For the rest of the evening he was extremely gentle to her, although still dining at her hotel. His intentions were no longer the same. The temperature had changed, as she noted. Perhaps in a quiet defeated way he was content to have abandoned his scheme. The air was purer. When at the train he asked her to come back every year he meant it, at least more than most English people who scatter those vague invitations so generously. There was this unusual affinity between their souls and their minds, but it could not have been complete unless her own soul had been in the body, perhaps, of the youth in the footman's livery which was too big for him.

Alice never went back to stay in Rome, and one wonders whether Aubrey threw her sovereign into the Fountain of Trevi. In his financial state it would have been painful for him to do so, and to know that it would be fished out by some urchin as soon as his back was turned. Or is this too low an imputation? Is it not better to believe that the Fountain of Trevi does not always work?

In spite of the above it is possible that my illness, combined with Aunt Diana's selfishness, saved Alice. If Aubrey had discovered, as he might have in another two days, that her income, though halved, was still about twenty times what he had left, he might have continued with his design. So I may now once more, and with greater complacency, invoke the ghost of my grandmother, receding into Paradise. Whatever I may be doing now, think what I did for you then, offering the sufferings of that frail flower, my tiny body, to save you from dreadful scandal. It is true that I may also have deprived you of years of autumnal bliss, but does autumnal bliss of that kind happen unless there has also been a summer, not merely a single, distant spring day?

And by this infantile sickness I saved not only my grandmother, but the entire family from ruin. For if she had gone off with Aubrey he would certainly have squandered her fortune, as he had squandered his own. My father, uncles, aunts, cousins and their wives and children would have been left penniless, all fishermen and tobacconists. I, instead of buying brocade and aubusson for Westhill, would be selling daphne and boronia at the corner of Little Bourke Street. Aunt Mildy alone would have realised her ambition, as she lurked in a doorway or paced her beat nearby.

I was once at a detective play in London. At the end, when the villain was discovered and arrested, a woman in front of me said: 'Well, I don't believe he did it.' Whoever reads this is at liberty to take the same attitude, to disagree with the author about his characters. As I have written earlier, if Mildred or Dominic had compiled this book, the story would be very different. Mildred would have magnified the bouquets to beds of roses, as in the novels of Mrs Glyn, while Dominic would have seen Aubrey as spending agonised nights of prayer, wrestling with his temptation. Perhaps we would all be wrong. Aubrey may simply have been an ordinary man of good principles, immensely enjoying Alice's company, but as determined as she that their friendship should be above reproach, though nowadays it is unusual to contemplate such a possibility.

The trek began again, farther south, but first my father and Uncle George went back to Waterpark to pack up the smaller personal belongings left there. Alice must have intended to be away a year or so. Dust covers were put on the furniture and a caretaker and his wife installed. The way they drifted apart from this house is curious. When they left for Brittany a year earlier, there was no suggestion that they would not be back in a few weeks. A kind of spell seems to have come upon them, drawing them farther and farther towards the south in aimless wandering. They were like those peasants of whom Tolstoy writes, who suddenly abandon their homes and all that they have, to journey to 'the warm rivers' which exist only in their imagination. Alice was at least twice in Paris during this year. It would have been nothing to her to run across to England and see how things were at Waterpark. To be so close to one's home and not to go to it is almost uncanny, like something that happens in a nightmare. When I read in her diary that Steven and George had gone to Waterpark, if only to pack, it was a relief, as if a breach had been made in some thick and maddening cobwebs.

There is no explanation of why they stayed away for so long. It was surely not cheaper to keep the whole family in foreign hotels, and I cannot help resenting the fact that I was allowed to be born in one, instead of in the ancient home of our family, in spite of my Venetian lace cap and Madame Miradoux de la Primaube's bouquet. My parents, although nowadays in Australia they would be thought typically English, were Australian enough not to give the same importance to things of this kind, as people in whom tradition is quite unbroken.

It is possible that something had happened to make them feel uncomfortable at Waterpark. Did they think it a disgrace not to have signed Dolly Potts's marriage settlement? Or had Austin said something outrageous to a duchess in the hunting field? As Australians they may have felt more under criticism than if they had been at Waterpark all their lives.

A Cornishman once told me that when he was a boy he caught a seagull, and clipped its wing so that it could not fly away. After a while the feathers grew and he forgot to clip them again. It flew back to its companions who killed it. In its captivity it had acquired some human taint which they sensed was hostile. My family were captive seagulls, both at Waterpark, and even more, as time went on, in Australia.

Again there is another explanation for this long absence. After they had 'chummed' Austin and Mildred to Marseille, they thought that they might as well stay in the South of France for the winter. Then, when the summer came, Alice could not bear to return to England until she had been to Rome. But she could not go to Rome in mid-summer, and Aubrey might not have been there. Perhaps only half-conscious of her motive, she planted the whole family at Lucerne, as a kind of chaperone in the centre of Europe, whom she could accustom to her innocent flights to various capitals, until on that triumphant day, the Feast of S. Izarn, she wrote to Honble. A. Tunstall, telling him she would be in Rome on Thursday.

However, at last, after five months, the party left Lucerne. Although the season was well over, quite a number of people came to see them off, this strange little contingent of colonials, who had settled amongst them, added myself to their number, and now passed on. They stayed a few days in Milan and Florence where Bobby seeing a procession of young noblemen in evening dress, said: 'Look at the waiters going to school.' The next halt was Rome. My parents and the Flugels had never seen Rome and wanted to stay there. Alice with George went straight through to Naples.

It was a pardonable vanity. To have reappeared in Rome, accompanied by three children, a son-in-law and daughter-in-law, five grandchildren, two nurses and three perambulators, would have been an intolerable anticlimax. After a week the family joined her in Naples, and they all went on to Brindisi, where she makes an odd little entry in her diary:

'*19 Novembre*. Dimanche. Ste. Elisabeth. The *Arcadia* came in at eight o'clock this morning. I bought a fan, some silk caps and a picture and we all went on board before luncheon. Had a telegram from A. T. "Arrivederci a presto." The last time I was here I had some chocolate in the hotel with Mr Rudyard Kipling.'

This name, suddenly unfurled like a Union Jack at the exit from an enchanted garden, closes Alice's European experience for ever.

14

Six weeks later they were back at Westhill, the bolt-hole. They had first spent a week in Melbourne. Alice is seldom ill-natured in her comments, and one can only guess her feelings from what she does not say on arriving at the final goal of that trek which began with the flight to Brittany fifteen months earlier. Austin met them at Adelaide. 'The children remembered him quite well.' Who could forget him? Mildred, dressed more for a garden party, than for Port Melbourne pier at ten o'clock in the morning, met them there. They drove through a pouring shower and a cold wind to Lady Langton's house in East St Kilda. In the evening Arthur gave a family party to all the relatives to welcome them back.

'It wasn't a success,' he told me. 'Alice had been away so long that all the untravelled relatives expected her to put on airs—a thing she never did in her life—but she was a little depressed at the sight of them, and by God, I don't blame her. Your mother and Diana, with all her high-souled rot, did look and behave like ladies, but you couldn't say the same for Mildred, and even Maysie had become very bourgeoise. If women are happily married they just become second editions of their husbands. Mildred and Maysie weren't by any means the worst. There were some ghastly Mayhew wives, and Walter's girls had that provincial refinement which considers *le monde qui s'amuse* vulgar, like University people and New Zealanders. They looked at Diana as if she were a barmaid. Diana did provoke them with her Paris clothes and her air of bewilderment. Then Hetty was there looking like the propri-etress of a Methodist *maison tolerée*, with her pugilist's shoulders and her jutting jaw, and her black opaque eyes. I didn't ask her. Mama did, but it was sheer effrontery for her to come. Nobody talked of anything but the financial crisis. Alice must have felt inclined to go upstairs and burn her cheque-book. She had just come back from years spent in the most beautiful and interesting places in Europe, but no one would let her utter a word. They were determined that she should not be allowed to patronise them. As if she wanted to!'

Alice only makes a brief reference to this party: 'A great many relatives present. They all seem to have lost money. Percy Dell asked me to lend him £45 for two months. I said I would. His son Horace looks very unpleasant. It is strange to be here.'

The captive seagull had been away too long. Not only had it become suspect to the flock, but the flock itself had become alien to the seagull. Before they came up to Westhill she filled in the last page of that diary with the French headings. It must have been like using the last jewel of some precious chain of which the principal stones were lost.

'*31 Decembre*. Dimanche. S. Sylvestre. Went with Austin to the new cathedral. I do not like it at all. It is so hard, striped and confused. No repose for the eye anywhere. They should whitewash it and hang up some good tapestries as at Arles. It needs softening. Sermon on the financial difficulty and trouble of this past year.' As she listened to this financial sermon in the new striped cathedral, did she find that it was the heart and not the eye for which there was no repose, and did she try to imagine that she was in the duomo at Milan, or in Santa Croce, or in St. Peter's where the cardinal walked in procession in his petunia cope, and Aubrey waited outside between the colonnade and the fountains?

Everyone but the Flugels came up to Westhill. Alice behaved rather like a modern government in times of crisis. Her own income was halved so she halved all the allowances. It was theoretically just, but it was disproportion-ately hard on Wolfie and Diana, who had nothing else to live on, and who for the past two years or more had been used to having their living expenses paid for them. They took a tiny wooden cottage in Balaclava, where even Diana's Paris clothes and diamonds did not give her much chance to patronise her cousins. They were so poor that their poverty became a legend in the family, and though later they were quite comfortably off, the Craigs always pretended to believe that they had not enough to eat. Wolfie had to begin music lessons again, but after the boom he could find few pupils, and for awhile he did actually tune pianos, though he said: 'It is not good for a composer to tune pianos.' Arthur when he told me this, had been guilty of that subtle form of falsification of history which consists of giving wrong dates to true events. When I questioned his statement he was ashamed to insist on the point.

It is strange that Alice allowed her favourite daughter to become so poor. History again becomes irrational. Her too rigid sense of justice may perhaps have prevented her from treating Diana differently from the others. She may have been rather disgusted with the selfishness the Flugels had shown in London and elsewhere. Or is it possible that she had not forgiven Diana for hurrying her back from Rome to Lucerne, two days before it was necessary?

The household at Westhill for the next few years must have been extraordinary if Arthur is to be believed. Austin and Alice would have been happiest living like one of those Italian families, of which the different branches all occupy apartments in the same palazzo. Westhill was not big enough for that. Even so in the summer time it was always bursting with relatives. Beds were made up in the room for developing photographs, in the studio my father built, and even for odd young men in the loft above the harness room, while the Flugels occupied the spare cottage. On one Sunday the party from Westhill filled an entire side of the local church. The cooks were always leaving as the hordes of grandchildren invaded the kitchen. My father had built a forge where he did wrought iron work. According to Arthur anyone standing on the lawn would hear, in addition to the crying of babies, the noise of hammering from the forge, of bassoons from Austin's music room, of Wolfie at the drawing-room piano, and more distantly an irate cook raging at the children in the kitchen. Then from the stableyard of this slightly shabby house in the Australian bush would appear a grand carriage with blazons on the panels, driven by a groom in a bowler hat, or else a six-in-hand drag with delighted shouting postillions of seven years old.

This picture cannot be quite true, as all those sounds would not be heard from the same point, children of seven could not ride carriage horses at anything more than an amble, and myself and my cousin Deirdre von Flugel were both placid babies, and could not have been crying all the time. All the same there must have been some truth in it. Only the other day I called on a Miss Violet Chambers, a lady of eighty-three. She told me that she had stayed here in 1895. 'It was such a happy house,' she said. 'There was so much life and fun there. Your grandfather was the most amusing man I have ever known. And the cherry plums!' I came home and looked up the diary for that year, and found: 'We all went to meet Vio Chambers at Narre Warren. Schmidt drove Laura and me in the landau. The rest went with Austin in the drag. He had harnessed six horses in a pyramid and was wearing a pink hunting-coat and a solar topee. The children rode their ponies. I thought Vio would prefer to drive with me, but she climbed up on the box beside Austin and blew the coaching horn. A hot but amusing day.' The next day she writes: 'Ernest Dell seems to be very taken with Vio. They spent the afternoon together picking cherry plums while we went for a picnic. She is a little old for him.' Is there another sad Dolly Potts romance behind this laconic entry?

Alice for the most part was contented with the lively and amusing, if occasionally freakish life at Westhill, with her interest in her grandchildren and in the attractions between the young people like Ernest and Vio. She imagined that the fates which shaped her destiny and her character had about finished with her, that her role was now one of a looker-on, or of the onion woman, stationary in mid-air, not ascending to Heaven but performing a useful and not too uncomfortable function in sustaining her large family at a good height above the infernal regions of poverty.

Austin clearly did not want to return to Waterpark, and when after she had been back a year and he showed no sign of changing his mind, she had the carriages, and also some of the furniture and pictures sent out from England. A lingering hope had died. One day she wrote:

'Today the carriages arrived from Waterpark. I sometimes think I see what the pattern of our lives ought to be. I believe I saw it clearly when I was first married. It seems impossible for us to carry out the design. Circumstances outside ourselves or our own natures pull it crooked. I cannot think of one person to whom this has not happened to some extent. Are we only put into the world to see what the design ought to be? In another life we may realise the possibilities we saw. Yet the design for me was not impossible. It was only prevented by circumstances.'

A few days later she had 'a very nice letter from Lady Dilton. She said we were missed at Waterpark and hoped we would return. Sometimes I feel that it is quite foolish if not wrong to stay out here. We are amusing ourselves too easily. Lady D. said that A. T. had left his Rome apartment and had gone to live in Taormina. C'est tout fini.'

She could not think of Aubrey in any other place than Rome. If he was not there he was nowhere. Even at the meet at Boyton, when he laughed into her eyes, she saw behind him not the bare winter oaks, but the ilex trees on the Pincio, not the wide English pond, but the hanging water gardens of the Villa d'Este.

The fates had not finished with Alice. They had two more blows to deal her to reduce her to complete submission, to complete renunciation of the idea of any positive pleasure for herself, to the condition she was in when I first remember her, the white-haired old lady, the onion woman static in mid-air, bearing dutifully on her skirts the weight to which she was accustomed.

As ambition for herself faded, and then for her children, she transferred it to her grandchildren, and mostly to Bobby. She quotes his sayings more than any of the others. She hoped that one day he would reign at Waterpark, with all the best qualities of an English squire, but with extra adornments of wit and taste. She may too have dwelt with pleasure on the fact that he was not so very distantly related to Aubrey Tunstall.

But the day came when she wrote:

'This morning I was gathering apples in the orchard. Bobby saw me and ran to help me. I was carrying them in my skirt and he said: "Grannie you will spoil your skirt," and he went to fetch a basket. He climbed the tree and we gathered quite a lot and brought them in together. At luncheon Steven told him that he might ride Pride this afternoon, when I went to Harkaway to take some plants to Mrs Daly. Pride is bigger than his own pony and he has not been allowed to ride her before. I have never seen a boy so happy. His eyes were alight with happiness and his face was so rosy with its clear and flawless skin. He looked really beautiful. We were all pleased and amused to watch him, and he said such funny things. I drove with Schmidt in the dogcart. Bobby rode beside us, and sometimes he rode ahead and called to me to see how well he could sit on Pride. When we arrived back here and had pulled up at the front door, I told him how his father and the other children used to ride their ponies into the house and out through the lobby to the stables. I wish I had bitten off my tongue. He said "I will do it" and he put Pride at the steps, but she shied, and he fell off on the gravel. I expected him to get up, as the children are often thrown, but he lay there quite still. I carried him into the house and laid him on my bed. Tom Schmidt galloped for Dr Rayner. Steven and Laura had gone out sketching and I sent Schmidt to look for them. The doctor came and said he thought Bobby had a fractured skull. He did not recover consciousness and died before Steven and Laura returned. They said nothing. I went out and left them in the room with him. I sent Tom into Berwick with a telegram to Austin who was in Melbourne.

'The children do not understand what has happened. They are very quiet and trying to be helpful to us. When they asked where Bobby was I said that he had gone to Heaven. Dominic said: "When will he be back?" I said that he would see him there some day. Dominic said: "Can he see God?" and I said "Yes" because I am sure that his angel does behold the face of the Father, as we are told. Dominic said: "I will ask him what He's like when he comes back." Brian patted my hand because he saw that I was upset. Austin arrived after dinner. He looked terrible.'

The above is an entry which I feel in a way that I should not have included, but Julian expressed surprise when I said that we were cursed. Even so this was a simple tragedy compared with what happened in later years. Or was it so simple? Was Bobby making expiation for one of the duque de Teba's altar boys? We do not know, assuming a *damnosa hereditas* to exist, how it may work, whether the malefic stars strike the innocent natures from without, or rot the guilty from within. Bobby and Dominic, their two most evident victims, are buried in the same grave in the Berwick cemetery, the old man the younger brother of the boy.

Austin did not recover his spirits. He no longer took any pleasure in his horses, or in teaching the children to ride. He complained of feeling unwell, and got up in the middle of the night. He told Alice that he did not want to go on living at Westhill, and she agreed to take a house near Melbourne. No one suggested returning to Waterpark. Austin went off house-hunting the next day. Another historical mystery— Alice let him sign a lease without first seeing the house herself. There was a week of packing, and then some of the furniture, with more that they had stored in Melbourne, was sent to their new home.

I think it was at this time that I was moved into the night-nursery with my brothers, so that my mother would still see three sons sleeping there, and not be harrowed by the sight of an empty bed. Every night we used to sing a hymn, often

Bishop Ken's evening hymn, which she told us was written at Heaven's Gate, a wooded hill above Longleat, only a few miles from Waterpark. Often too we sang 'Now the day is over' which I think is beautiful in the absolute simplicity of its petitions, and its picture of the sleeping world. Perhaps these words of goodwill towards mankind, sung every night from his earliest years, awakened Dominic's sensitive soul to its repudiation of the inhumanity of the modern world. Ten years or so later I was once with my mother at the evening service at Waterpark, when they sang Cardinal Newman's famous hymn. Her eyes were full of sorrow and I was sure that the angel faces she had lost awhile were those of her children at Westhill, one through death and the others through growth and the inevitable changes in their natures. There was always too, in our ever *depaysée* family, the nostalgia for the other home, ten thousand miles away. In the Northern or the Southern Hemisphere there was no abiding city.

The house that Austin had taken was on the sea-front between Brighton and Elsternwick. Not long ago I drove an English visitor past it, and he burst out laughing. I did not dare to tell him that my grandparents had lived there. If I had told him, I would have wanted to explain how they came to live there, and it would have meant telling him nearly everything that is written in this book. It was of bright red brick. There were terraces and statues, oriel windows, battlements and turrets. It was called 'Beaumanoir.' It is inconceivable that Austin who owned both Waterpark, a genuine country 'seat,' and Westhill, a modest and pleasant house, could bring himself to end his life in this bogus baronial mansion, even more so how Alice could agree to live there.

Austin did not want to be eccentric, but he often saw only one aspect of a situation. If for example he wanted to cart turnips and the only available horse vehicle was a brougham, he would use it rather than make several laborious journeys with a wheelbarrow. A mischievous fate too often presented him with a brougham as the sole alternative to a wheelbarrow. He now thought it would be pleasant to bathe in the morning directly from the house, and the only available house with a sea-frontage was 'Beaumanoir.' Alice too may have thought it would be nice to walk out on to the sea-shore, and the house may have appeared less grotesque to her in the nineties, than it does to us, half-way through the next century. As children we thought it was glorious, and loved to climb into the dusty turrets, and to turn on the fountains in the fernery. When she wrote to her friends in Europe she must have felt that after 'Waterpark House, near Frome' it was somewhat humiliating to have her writing-paper headed: 'Beaumanoir, Higgins Street, North Brighton, Vic.'

It was under the heavy ornamental plaster ceilings of Beaumanoir that she was reconciled with Hetty. Arthur was present. 'They had of course met often in other people's houses,' he said, 'but Alice had never received Hetty, who had not been to Westhill for twenty years. Now she wanted to see what Beaumanoir was like. When she wanted a thing she always went for it. She did not even do it as an outrageous lark. She was entirely without humour, which made people think she was very amusing. She did everything like a steam-roller. I was with Alice one afternoon when a servant came in and announced Mrs Dell and Miss Mayhew. She was clever enough to bring Sarah, whom Alice could not very well refuse to see, and who shortly afterwards came to live with them again. Hetty came in on the servant's heels. She was quite unsmiling and her eyes were like black agates. She looked at Alice suspiciously to see how she was taking it. A momentary flash came into your grandmother's eyes, as she was not the kind of person with whom one took liberties. Then I saw an extraordinary, really quite beautiful expression come into her face, and she took Hetty's hand and led her to the sofa. When we are old, and things have not gone very well, we feel kindly towards the people we knew when we were young, even if they were then our enemies. And Hetty, though at that time she still had a sort of champion wrestler's physique—really Austin must damn nearly have risked his life—she looked so hang-dog, that Alice wanted to give her back her self-respect. After that she lunched with your grandmother every Friday.'

At Beaumanoir also, one day Alice wrote: 'George arrived at tea-time. He had heard from Dolly. She says she cannot go against her father's wishes.' It was then five years since they had parted at Nantes. Not very long afterwards Major Potts died, leaving Dolly, for whom he had demanded such a large settlement, with a tiny pittance, as he left nearly all he had to his son, to 'keep up' his name. By that time Aunt Baba had married George for his money.

In the last summer of the century Austin had reached the stage of complete indifference to public opinion. Every morning he walked across the garden to bathe. He wore only his pyjamas to the beach, and nothing into the sea, even when he bathed on horseback, which he liked to do. The unwarrantable assumption was that no one could see him. He then came back to the house and still wearing his pyjamas had grilled steak and beer for breakfast. He drove about a good deal and arrived at awkward times at other people's houses. All this year there was a look of excitement in his eyes, and the red of his face was not very healthy. Again he began to complain of feeling unwell and he walked about the house at night. The doctor advised that he should go for treatment into a private hospital, as nursing homes are called here. His condition did not improve and they decided to perform what in those days was a very difficult operation, under which he died.

Slowly, as Alice recovered from the shock, she began to realise that she was completely free. Throughout the months following Austin's death are many allusions to plans forming in her mind. She thinks of taking Diana and Wolfie back to Europe to compensate them for the hard time they have had. She has more money now. Or should she take Steven and Laura and settle again at Waterpark?

She tries to imagine what it would be like to arrive in Taormina. How would Aubrey welcome her? She examines her face in the glass, and writes: 'I look much older than I did six years ago.' It was no good. She could not go back in time. She could not repeat an experience. Too often we are given what we asked when we no longer have the power to use the gift. She had to go on to the next phase, for her the last, that of the static onion woman, waiting for the angel himself to remove the weight from her skirts, and to pull her up into the skies. For her there was no more vital experience. All that had ended on the evening when she wrote:

'Mr Hughes, the surgeon, rang up to say that they were

going to operate on Austin early this afternoon. Steven had come down and we waited anxiously to hear the result. The operation was unsuccessful and A. died under the anaesthetic. Mildred went in a hansom to break this news to Diana and to Maysie. Steven rang up George at his club. Mr Hughes came out to see me. I asked him what were A.'s last words—if he had said anything. Mr Hughes smiled, and said he could not tell me. He told Steven. A. said that if the surgeon did something to him under the operation he would punch his nose when he came out. I had to smile at the last funny thing he said. It was so shocking, and so courageous. Goodbye my dear, Goodbye.'

Text Classics

The Commandant
Jessica Anderson
Introduced by Carmen Callil

Homesickness
Murray Bail
Introduced by Peter Conrad

Sydney Bridge Upside Down
David Ballantyne
Introduced by Kate De Goldi

Bush Studies
Barbara Baynton
Introduced by Helen Garner

A Difficult Young Man
Martin Boyd
Introduced by Sonya Hartnett

The Cardboard Crown
Martin Boyd
Introduced by Brenda Niall

The Australian Ugliness
Robin Boyd
Introduced by Christos Tsiolkas

All the Green Year
Don Charlwood
Introduced by Michael McGirr

The Even More Complete
Book of Australian Verse
John Clarke
Introduced by John Clarke

Diary of a Bad Year
J. M. Coetzee
Introduced by Peter Goldsworthy

Wake in Fright
Kenneth Cook
Introduced by Peter Temple

The Dying Trade
Peter Corris
Introduced by Charles Waterstreet

They're a Weird Mob
Nino Culotta
Introduced by Jacinta Tynan

The Songs of a Sentimental Bloke
C. J. Dennis
Introduced by Jack Thompson

Careful, He Might Hear You
Sumner Locke Elliott
Introduced by Robyn Nevin

Terra Australis
Matthew Flinders
Introduced by Tim Flannery

My Brilliant Career
Miles Franklin
Introduced by Jennifer Byrne

The Fringe Dwellers
Nene Gare
Introduced by Melissa Lucashenko

Cosmo Cosmolino
Helen Garner
Introduced by Ramona Koval

Dark Places
Kate Grenville
Introduced by Louise Adler

The Long Prospect
Elizabeth Harrower
Introduced by Fiona McGregor

The Watch Tower
Elizabeth Harrower
Introduced by Joan London

textclassics.com.au